All He Saw Was the Girl

Peter Leonard is the author of two previous novels, *Quiver* [illegible] *Trust Me*. He lives in Birmingham, Michigan.

Praise for Peter Leonard:

"[illegible]eter Leonard gets better and better . . . The book has all the hallmarks of vintage Elmore. There's the hot-plate sizzle of brilliantly written dialogue, succinct description, all you need to know about where you are in a few telling sentences, no fat at all on these words, crisp characterisation that tells you ev[illegible]ng about the book's colourful cast and brings them to [illegible]uality in a few neat strokes and an impeccable eye for [illegible] Tremendous stuff, really." **** *Uncut*

"E[illegible]rtly plotted and fast moving, the twists and turns keep the [illegible]ader on a thrilling roller coaster ride right to the gripping [illegible]nd . . . A great thriller for a holiday." *Irish News*

"T[illegible] Leonard's third novel confirms the enormous pr[illegible]e of its predecessors. While he has Elmore's wit a[illegible]ll at writing razor sharp dialogue, he has highly in[illegible]l qualities that set him apart . . . Leonard weaves a c[illegible]vating yarn . . . A terrific read shot through with humour, ge[illegible]nely scary moments and jaw-dropping surprises." *[illegible]otsmag.co.uk*

"Razor Sharp." RJ Ellory

"A huge talent." Mo Hayder

"Clever plotting and blood and guts characters." Michael Connelly

"Great storytelling." Carl Hiaasen

Also by Peter Leonard

QUIVER

TRUST ME

All He Saw Was the Girl

PETER LEONARD

faber and faber

This is a work of fiction. All of the characters, organizations, and events portrayed in this novel are either products of the author's imagination or are used fictitiously.

First published in 2011
by Faber and Faber Limited
Bloomsbury House, 74–77 Great Russell Street,
London WC1B 3DA
This paperback edition first published in 2011

Typeset by Faber and Faber
Printed and bound by CPI Group (UK) Ltd, Croydon, CR0 4YY

A CIP record for this book
is available from the British Library

ISBN 978-0-571-25575-7

2 4 6 8 10 9 7 5 3 1

For the boys, Tim, Alex and Max

One

McCabe watched Chip offer the long-haired guy a cigarette, the guy surprising him, taking the pack of Marlboros out of Chip's hand. Chip tried to get it back and the guy pushed him. He was six feet, maybe a little taller, with dark hair, shoulder length and reminded McCabe of Fabio, the romance-novel model. McCabe watched him tap a Marlboro out of the pack, put it in his mouth and light it with a plastic lighter, blowing smoke in Chip's face, and slipping the cigarettes in the front pocket of his shirt. Now a stocky guy with close-cropped red hair, like a Marine, came up next to him and Fabio said something in Italian and they both glanced at Chip and laughed.

Chip came toward McCabe and McCabe said, "You let him take your cigarettes?"

"I didn't let him, he just did it," Chip said.

McCabe looked down at his black $400 Cole Haan boots with a zipper on the side. "He's going to take your shoes next and then he's going to take anything else he wants."

Chip looked over at the guy and back to McCabe. He looked nervous now, afraid. "No he isn't," Chip said, like he was trying to convince himself.

"You better hope not," McCabe said.

"What do you want me to do? There're two of them."

McCabe was pissed at him for getting them in this situation in the first place.

Chip said, "You think I'm going to get in a fight over a pack of cigarettes?"

"I wish you luck," McCabe said.

An hour earlier they were coming out of a bar in Santa Maria di Trastevere, fountain in the middle, church at one end. It was a little after midnight, Chip walking drunk toward a taxi that was across the piazza, a dark silhouette shape in the moonlight. Chip ahead of McCabe, stopping now, stumbling, arms outstretched, gaze fixed on something in the distance.

"'There, Spartacus, is Rome,'" he said in a theatrical British accent, voice echoing off the buildings that surrounded the square. "'The might, the majesty, the terror of Rome. There is the power that bestrides the known world like a colossus.'"

McCabe grinned, he'd heard it all before, but it was still funny the way Chip got into, the way he delivered the lines. Chip started moving again, walking to the taxi, a yellow Fiat, leaning against it, facing McCabe as he approached.

"'There is only one way to deal with Rome,'" Chip said. "'You must serve her. You must abase yourself before her. You must grovel at her feet. You must love her.'"

"Dinner theater ever comes to town," McCabe said, "you're all set."

He got in the rear passenger seat of the cab, looked forward and noticed the driver wasn't there. He leaned his head back, closed his eyes, feeling the buzz from eight Morettis, resting for a few seconds. He heard a door open and close. Heard the engine start up and rev. He opened his eyes, Chip glancing back at him, grinning. Chip putting it in gear, accelerating around the square, picking up speed, doing a donut, tires squealing.

McCabe said, "This how Connecticut rich kids get their kicks?" He figured Chip would lose his nerve or lose interest, but he didn't.

He looked at McCabe in the rearview mirror and said, "'Are you afraid to die, Spartacus? When one man says no, I won't, Rome begins to fear.'"

McCabe saw the taxi driver come out of a restaurant now, old dude running into the piazza after his car, yelling and shaking his fist. "*Basta! Aspetta!*"

McCabe felt bad for the guy and said, "Come on. That's enough."

Chip ignored him and drove out of the square, made a wide right-hand turn, going into the oncoming lane, forcing a car to swerve out of the way.

McCabe reached between the seats, grabbed Chip's arm and said, "Pull over, you dumbass, you're going to kill somebody."

"We're going to Harry's for a nightcap," Chip said, slurring his words.

They were in Trastevere, a maze of narrow cobblestone streets and medieval buildings on the west bank of the Tiber. They blew through an intersection, took a right on Via Garibaldi, passed a cop car parked on the side of the road, the word Carabinieri in white type on the side of a blue sedan, two cops in the front seat, looking at them. The scene felt like it was happening in slow motion. McCabe glanced back through the rear window as the police car, lights flashing, took off after them. He saw Chip's face in the rearview mirror, the happy drunk grin gone, replaced by a worry, concern.

Chip said, "Jesus Christ."

McCabe said, "I can't wait to see what you're going to do next."

Chip braked hard and went left down an alley that didn't look wide enough for a car, laundry hanging overhead on ropes strung between the buildings. Chip turned the wheel, taking a left on Via dei Riari, the back end of the taxi sliding, then going all the way around, spinning out of control, crashing into a parked car. McCabe was on the floor when the police pulled him out and cuffed his hands behind his back.

~

Now they were in the center of a holding cell at police headquarters in Rome, wondering what was going to happen. Prisoners spread out across the room that looked to be sixty by forty, bars along one side, guys staring at them, two American students looking out of place among the Italian drunks, thieves and cons. The long-haired guy and his friend were still looking at them, grinning, mocking them.

McCabe said, "I'll be right back." He turned, heading for the two Italians.

Chip said, "What're you going to do?"

McCabe could feel all the eyes in the room watching him as he approached Fabio, walked up to him and said, "I see you looking over laughing at us like a little girl. Is that what you are? With that hair, I can't tell if you're a woman or a sissy." He didn't know if the guy understood what he was saying or not, but his arm muscles tightened like he was going to throw a punch. McCabe stepped in, grabbed the cigarette pack, ripping the pocket off his shirt. Fabio stood there, looking surprised. "You took this from my friend, forgot to give it back." McCabe turned and went back over where Chip was and handed the pack of Marlboros to him. "Somebody else takes them," he said, "you're on your own."

Chip gave him a big wide-eyed look. "Unbelievable. What did you say to him?"

"I don't remember."

"You don't remember? Come on."

They were taken to a room and interrogated by a no-nonsense cop, a detective in a black sport coat. He was built like a soccer player, stocky and still muscular in middle age, thinning salt-and-pepper hair combed back. He introduced himself as Captain Ferrara. McCabe told him their names and told him they were students at Loyola University.

Chip said, "We weren't actually stealing the taxi."

Ferrara said, "No? What were you doing?"

Chip said, "We were drunk. It was a joke. *Scherzo*."

Captain Ferrara said, "*Scherzo*? This is how a man makes his living and you dismiss it as something trivial, unimportant. You have too much to drink and use this as an excuse? The man's automobile is damaged. Now he has no way to earn a living, support his family."

Chip said, "I'll buy him a new one."

He held Chip in his laser gaze, eyes locked on him.

Chip said, "You know who Senator Charles Tallenger is, right?"

He sounded drunk.

Captain Ferrara stared at him, studying him.

Chip said, "Well I'm his son, Charles Tallenger III."

Captain Ferrara didn't say anything, didn't seem impressed, gave him a stern look.

Chip was a smartass, but McCabe had never seen him turn on this arrogant superiority. Based on the captain's expression it didn't seem to be going over very well.

Chip said, "I have to make a phone call."

He said it like a spoiled Greenwich rich kid, which McCabe decided was redundant, maybe even tri-dundant if there was such a word.

"It's my right as an American citizen," Chip said.

Captain Ferrara said, "You are a prisoner, you have no rights. In Italy, you are guilty until proven innocent."

Chip said, "I don't think you understand what I'm saying."

The captain's face tightened, like he wanted to go over and knock Chip on his ass.

He said, "No, I think you are the one who does not understand, but you will."

He turned and walked out of the room and closed the door.

McCabe said, "Do me a favor, don't say anything else, okay?"

Chip said, "What's your problem?"

"You're being an asshole. Every time you open your mouth the situation gets worse." He'd never seen Chip act like this before. Jesus.

"You want to get out of here?" Chip said. "We've got to tell these idiots who they're dealing with."

"All you're doing is pissing him off," McCabe said, "making things worse. I'm in this thanks to you, and I don't want you talking for me."

Captain Ferrara never came back, and a few minutes later a cop in a uniform came in and cuffed McCabe's hands behind his back and took him to the garage and pushed him in the rear seat of a Fiat. Two heavyset cops squeezed in on both sides, flanking him like he was a hardened criminal, a flight risk.

The cops sitting next to him had breadcrumbs on their jackets and there was a comic-opera quality about them, big men in fancy, over-the-top uniforms with red stripes running down the sides of the pants and white leather sashes worn diagonally across their jackets, and matching white leather holsters. They held their brimmed blue hats in their laps. McCabe thought they looked like cops from some made-up Disney dictatorship.

They pulled out of the garage and turned right and drove down Via del Corso past Victor Emmanuel, the Wedding Cake, also known as the Typewriter, past the Colosseum and the Forum and Campidoglio, the cops talking about Italy playing in the World Cup.

The cop on his left said, "Did you see Grosso score the winning penalty?"

The cop on his right said, "How about that crazy Frenchman?"

"Unbelievable," the cop behind the wheel said. "Zidane's a madman. Ten minutes to go, he headbutts Materazzi. That was the game."

"It was a factor, sure," said the cop to his right.

The cop to his left said, "A factor, it was the difference."

The driver glanced in the rearview mirror and said, "What are you, head of the Zidane fan club?"

"I don't like him," the cop to his right said. "But you have to admit he is one of the all-time greats – up there with Vava and Pele."

"How much have you had to drink?" the cop to his left said.

When they got on the autostrada, McCabe said to the cop

on his right, "Where're we going?"

The cop looked at him and grinned like something was funny.

Twenty minutes later McCabe understood why, the walls of a prison looming in the distance, 3:30 in the morning.

The cop on his right said, "Rebibbia. Your new home."

He'd heard of Rebibbia, the prison for hardcore cons, and wondered why they were taking him there. Stealing a taxi didn't seem serious enough. They drove along a fence topped with razor wire, the prison set back on acres of flat open land.

They entered the prison complex and McCabe's carabinieri escorts took him into the processing area, released the cuffs and handed him over to the Polizia Penitenziara, a prison cop signing a form and giving it to one of the carabinieri cops, making the transaction official.

Then he was standing in line with at least twenty other prisoners – some he recognized from the holding cell – waiting to be processed. Each prisoner was photographed and fingerprinted. Then they went through a room where they were given a blanket, a tin cup, a spoon, a bar of soap, a towel.

McCabe heard Chip's voice and saw him at the far end of the line. "I'm an American. My father is a US senator. *Capisce?*"

The guard looked bored, his expression saying he had no idea what Chip was talking about, but there was no way he could mistake Chip's attitude, his arrogance.

McCabe said, "Hey, Tallenger, with your connections I thought you'd be out by now. Don't they know who you are?"

He spent the night in an eight-by-eight-foot cell, solitary confinement. As he was waking up, he was thinking about

Chip and the taxi and being taken to Rebibbia, wondering, before he opened his eyes, if it was a dream, and then opening them and seeing sunlight coming through the barred window, making a distorted pattern on the floor.

He sat up studying the room in daylight for the first time. The door was made out of steel, painted blue. It had a little square window about three quarters of the way up, so the guards could look in, check on him, which they did on a fairly regular schedule.

There was a metal sink against the wall, and the bunk he was sitting on, the frame painted orange, bolted into the wall. There was a stainless-steel toilet without a seat, squares of newsprint cut for toilet paper. The walls were cracked and scarred with graffiti. Some guy named Ricki professing his love for Anna in black marker.

McCabe got up, went to the sink, turned on the faucet and scooped water in his hands and splashed it on his face. He dried himself with the towel they gave him, gray-white and stained. He wondered how many inmates had used it before him to dry their own parts. He moved to the window and held the bars, looking out at the prison walls and guard towers, and below him the exercise yard, an expanse of concrete surrounded by a high fence topped with razor wire, the yard empty first thing in the morning. It looked like ghetto playgrounds he'd seen in the projects around Detroit.

A guard came to his cell and got him, 3:30 in the afternoon, took him through the cellblock, passing blue steel cell doors just like his, to a barred gate at the end of the hallway. It felt good to get out of the little room, stretch his legs. He'd never been in a confined space for that long without being able to leave and it was getting to him, messing with his head.

Adding to the problem, McCabe was on an academic scholarship, thirty-five grand's worth of tuition, room and board. He'd lose it if he was involved in a disciplinary situation, school rules listing a dozen things that would get a student kicked out: drinking, drugs, fighting, cheating, missing classes, not maintaining an acceptable grade point average and a few more infractions he couldn't remember, but stealing a taxi was definitely not one of them.

The school would bend the rules where Chip was concerned. He wasn't on scholarship and his dad was a US senator who had generated a lot of positive PR for the Rome Center Year Abroad Program.

Mazara watched him walk across the yard and stand with his back to the fence, face tilted up feeling the sun after almost twenty-four hours in a cell, the white box as prisoners referred to it. Mazara studied him, one of the Americans from the holding cell. He was not big, but looked like he was in shape, about his age. He had surprised Mazara, taking the cigarette pack out of his pocket, surprised him and caught him off guard by the boldness of the move, not expecting it. Now Mazara wanted to see how good he was, see if he could back it up.

He dribbled the basketball over to the American, inmates watching him, wondering what he was going to do. Mazara bounced the ball off the concrete at him, the ball thudding into his chest. The American opened his eyes, reached over, picked it up and held it, eyes on him.

"I don't have any cigarettes, if that's what you're looking for."

Mazara said, "Want to play? You and me. The winner walks through the gate a free man."

The American smiled, looking up at him, eyes squinting in the sun.

Mazara said, "They catch you selling drugs?"

"Stealing a taxi," the American said.

"*Va bene*," Mazara said. "They keep you here eight, ten months, no more than a year."

The American said, "What about you?"

Mazara said, "Is a misunderstanding." He pulled his hair back and wrapped a rubber band around the ponytail.

"They put you in Rebibbia for a misunderstanding, huh?"

"It can happen," Mazara said.

The American bounced the ball to him and got up.

Fabio, as McCabe thought of him, took it out. He started with the ball straight up over his head. Moved it down to his chest and waist, then his knees and back up. He faked left with his eyes and McCabe went for it. Fabio dribbled to his right and went up for a shot, arms bent, snapping his wrist as he released the ball, the ball arcing up and swishing through the cylinder. He raised his fist, looked at McCabe, nodded his head a couple times. There were hoots and cheers from the inmates that had formed a circle around the half court.

Now McCabe brought it in. He went right, crossed over, drove for the hoop, Fabio all over him, bumping him with his body. McCabe hesitated, faked left, went left, threw up a half hook that kissed the glass and went in.

The prisoners went crazy.

Fabio brought the ball in, faking left with his eyes, going to his right with his right hand, knees bent, made his move, juked McCabe with a shoulder fake, crossed over, right to left, and back, had him off balance as he went up for a fifteen-footer, but McCabe regained his balance and stripped the ball.

McCabe brought the ball in, went full tilt for the basket, stopped, pulled up and launched a twenty-five-footer. Fabio tried to block the shot, but he was too late. The ball bounced around the rim and in.

Fabio was pissed off now, McCabe could see the strain on his face, McCabe making him look bad in front of his boys. Fabio brought the ball in, did a shoulder fake, froze McCabe and launched a high thirty-footer that landed on the rim and bounced off.

The prisoners were really getting into it, shouting, taunting.

McCabe worked his way toward the basket, keeping his dribble low, protecting the ball. He went in for a short jumper, left his feet and Fabio hit him, fouled him in mid-air. The ball hit the glass and went in. McCabe went flying, landing hard on the concrete. He got up slowly, gaze locked on Fabio, "This the way you want to play? Okay."

Fabio held the ball close to his chest under his chin. He drove left, went behind his back with his right hand, left McCabe standing there. Drove hard for the hoop and went in for a lay-up, a sure thing, but McCabe caught him, stuffed him from behind, and knocked him down; the inmates were yelling, going crazy.

Fabio got to his feet, squaring off with McCabe, fists raised, ready to go at it as a guard appeared, pushing his way through the crowd.

Two

"I didn't see McCabe again till we were taken over for trial," Chip said. "There were thirty of us packed in a holding cell, waiting to be transported to the courthouse. I look over, see McCabe handcuffed to this little dude, I thought he was a midget."

"He was Sardinian," McCabe said. "Scared to death. Kept throwing salt over his shoulder and picking his nose."

"Why salt?" Brianna said.

She was Chip's girlfriend. Brianna Labitzke, a nice-looking brunette with perfect teeth, from Santa Clara, whose father owned a vineyard named after her. They made a premium Chardonnay and an award-winning Pinot.

"For good luck," McCabe said.

"Why'd he pick his nose?" Brianna said.

"I don't know," McCabe said. "Maybe it's a Sardinian custom." He flashed back to the transport van, the size of an airport shuttle, narrow two-sided bench that ran down the center, six prisoners sitting back to back with six others, McCabe handcuffed to the nervous little dude with tiny feet in scuffed brown shoes dangling over the floor, the bodies of twelve men jerking back and forth to the sway of the van. He remembered the view approaching the city, Rome spread out in the distance, seeing six of the seven hills.

Now they were sitting at a table at Pietro's, a neighborhood café two blocks from school, eating bread and cheese and olives, drinking wine, the house Chianti, McCabe across from Chip, Brianna on his left. The room was big and open and only a third full at 7:00 in the evening. There was an Italian newspaper, *Corriere della sera*, open on the table, McCabe reading a headline that said:

US SENATOR'S SON ACQUITTED IN TAXI THEFT

There were photographs of McCabe and Chip, shot when they were standing on the steps of the courthouse after the trial, their names transposed. A line under McCabe's photo said, *Charles Tallenger III, son of US senator Charles Tallenger II.* The line under Chip's picture said, *William McCabe, a student at Loyola University.*

Chip said, "There must not be much happening in Rome if this qualifies as news."

McCabe said, "Are you kidding? Any time a famous rich kid screws up, people want to know about it. Makes them feel good. Makes them think they're better than you."

"Well, I've got news for you, they're not," Chip said.

"Remember when Paris Hilton went to jail? The media interrupted coverage of the G8 summit to tell us what was happening in her life."

Brianna glanced at McCabe and said, "It looks so strange to see your name under Chip's picture." She took a sip of wine, eyes staying on him. "You don't look like a Charles Tallenger III."

Chip said, "McCabe couldn't be me if he had to."

McCabe said, "I'm not dumb enough." He picked up an olive and popped it in his mouth, chewed it and spit the pit into his napkin.

"You're not refined enough," Chip said. "It comes down to refinement and breeding."

McCabe said, "You sound like a French poodle."

Brianna said, "Or what's that dog that looks like a Chinese person?"

Chip said, "A shih-tzu."

"No," McCabe said, "a shih-tzu looks like a miniature lion. You're thinking of a Lhasa apso."

Chip said, "How's a guy from Detroit know what a Lhasa apso looks like? A Rottweiler or a pit bull, I can understand."

He picked up his wine glass now, drank too much and splashed down his chin onto his shirt. Chip dipped his napkin in his water glass and rubbed the wine stain on his shirt, blotting it, making it worse.

"Look at him," McCabe said. "It comes down to refinement and breeding."

Chip grinned showing a mouthful of olive paste.

"He's a class act," McCabe said, "isn't he?"

Brianna said, "McCabe, look at the positive side. If you were Chip, you'd get the trust fund, and I'd be going out with you."

McCabe said, "So you're in it for the money, huh?"

Brianna winked at him and smiled flashing her perfect teeth. "'Course I am."

"Be nice, wouldn't it?" McCabe said. "Somebody hands you a million dollars for doing nothing."

"Add two more zeros," Chip said, "you'll be in the ballpark."

Brianna said, "I want to hear about jail. Were you afraid?" She put her sexy gaze on Chip.

"I wasn't," Chip said. "Prisoners I met were a bunch of pussies."

McCabe glanced down at the newspaper, the next page, and saw two black-and-white photographs of faces that looked familiar. "It's your buddies from jail."

Chip said, "What're you talking about?"

"Guy who took your cigarettes and his friend."

Chip said, "Yeah, right?"

McCabe picked up the newspaper and turned it around so Chip could see the pictures. Chip picked it up and read the article, and when he finished, looked up at McCabe.

"The prison transport they were riding in was ambushed as it came into the city. It was stopped at a traffic light. Men dressed as construction workers got out of a truck that was parked on the side of the road. Shot out the van's tires, gained entrance and overpowered the guards. The two prisoners and their accomplices escaped." He held up the paper. "Look at this."

There was a photograph of the van, tires resting on their rims, bullet holes in the windshield.

"The two prisoners, Sisto Bardi and Roberto Mazara, had been arrested for extortion and were going to trial when the van was intercepted."

"Who are they?" Brianna said.

"We were in a holding cell at police headquarters," Chip said. "I asked the long-haired guy, Mazara, for a light. He asked me for a cigarette. I took out my pack and he grabbed it."

Brianna said, "What'd you do?"

"Nothing. It wasn't worth it." He picked up his glass and sipped his wine. "McCabe went over and got it back. I couldn't believe it. You should've seen these guys. They looked like extras in *The Sopranos.*" Chip glanced down at the paper.

"It says they're allegedly involved in extortion, kidnapping, weapons trafficking and racketeering."

Brianna said, "What's racketeering?"

"Being involved in illegal activities," Chip said. "They're armed and dangerous." He was reading the article. "You see them, call the ROS." He looked up. "Like we're going to see them again."

Brianna said, "What's the ROS?"

Chip said, "Raggruppamento Operativo Speciale," reading the article, "an elite unit of the carabinieri formed to fight organized crime."

McCabe saw Pietro, the owner, wave him over, Pietro sitting at the bar, having a glass of grappa before it got crowded. McCabe stood up and said, "I'll be right back." He walked over and sat next him.

Pietro was in his mid-forties, short and heavy with a thin tapered mustache and dark hair combed back.

"McCabe, what is this I hear about you in Rebibbia?"

For whatever reason, Pietro had taken a liking to him, introduced him to his family, invited him to his house for dinner, offered him the use of his summer home in Lazio. McCabe told him what happened.

Pietro shook his head and glanced at Chip. "Him I can see, but not you, McCabe. You should have phone me. I know a few judges. They come here for cannelloni." He patted McCabe on the cheek. "Stay out of trouble, uh?"

McCabe went back to the table.

Brianna said, "You guys were lucky. Anything else happen? Anybody try to . . ."

McCabe said, "You mean did we end up being somebody's girlfriend? I don't know about Chip, but I walked out with my virginity intact."

Chip said, "I was in a cell with a South American pickpocket and an old dude who'd been there since the early seventies."

Brianna said, "What'd he do?"

"I don't know, but he slept with his clothes on, thinking he was going to be released any time and wanted to be ready."

Brianna said, "How'd you get out?"

Chip said, "The Senator bought the taxi driver a new Fiat and gave him money for his trouble."

"You call your dad the Senator?"

"No, I call him Chuck."

"Come on?" Brianna said.

"That's my name for him because it's so out of character. He's Charles. Not Charley or Chuck or Chucky. He's too straight to have a nickname."

Brianna said, "You don't call him Chuck to his face, do you?"

"Not if I want to collect the trust fund. Chuck also hired attorneys who knew one of the judges. A deal was made, although I don't know the particulars."

Brianna said, "You mean a bribe?"

Chip said, "We don't use words like that, it's politically incorrect."

Brianna said, "Judges? How many were there?"

"Three,' McCabe said, "and a prosecutor who wanted to make an example of us. Teach American students what happens when they steal a taxi in Rome. He wanted to give us eighteen months."

Chip said, "Then one of the judges said something, and it was over and we were shaking hands with our attorneys."

McCabe flashed back to the courtroom, he and Chip in coats and ties, sitting next to their lawyers, facing three serious men wearing white powdered wigs and black robes, listening to the prosecutor yelling at them in Italian.

"On the way back to school," McCabe said, "Chip told his dad I stole the taxi and he tried to stop me. What a friend, huh?"

"Dude," Chip said. "We're out, who cares? If the senator knew I drove the cab, I'd be home right now. You don't know him. He's perfect, never made a mistake in his life. Ask him."

McCabe remembered the ride home from the courthouse. They were in a Mercedes-Benz Maybach driven by the senator's aide, a yes-man in a seersucker suit and bow tie, named Todd, who kept looking at them in the rearview mirror.

Charles Tallenger was impressive. He looked Hollywood's idea of a US senator, tall, good-looking, well-dressed, with dark hair, graying at the temples, sixty years old, the build of a tennis player, six two, 180, a two-term Democrat from Connecticut. Played lacrosse at Princeton. Was a Rhodes Scholar. Went to Harvard Law. Started a software company he took public ten years later and cashed out for $500 million.

Chip was right, he was perfect. Yeah, McCabe thought, he'd be a tough act to follow. Tougher if your name was Chip. They were driving along the Tiber past Castel Saint Angelo, the dome of St Peter's in the distance. The senator was turned sideways in the front seat, looking back at them.

"Do you guys know how lucky you are?"

Chip wouldn't look at him, eyes on the floor.

The senator said, "Whose bright idea was it to steal the cab?" Chip looked up and glanced at McCabe.

The senator said, "What were you thinking?"

McCabe didn't know what to say, so he didn't say anything.

The senator fixed his attention on Chip now and said, "And you went along for the ride, huh? That's just as bad. Why didn't you do something, try to stop him?"

Chip squirmed in his seat. "I did."

McCabe couldn't believe it, Chip throwing him under the bus like that. He could see Chip was afraid of the guy.

"You didn't try very hard, did you? You guys are what, twenty-one years old? Still acting like kids. It's time to grow up." He looked over at the driver. "Todd, you're only a few years out of college, you understand any of this?"

Todd glanced at the senator and said, "No, sir, I honestly do not. I couldn't fathom doing something like that."

McCabe wanted to pull the little weasel with the bow tie out of the car and pop him.

The senator said, "You know what I was doing when I was twenty-one?"

Todd said, "If I may, Sir? I believe you were Princeton's Rhodes Scholar attending Oxford University, the world's most prestigious international fellowship."

Todd flashed a weasel grin.

Charles Tallenger glanced over his shoulder at McCabe.

"You hear that? I was trying to learn and grow as an individual – what you should be doing in this spectacular city."

He had a disc jockey's voice and liked to hear himself

talk. McCabe felt sorry for Chip, having to live up to this overachiever's expectations.

"McCabe, do you have any idea what it cost to make this go away?" the senator said, eyes on him.

"Senator, I appreciate your help," McCabe said. "Tell me what I owe you and I'll pay you back. I just can't do it right now."

"I like your attitude. You sound like a stand-up guy." He'd made his point, turned away from them, square in his seat now, looking out the windshield.

They drove along Corso Vittorio Emanuele. Looking past Chip, McCabe could see the dome of the Pantheon to his right and then got a quick glimpse of Fontana del Moro in Piazza Navona. They crossed the river, drove through Vatican City to Piazza Risorgimento, and started the climb up Monte Mario, no one talking, the Maybach solid and quiet like a bank vault.

They turned on Via Trionfale, in the neighborhood now, moving past Pietro's, a café, and Max's Bar, another student hangout, pulling in the entrance to the school that looked like a country club with its stucco pillars and ornate iron gate. Cruised up the winding drive past sculpted shrubs and rows of cypress trees evenly spaced, to the three-story villa painted a pastel color called umber.

The senator glanced back at them and said, "Tell me you learned something from all this."

"I did," Chip said with a solemn expression. "I'm sure McCabe did too," Chip said, glancing at him.

McCabe had never seen Chip intimidated by anyone. He'd been cocky and overconfident till his dad showed up, and now he was a different person, nervous and unsure of himself.

There was a group of students standing at the entrance as the Maybach pulled up, students glancing over to see what visiting dignitary had arrived in this $300,000 car. Chip got out first, approaching the group.

"We're baaack," he said, playing to his audience.

When McCabe got out, he looked over and saw Frank Rady, the dean of students, staring at him from the window of his first-floor office.

McCabe hadn't been in his room ten minutes when the RA, a straight-arrow former student named Mike Fagan, knocked on the door and said Mr Rady wanted to see him ASAP. Now McCabe was sitting across the desk from him, Rady shuffling through papers, keeping him waiting, a pair of reading glasses balanced on the end of his nose.

There was a nameplate on the desktop that said, *Frank Rady Dean of Students*. McCabe wanted to say, what's that for? In case you forget who you are. There was a pen and a pencil holder and assorted photographs of his family in matching gold frames on his tidy desk. Frank had been a high-school football coach for fifteen years and looked the part: a big, freckle-faced guy with a strawberry-blond flat-top. He took off the glasses, leveled his gaze on McCabe.

"I assume you know why you're here."

McCabe didn't say anything.

"Well, let me enlighten you." He picked up a sheet of paper and started to read: "On September 10th you were caught sneaking out of the women's dorm after 2:00 a.m., a strict curfew violation. On October 7th you got in a fight with an

Italian soldier on a 913 bus."

McCabe said, "Guy was smashed, trying to take Celeste Laveccha's clothes off."

"Come on, a little harmless touching? It's the national pastime."

"He was humping her. Does that sound like harmless touching? You talked to Celeste, didn't she tell you what happened?"

"That could've caused an international incident."

"Come on?" McCabe remembered grabbing the soldier, pulling him off Celeste, telling him if he bothered her again he was going to throw him off the bus. That was it, the soldier sat down, kept to himself after that.

"And your latest move, stealing a taxi. What were you planning to do with it? Will you tell me that?"

"I didn't steal it."

"You didn't steal it, huh? That's why you spent five days in prison?"

Rady was dumb, there was no doubt about that, but it was his self-righteous tone that really annoyed McCabe.

"You have any idea how this reflects on the university?"

McCabe could see the maintenance crew trimming trees and cutting grass through the window behind Rady's desk.

"Seen the newspapers? Your story picked up in every one of them."

McCabe said, "You think the fact that a US senator's son was involved might have something to do with it?"

Rady stared at him but didn't say anything.

McCabe said, "Think you're overreacting?"

"Let me try to make it easy for you to understand. Screw

up again, your scholarship's done and gone, and you're on a plane back to De-troit. Still think I'm overreacting?" He grinned at McCabe.

McCabe was going to say you can't help yourself, but decided to not say anything, keep his mouth shut for once.

Rady stood up. "I'm going to be watching you, McCabe. One more mistake and you're through."

Three

Sharon used her maiden name when she went out at night. She sat at the far end of the bar with the windows behind her, looking down the long stretch of granite and wood, studying the guys sitting there, scanning them in slow motion like a movie camera, stopping, holding on a face or passing it quickly, depending how old, interesting or good-looking the guy was.

Sharon had just completed her maintenances, had her hair colored and decided on a new style her hairdresser said was snappy. He said it with a lisp so she believed him, figured he knew what he was talking about and he did. Looking in the mirror when he was finished, she didn't feel "snappy" though, she felt sexy. She'd also had her nails done, a French manicure. She liked the satin finish and the white painted edge on the nail tips. It was classy. It was elegant. Sharon had been married for thirteen years – talk about bad luck – to a man she rarely saw and felt she hardly knew any more. He was out of town three out of four weeks, or more, and when he did come home he was usually stressed out. She'd be sitting at the kitchen table and see his car pull in the driveway and get nervous. She didn't know what kind of mood he'd be in, whether he'd be angry, drunk or what.

Over the years he'd been gone for her birthday, their anniversary – she doubted he even remembered when it was – Christmas, New Years, most national holidays. She'd gotten used to living without him around. Preferred it.

She hadn't had sex with him in nine months. When he was home, Sharon stayed on her side of the queen-size bed, her back to him, hoping he wouldn't touch her – thinking the last few times they'd tried to do it had been disastrous.

When he was home she felt like she was walking on egg-shells. They'd have dinner, sitting across the table from each other, eating in silence. She'd say, "Come on, Ray, talk to me. How's the job?"

"Are you making conversation? You really want to know how the job is. Come on . . ."

"You've got to get out of there," Sharon said.

"I do, I lose my pension, everything I've worked for."

"You don't," Sharon said, "you're going to lose your mind."

"What do you care?"

He was right, she didn't. She'd given up. He was drinking Scotch, Dewar's with ice. "Dewar's–rocks," he'd say when he ordered a drink in a bar. He looked drunk, face puffy, eyes bloodshot. She said, "How many is that?"

"You counting my drinks now?"

"Somebody better." She was trying to remember why she married him. Trying to remember why she'd stayed with him so long – determined to get a divorce every time he left the house. But then changed her mind. Not sure why. It was weird, like he had some strange hold over her.

She lit a cigarette, sipped her wine and looked down the bar. There was a good-looking guy smoking a cigar, talking on his cell phone. He saw her looking at him and smiled. He closed the phone, put it in his pocket, got up with his drink and his cigar and came over to her. He was a big man and she liked big men.

He said, "Know what my horoscope said?"

Sharon said, "You'd fall in love with a mysterious blonde." She'd gone from blonde streaks to full blonde a month earlier and got more attention from men than she ever had in her life. Her mother thought she looked like a $20 hooker. Sharon wondered how her mother knew what hookers charged, but she liked her new look. Had her eyebrows done too, waxed and colored to match her hair. Sharon worked with a girl who dyed her muff with a product called Fun Betty that came in three colors. You could be red down there, brunette or blonde. Sharon thought that was going too far. She didn't care if the carpet and drapes didn't match. No guy she'd been with had ever mentioned it.

He said, "You're close. It said, 'You're starting to design a life for yourself that is truly custom-fit to your proclivities.'"

Proclivities, huh? She wondered if he had any idea what it meant. Sharon hadn't heard a guy use his horoscope as a pick-up line in fifteen years. Maybe it was back in style. She said, "You just get a divorce?"

"No, I just met you." He puffed on the cigar and blew a cloud of smoke over the bar top. "Where're my manners?" He held up the cigar, pinched between his thumb and index finger. "This bother you?"

"I like it," Sharon said. "Reminds me of my father and uncles."

He said, "Good, we'll get along great. My name's Joey, by the way. Joey Palermo."

He offered his hand and she shook it. It was warm and dry and wrapped around hers.

She wondered why a grown man would want to be called

Joey. "I'm Sharon Vanelli," she said.

"How do you like that? Two Italian kids meeting by chance, or is it fate?" Joey still working the horoscope angle, that being there at the same time was somehow pre-ordained.

Joey said, "Where'd you grow up at?" He gestured with his right hand, kept it going while he talked, like he couldn't talk without it.

"Bloomfield Hills."

"So you're rich and beautiful."

"My dad was in PR at Chrysler." She almost said Chrysler's, out of habit.

"You in PR?"

"I sell ad space in magazines." She finished her wine.

"How about another one?"

"Chardonnay," Sharon said. "Sonoma-Cutrer."

Joey raised his hand, got the bartender's attention, pointed to his glass and Sharon's. The bartender nodded and went to work.

"What magazines?"

"Heard of *Rolling Stone*?"

"No. What's that?" He grinned. "'Course I heard of it. Bought the issue had Jessica Alba on the cover."

"You like beautiful, tall, thin movie stars, huh?"

"Who doesn't?"

He puffed on the cigar, pinching it between his thumb and index finger.

"Not everyone," Sharon said and winked.

"She don't got nothing on you," Joey said, and winked back.

He wasn't going to be mistaken for a poet laureate, but she appreciated what he was trying to say.

Joey said, "What do you listen to?"

"On the way here, the new Wilco CD." She had 3,500 songs on her iPod.

"I've heard of them," Joey said.

"What do you like?"

"Old stuff, Frank and Bobby."

Frank and Bobby. Using their first names like they were friends. He wore a blue button-down-collar shirt with the top three buttons undone showing chest hair and a gold chain with the letters "SJ" hanging from it. "What's SJ stand for?"

He grinned and put the nub of his cigar in the ashtray. "Swinging Joey."

"That's your nickname, huh? What's it mean, you like to dance, like to have a good time?"

"Something like that."

The bartender put fresh drinks in front of them. Joey picked his up, and clinked her glass and said, "*Salute.*"

Sharon sipped her wine and said, "You from Sicily?"

"Huh?"

"Your name's Palermo," Sharon said. "Isn't that the capital?"

"I'm from St Clair Shores. Used to go to Tringali's with my mother, she'd buy her tomatoes, or Pete & Frank's."

She said, "Ever go to Club Leo?"

"Club Leo? We were there like every other weekend, weddings and parties. My dad and the owner were buds. We called him Uncle Phil. You went there too, huh? I wonder if we met before."

"It's possible," Sharon said. She pictured the place, an old Knights of Columbus hall, spiffed up, cinderblock on the outside, fake stucco inside. A dance floor and long tables and buffet food, three meats: baked chicken and pork chops and sliced beef that looked like shoe leather. The men drinking wine out of little juice glasses. "Remember dancing to Louis Prima? I can hear him doing 'Felicia No Capicia' and 'Buona Sera'." She remembered dancing with her uncles who smelled like cigars and BO.

Joey said, "When'd you graduate high school?"

"You want to know how old I am? Ask me. I'm thirty-eight."

"How old are you really?"

Sharon gave him a dirty look. "What's that supposed to mean?"

"Hey, take it easy, I thought you were like twenty-nine, thirty tops."

It was a line but Sharon liked hearing it.

"Ever been married?"

"Once. I'm separated." In Sharon's mind it was true. That's how she felt.

"Now I live in Harrison Township," Joey said. "Place on the lake."

Sharon could picture it, mammoth house on a postage-stamp lot, nouveau-retro. "Let me guess," Sharon said. "You've got a thirty-foot Wellcraft docked behind it."

"It's a Century," Joey said, "and it's a thirty-two-footer. How'd you know?"

How'd she know? He was a wop from the east side. "What do you do?"

"Little of this, little of that." He sipped his drink, looked like vodka on the rocks with a twist. "Want to go somewhere?"

~

Sharon was thinking, who was this guy lived in a five-thousand-square-foot house – not that his taste was any good – on Lake St Clair, had nothing but leisure time or so it seemed?

He called her four, five times a day, said, "How you doing?"

And Sharon would say, "Same as I was when you called fifteen minutes ago."

"Baby, I miss you. Tell them you're sick, we'll go to the casino." Or he'd be at the track or a Tigers day game, he'd say, "I gotta see you. Take the afternoon off, I'll send a car."

She'd been going out with him for three weeks and it was getting serious. They'd meet at noon, check into a hotel a couple times a week and spend two hours in bed, screwing and drinking champagne. It was something, best sex she'd ever had in her life. He did things to her nobody had ever done before. She'd say, where'd you learn that? And he'd say, you inspire me, beautiful. The only bad thing, he called her Sharona, or my Sharona. Everything else was great so she let it go.

They'd take his boat out on Lake St Clair and she'd sunbathe topless. Something she'd never done in her life and never imagined herself doing. She felt invigorated, liberated. He always told her she looked good, complimented her outfit. Showered her with gifts, bought her clothes and jewelry. She felt like a teenager again. They'd meet and talk and touch each other and kiss. She was happy for the first time in years. She had to be careful. Ray, the next time he came home, might notice something and get suspicious. Why're you so happy? she could hear him saying – like there was something wrong with it.

But this relationship with Joey also made her nervous.

Things were happening too fast. She was falling for him and she barely knew him, and she was married.

Joey drove a Cadillac STS with the big engine. He liked to drive fast, too, like a high-school kid, always flooring it, burning rubber. He'd have a few drinks, nail it and the tires would squeal and he'd get a big grin on his face.

She said, "What're you running?"

"469-horsepower V8," he said.

She said, "What's its ET?"

"Jesus, you know cars, huh? I don't know what its ET is. Never been timed."

Her dad used to take her to Detroit Dragway when she was a kid to see the nitromethane-burning fuel dragsters, fuelies that went zero to sixty in two tenths of a second. Nine seconds in the quarter mile, its ET, elapsed time.

Her dad said you could tell the guys that burned nitro. When they took off, it smelled like acid. Nitro isn't a fuel, it's an explosive. It would blow off cylinder heads like a hat off your head.

Her dad's interest: most of the stock blocks were 426 Hemis, an engine Chrysler made.

One day they went to Nino's for groceries and then drove to Joey's place, this atrocious-looking, fake brick neo-colonial. He popped the trunk and as they were unloading the bags of groceries, Sharon noticed a baseball bat, a Louisville Slugger that was stained with something red. She said, "What's on your bat? Is that blood?"

He told her he played on a softball team and one of his

teammates got hit in the face by a pitch. That's where the blood came from. She knew you didn't use a wooden bat to play softball, but didn't really think about it at the time. But then Joey had his friends over and everyone had a nickname.

There was Hollywood Tony.

Joey said, "Ain't he a good-looking kid?"

There was "Big Frankie" and "Cousin Frankie." They were cousins who looked like twins. Sharon said, "How do you tell them apart?"

"What do you mean?" Joey said. "It's easy."

There was "Joe the Pimp" and "Skippy" and "Paulie the Bulldog." "Fat Tony," who was thin, and "Chicago Tony," who was fat, and "Tony the Barber" who didn't cut hair. They all drove Caddys and had money and hung out with hot young girls who looked like models or strippers. Sharon had heard of some of the guys, knew they were mobsters.

She remembered Jack Tocco, the don, coming in Club Leo one time with his entourage, and the whole place stopped, people looked like they were frozen, the men, her father included, paying homage to the man, the boss of all bosses.

She said, "Joey, what the hell do you do? You connected?"

He said, "To what?"

"The Mob?"

He never answered the question. They were on his boat called *Wet Dream*, that's how imaginative he was, looking out at the lake, a couple miles offshore, Canada somewhere in the distance, sun setting, red highlights on the horizon, Sharon thinking she'd gotten herself in too deep and shouldn't see him any more. He got up and went below and she was trying to think of what to say to him.

He came back on deck with a bottle of champagne and two flutes three-quarters filled and handed one to her.

She said, "What's the occasion?"

Joey said, "I've been thinking about this for a while. I hope you have, too."

He put the bottle in a cooler that was on deck. He got down on one knee and looked up at her.

"Will you marry me?"

He clinked her glass and took a sip. She did, too.

"Be careful," he said. "There's something in there."

Sharon saw it at the bottom of the flute, floating just above the stem. She knew what it was.

"It's our anniversary," Joey said. "Five weeks from the day we met."

Joey was a party boy. This was the last thing she would've expected. She said, "I've got to tell you I'm a little surprised. I thought you were seeing other girls, too."

"Not since I met you, babe. When I saw you I got hit by a tornado, a fucking hurricane."

She didn't know what else to do so she drank the champagne and felt the ring tickle her mouth, bobbing in the bubbles. When her champagne was gone, she turned the glass upside down and caught it, a diamond ring, a big one.

He said, "Put it on."

And she did, the biggest engagement ring she'd ever seen.

"Three fucking carats," he said.

He was grinning, holding his champagne glass by the stem. "Had it made special. What do you think?"

Four

McCabe waited at the bus stop on Via Trionfale with a heavyset gray-haired woman wearing a black dress. She was holding hands with a young girl in a school uniform who looked nine or ten. The woman wore dark translucent stockings and he could see the hair on her legs matted against the fabric.

Two tradesmen in blue coveralls were smoking, a slight breeze blowing it toward the woman. She glanced at the men, fanning her face. They dropped their cigarettes on the sidewalk and stepped on them as the bus pulled up. The doors opened and people got off and McCabe and the others got on.

The bus was packed, siesta over, people going back into the city to work. McCabe stood leaning against the rear window, looking down the aisle, the air thick with the smell of body odor. At times it was so heavy he had to breathe through his mouth.

He watched traffic approach, looking out the rear window, helmeted riders on Vespas and Lambrettas coming up close to the bus then gunning their motorbikes, hearing the throaty whine of their engines at high rpms as they whipped by. The bus drove down Via Cola di Rienzo, over the river and through the giant arches of Flaminia and stopped in Piazza del Popolo. McCabe got off and walked across the square to Rosati.

He sat at a sidewalk table, sipping a Moretti in a stemmed

glass, taking in the scene, studying the obelisk that was brought to Rome by Augustus after the conquest of Egypt, appreciating the simplicity of it. Beyond the obelisk was the Porta del Popolo, a giant arch carved out of the Aurelian Wall, the original perimeter of the city.

He watched pigeons land in the piazza in front of the churches, strutting and bowing on their little red feet, blue-gray feathers flecked with red. He once saw a show on pigeons on the Nature Channel and remembered some amazing pigeon facts: they could fly fifty miles an hour and they came in seven different colors and when they had sex, the female bent down and the male climbed on top, flapping his wings for balance, saying "Coo roo-croo coo."

At a table to his right, a balding old dude in a suit was having a conversation with a young girl who looked like a model, a bottle of wine in an ice bucket next to the table. Rosati was known as the place wealthy Italian men brought their mistresses during the week, and their wives on weekends. He watched two stylish girls, early twenties, get out of a taxi and move past him on their way into the café. He turned and checked them out and they turned back and smiled, and sat a few tables behind him. He was thinking about buying them a drink when he saw a girl coming across the square.

Fixed his attention on her moving toward him from Canova. And although cars and motorbikes zipped around, all he saw was the girl coming toward him like a scene in a movie. The girl wearing sunglasses and tight black capris and a white tee-shirt, hair combed back, tied in a ponytail. She reminded him of Manuela Arcuri, Manuela with streaked hair. McCabe held on her, gaze locked on her as she came closer, maybe fifty yards from where he sat at a front table.

He saw a motorcycle appear, entering the square from Via del Babuino conscious of the throaty *brat-brat* of its exhaust, muffler going bad. It made a ninety-degree turn, coming fast behind the girl, two riders on it. She heard it too, and switched her bag from her left shoulder to her right, the motorcycle coming up behind her now, going right, surprising her, the passenger on the back grabbing the bag, yanking it off her shoulder, the girl trying to hang onto it, and then letting go.

McCabe got up and moved between two BMWs parked in front of the café, and went into the square as the motorcycle approached. It was heading for Via di Ripetta. He stepped in front of it, and as the bike tried to swerve around him, he reached out and grabbed the passenger's arm and pulled him off the back and took him down on the cobblestone surface. The guy was trying to get up, but McCabe was bigger and stronger, knees on his chest, holding him down, a skinny teenager with a big nose, wearing a striped soccer jersey, looking up at him, stunned and afraid.

McCabe pulled the girl's purse out of his hand and now the girl ran up and started kicking him in the ribs, swearing in Italian. McCabe got off him and watched her. The kid tried to cover up and then scrambled to his feet, running, the girl going after him, letting him go. She yelled something in Italian, but the kid didn't look back.

McCabe handed her the purse, a black shoulder bag that said Prada Milano, silver metal in a black triangle on the side. She stared at him, studying him.

"What you did was very courageous. How can I repay you?"

McCabe could think of a few ways. He said, "Have a drink

with me." She was better-looking up close, about his age, early twenties.

She said, "Only if you let me buy one for you."

Her English was perfect and she spoke with a sexy Roman accent.

"I've got a table," he said.

"Not here," she said. "I know a better place. Do you mind?"

Did he mind? He couldn't believe his luck. He stepped over and put a five-euro note on the table and the people sitting there applauded him. He moved back to the girl, surprised by the reaction.

She said, "See, you are a hero."

They walked across Piazza del Popolo and down Via del Babuino toward the Spanish Steps, passing storefronts: Gente, Bonora, Feltrinelli and Carlucci.

She said, "What do you do when you are not pulling thieves off the back of a motorcycle?"

"Have drinks with good-looking girls," McCabe said, walking past St Attanasio, a small church tucked in among the designer shops, an odd contrast he thought. "I'm a student, and the only reason I saw the motorcycle was because I was watching you."

She gave him an innocent look.

"What school do you go to?"

"Loyola University. It's on Via Trionfale in Monte Mario."

"What do you study?"

"Art history."

"You are in the right city, uh?"

They were on a narrow sidewalk crowded with pedestrians, lined on one side by boutiques and restaurants, and on the other side by parked cars. They had to stop occasionally to let people pass, McCabe checking her out, trying to be discreet.

She caught him and said, "What're you looking at now?"

"The sights of Rome." He smiled and she did too. "What about you?"

"I can't tell you. It would spoil the mystery. You have to guess."

"You're a model?"

She gave him a look. "No."

McCabe said, "Okay, you're an actress."

"Why do you think that?"

"You remind me of Manuela Arcuri."

She shook her head. "I don't think so." And seemed embarrassed by the compliment.

"I give up," McCabe said.

She gave him her sexy look again.

"No, you can't."

"Let me think about it."

They walked along Via Condotti, congested now after siesta, strolled past designer storefronts: Missoni, Prada, Gucci, D&G, Valentino and MaxMara.

She stopped in front of Armani. "Is this where you shop?"

McCabe, in faded Levis and a blue Nine Inch Nails tee-shirt with red type, said, "You can tell, huh? Yeah, I'm very fashion-conscious."

'You do have your own style," she said, grinning now, "I have to say."

She was making fun of him and he liked it. She took him to an *enoteca* in the neighborhood. They sat outside, drinking glasses of Brunello di Montalcino, her choice, and watched people go by. She held up her wine glass, looking sexy, her brown eyes and skinny arms and nice rack, a line of cleavage visible where the tee-shirt tapered into a V.

She picked up her wine glass. "Do you like Tuscan wine?"

"I must 'cause I'm drinking it like it's beer," McCabe said.

"Take your time, savor it." She showed him how, put the glass up to her lips. "You take a little in your mouth, chew it, let it slide under your tongue and down the inside of your cheeks, taste the different flavors: black cherry, spice, a little of cinnamon."

McCabe was staring at her mouth, with those lips, an urge to lean over and kiss her. Jesus.

She said, "*Parla Italiano*?"

McCabe said, "*Un poco*. Enough to confuse myself. I go into a store to buy something and say *quanto costa*? The person gives me the answer in rapid-fire Italian. I have no idea what he's saying."

"It was the same with English."

"You sound fluent," McCabe said. "Perfect."

"I grew up speaking English. Used to spend summers in Michigan.'

"No kidding," McCabe said. "Where?"

"The east side of Detroit. Have you ever heard of St Clair Shores?"

"I was born right near there," McCabe said.

She said, "I would have guessed Connecticut, or maybe New York."

"Why's that?" McCabe said. "You think I have an east-coast accent?"

"You know how it is. You look at someone and imagine where they're from? That's what I did."

Sure. Like he did with her. Thinking she was a fashion model from Milan. He said, "Why Detroit?"

"I have an aunt and uncle who live there. They would drive us north to Harbor Springs. They have a house on Lake Michigan. We would build a fire on the beach and cook marshmallows and watch the sunsets."

McCabe said, "What's your uncle's name?"

"You don't know him." she said.

"Maybe I do."

She looked at her watch again, the second time in the past ten minutes.

He said, "You have to be somewhere?"

"I am meeting a friend in Villa Borghese."

Her cell phone rang. She took it out of her purse and said, "*Pronto.*" She listened and said, "*Ciao,*" and put the phone away.

She said, "*Mi dispiace.* I have to go."

He said, "Maybe I should go with you. You never know, someone might try to steal your purse." He knew if she left now he'd never see her again.

"It is a long walk. Stay here. Let me buy you another glass of wine."

She was blowing him off, but in a nice way. He finished his Brunello and said, "Black cherry and cinnamon, huh? Yeah, I see what you mean." He stood up and offered his hand. "It was nice meeting you."

She got up too and moved toward him and kissed him on the cheek.

"Maybe I should take you up on your offer," she said. "You can protect me."

She smiled and he felt a rush of adrenalin, grinning, but trying not to, excited, but trying to hold it back. He'd miss Italian, his six o'clock class, but he was learning a lot in the company of this real Italian girl and figured he'd learn even more. He was going to Sicily with Chip and Brianna and a girl he was kind of interested in named Trish from New York. The train left at 8:06 that night. So he had an hour and a half to make a move.

As they walked through the narrow streets of the Condotti neighborhood, McCabe was thinking things like this only happened in movies, and he was going to take advantage of it, give it his best shot. Get her number and when he got back in town, call her and set something up. They moved past a café with outside tables. A waiter in a white jacket was serving drinks to a tourist couple. He glanced over, seemed to recognize her and said, "*Ciao, bella.*"

The girl said, "*Ciao*, Enzo," waved but kept walking.

Five

Twenty minutes later they were at the Pincio, looking down at Piazza del Popolo where they'd met an hour earlier. This was an even better view of Rome, the city spread out, a dusty haze hanging over the skyline, the giant dome of St Peter's looming in the distance. There were telescopes set up along the balustrade, tourists taking aim at points of interest. McCabe thinking this would be the perfect setting for Chip to deliver his lines from *Spartacus*.

They strolled through Villa Borghese, her arm hooked around his, walking close as they passed stands of chestnut trees, holmoaks and stylish umbrella pines that looked like they were designed by Armani or Zegna. It occurred to him he didn't even know her name, had forgotten to ask or hadn't thought to. "What's your name?"

"Angela."

"That's nice. Angela what?" She didn't answer or ask anything about him. "Where do you live?"

"That way," she said, pointing north.

They passed the Temple of Diana and the Goethe Monument. They walked further and McCabe could see Via Veneto below the park. He and Chip would sit at an outside table in front of Harry's Bar, watching the prostitutes come down from Borghese, beautiful girls, knockouts in stylish outfits, walking by them, asking if anyone wanted company. Chip would ask how much and then try to negotiate even though he had no intention of buying their services.

Now they were on a path flanked by thick ten-foot-high hedgerows. McCabe stopped to look at a bust on a marble pedestal, the face of a man scarred with graffiti. Someone had drawn eyelashes, a mustache and goatee on him.

Angela glanced at the bust and smiled.

McCabe said, "Know who this is?"

"No, but I think you are going to tell me."

"Cardinal Scipione Borghesi, the guy who designed the park." McCabe realized he was showboating, trying to impress her. "I memorize a lot of meaningless historical facts, so I can impress good-looking girls I meet."

She said, "I can see that."

McCabe said, "Did you go to college?"

"For two years," she said, "the University of Turin."

McCabe said, "What did you study?"

"Business administration," she said.

They followed the path, crushed stones that wound through the park, a wooded area on the right, open space, a field of grass on the left. McCabe could see the marble facade of Casino Borghese in the distance. "Where're we meeting your friend?"

"Right here."

She let go of his arm, stepping away from him as four guys with bandanas covering their faces came through the trees, looking like Halloween bank robbers. They came at him, McCabe wondering if there was some connection between these four and the thieves on the motorcycle, coming back for revenge. But that didn't make sense. There was no way they could've followed them. Now his attention was on Angela, if that was really her name, Angela calm and relaxed, like she was waiting to see what was going to happen.

They circled around him, McCabe separating them in his mind: the big guy who was the size of an NFL nose guard, the short stocky one, the thin wiry guy with blond hair, a bad bleach job. Even with the bandana hiding his face, he recognized Fabio, the long-haired guy from Rebibbia, the one he beat on the basketball court, the one with Mafia connections they'd read about in the newspaper.

He glanced at the girl again, standing there relaxed. She wasn't afraid because she was in on it, she was the bait. But how'd they know he'd go after the thieves on the motorcycle?

McCabe was moving backward, turning in a circle, trying to watch them all. The nose guard came at him first, charging, coming straight at him. McCabe stepped right as he got close, and the big guy overran him. McCabe turned, going to his kidneys with a hard right. The guy turned and McCabe hit him with a right-left combination to the body that dropped him to his knees.

Now the other three charged him. The stocky guy threw a wild right hand that missed. McCabe juked and weaved and hit him with a right hook to the jaw that stunned him. Then somebody tried to tackle him from behind. McCabe throwing an elbow that hit him in the face and he let go. Then something crashed into the side of his head and he staggered and went down, looking up at the long-haired guy standing over him. He rolled over on his hands and knees trying to get up, still dizzy and fell over.

~

Chip said, "We better get on, get a seat."

Trish said, "If McCabe doesn't go, I'm not going."

Chip said, "He'll be here. Have I ever lied to you?"

"Probably," Trish said.

She gave him a dirty look.

"What kind of attitude is that? Let me get you a drink, take the edge off."

Chip finished his beer and held the bottle up, telling the bartender he wanted another one. "Last call," Chip said.

The girls shook their heads. They were packed in the loud, crowded bar in the Stazione Termini in Rome. The train for Messina was leaving in twenty minutes.

"Why don't we call school, see if he's there," Trish said.

"Maybe he's mad at you," Brianna said to Chip, "for telling your dad he stole the taxi."

"He doesn't care," Chip said.

"I would."

"You're a girl."

The bartender handed Chip a beer. He pulled two five-euro notes off a roll of bills and left them on the bar top. Now Chip and the girls picked up their backpacks, left the bar, crossed the main floor of the station and walked to Track 17. The sign said *Messina*. Departure time: 20:10. They found seats in a first-class car and Chip drank his beer, looking out the window. He watched a porter push a cart piled high with luggage. A conductor in a blue uniform walked along the side of the train, announcing its imminent departure. Chip looked down the boarding platform toward the station. He was sure he'd see McCabe running into the picture, but it didn't happen and the train started to move.

Six

In the dream Ray could hear a phone ringing, sounding far away at first, then close and loud. He turned on his side, opened his eyes and saw the message light flashing. It seemed like it was synched up to the pounding in his head. He looked at his watch. It was 6:50 a.m. He was on duty in ten minutes and he wasn't going to make it, Jesus, wouldn't make it if he had an hour the way he felt. His cell phone vibrated on the nightstand next to the bed. He watched it slide around in a circular motion and then stop. He was still in his clothes from the night before, lying on the bedspread. His cell phone vibrated again, telling him he had another message. He knew who it was and what it was about.

He tried to piece things together. Remembered being at the bar with Sturza. They were going to have a couple, but only a couple because they were both on duty the next morning, early. He remembered talking to a dark-haired girl sitting next to him, already on his third Dewar's and water when Sturza got up and said he was hitting it, and Ray better do the same. They had to be ready to go in seven hours.

The girl was from Indianapolis and said she was in New York for a dental convention. She was attractive in an ethnic way, and reminded him of Sharon when she was younger, dark shoulder-length hair, bangs, brown eyes and a nice body, what he could see of it.

Ray said, "Are you a dentist?"

The girl turned to her two friends who were sitting next to her at the bar.

"He wants to know if I'm a dentist," she said.

All three of them laughed like it was some inside joke.

The girl said, "I'm a sales consultant. I sell dental equipment, we all do."

Ray said, "Like what?"

'Like titanium implants, disposable fluoride trays and x-ray mounts." She perked up now. Talking about her job seemed to excite her, energize her.

"What about dental floss?" he said, having fun with her.

"That, too."

"Sounds exciting," Ray said.

"You think that sounds exciting, huh? What do you do?"

"I'm a federal agent," he said. The Dewar's loosening him up, relaxing him, making him feel good.

She gave him a skeptical look. "Yeah, right?"

Ray sipped his drink.

"If it's true, you must have a badge or something, right?"

Ray took out his ID and showed it to her, the five-pointed star that stood for duty, loyalty, justice, honesty and courage.

She turned to the other sales consultants and said, "Oh-my-god, he's in the Secret Service."

A few drinks later he remembered going upstairs with her, making out in the elevator, going to his room, she was sharing a room with Terry, one of the girls at the bar. She told him she'd never made it with a Secret Service agent. Can I see your gun? She pulled out a joint and said, want to get high? You're not going to arrest me, are you?

They smoked the joint and had another drink and he remembered the girl taking off her clothes, hugging him, great body, big breasts and olive skin.

She said, "I've been a bad girl, you better put the cuffs on me."

She held her hands out in front of her. Ray took the handcuffs out of the suit coat pocket and clamped them on her wrists. She gave him a naughty look and Ray pictured Sharon in the room at that particular moment, and it distracted him, Sharon his wife who he hadn't seen in six weeks, and felt guilty. He remembered the girl getting angry, telling him he was a fucking Secret Service homo. He unlocked the handcuffs and she walked out of the room and slammed the door.

Ray got out of bed and went to the bathroom, still drunk, splashing cold water on his face. He looked in the mirror at bloodshot eyes. He heard a horn honk and looked out the window at midtown Manhattan twenty-five floors below. He heard a knock, and then someone pounding on the door.

"Ray, you in there?"

He crossed the room and opened it a crack, saw Sturza in a dark-blue suit, burgundy tie and white shirt, looking ready for action, and swung it open. Sturza came in, eyes moving, scanning the room, holding the bottle of Dewar's. That's right, he'd called room service, and there was a roach in the ashtray.

Sturza said, "What're you doing, trying to get canned? You know what time it is?"

He knew, but didn't care.

"Are you flaking? Jesus Christ. I'll try to cover for you, but you know Tracey."

"You know Tracey, what?" Special Agent John Tracey, his detail supervisor said, walking in the room. "Forget protocol, Pope? I've been calling you for forty-five minutes. You don't get up, check in before detail? How long have you been with the Service?"

"Longer than you," Ray said. He'd never gotten along with Tracey who was anal, a control freak, an asshole, a few of the nicer things Ray and his fellow agents said about him.

He looked at Ray, looked around the room. "Pope, if you've been drinking alcohol again, you're through."

Ray saw him staring at the bottle of Dewar's.

"Look at you," Tracey said. "You think I'm going to put you on detail in your condition? Christ, you can barely stand up. What don't you understand about not drinking when you're on call? This is a strict breach of discipline, a violation of the Service professional code of conduct. Pope, the reason you never made SAIC, you can't follow the rules."

Ray said, "If you're finished, I'm going back to bed."

Sturza flashed a grin and shook his head.

"You're the one who's finished," Tracey said. "I'll tell you one thing, you won't be on another protective assignment for the rest of your career. That I can pretty much guarantee." His pale white face was flushed red now like he was going to explode.

~

Ray was called back to Washington and dressed down by the Director of Protective Operations who told him he was in trouble, a walking time bomb.

The director said, "What were you thinking? You know what on-call means. Secret Service regulations strictly forbid the consumption of alcohol at any time during a protective assignment. Violations or slight disregard for this rule are cause for removal from the Service."

He was a big man with a folksy style, talking down to Ray in that bureaucratic voice, like Ray was an idiot.

"I have Agent Tracey's report right here. In it, he states: When you didn't check in, and didn't answer numerous phone calls, he went to your hotel room. He said he found you in an intoxicated, disheveled condition. In Agent Tracey's opinion, you were not in full possession of your mental and physical abilities. He observed a bottle of Scotch whisky in your room, and he said you smelled like you had been drinking. Further, when he questioned you about it you were belligerent and uncooperative. Agent Pope, you've demonstrated a pattern of behavior that is extremely troubling. This is your third breach of conduct. You're what the Service defines as a risk. Your bad judgment could've put the protectee and everyone in your detail in serious jeopardy. We can no longer trust you in a protective capacity. We no longer have confidence in you as a field agent, and as you know, trust and confidence are the core values upon which the Service was built."

He sounded like he was reading it out of the agency manual. He told Ray his behavior warranted dismissal, but they would make an exception and let him finish out his career in the uniform division. Ray pictured himself at the entrance to a foreign embassy, bored out of his mind, watching cars go by. He told the director "no thanks" and that was it.

Seven

McCabe opened his eyes and had no idea where he was. His head hurt where he'd been hit, a lump the size of a fifty-cent piece over his ear. The room was dark and musty. His hands were cuffed to a chain that went over the edge of the bed. He couldn't see its end point. Not yet, eyes adjusting to the light coming from a window high up on one the walls, light beaming in sharp and bright at the margins where the dark paper or cloth didn't cover it.

He heard water dripping. Heard a train, the *ticket-ticket-ticket* sound as it passed close by, shaking the beamed ceiling above him, sending dust through the cracks. He thought he was in the country outside Rome, no idea where, which direction. He pictured the farmhouses he'd seen on train trips to Florence, tile roofs and stucco walls painted colors like umber and sienna, colors he'd never seen anywhere but Italy. The houses and their outbuildings were built close to the tracks and he wondered why with all the acreage they had.

He heard a dog bark somewhere outside. Heard a car pull up, tires crunching on gravel. Heard two car doors close. And voices. He pictured the scene in Villa Borghese. They had cuffed his hands behind his back and picked him up and carried him to a van parked nearby. Borghese had streets and walking paths crisscrossing through it.

He tried to remember how long he was in the van, how

long it took to drive there, but couldn't. He was dazed, in and out of consciousness. They blindfolded him and lifted him out of the van and led him across a gravel area through a doorway into the house and down an old wooden staircase that creaked and groaned, into the cellar.

He was lying on a stained mattress on a bed with a metal frame. The room was twenty by twenty, the walls made out of brick, reminding him of the ancient brickwork in the Forum, the same simple style. There was a chair ten feet or so from the bed. He saw something moving out of the corner of his eye, a rat walking along one of the walls, long tail dragging. The rat looking over at him. What're you doing here? This cellar is mine. The rat went through a hole in the wall and disappeared.

He'd felt something crawling on him during the night and swatted it off. Probably the rat checking him out. He thought of the movie *Papillon*, Steve McQueen in solitary confinement, making friends with a bug. If McCabe was down here long enough, he might hang out with the rat, give it a name. How about Caesar? That sounded like a good Italian rat name.

He was handcuffed to a chain that snaked across the floor and looped around one of the wooden support posts that held up the house. Picking the lock or breaking the chain wasn't going to happen, so he'd have to come up with another way to escape. Behind him he could see meat hanging from ropes attached to the ceiling, cylindrical rolls of salami and the skinned carcasses of game animals.

There were shelves against the far wall. He moved as far as the chain would let him and looked at the jars of canned fruits and vegetables, McCabe starving, thinking it had been close to twenty-four hours since he'd eaten, but the chain wouldn't go far enough. There were also wine racks against a wall, filled with bottles. He couldn't reach those either.

He went back to the bed and sat with his legs over the side, feet on the floor. He thought about Angela setting him up, if that was really her name. Did this have something to do with the newspaper article that transposed his name with Chip's? The kidnappers thinking they had the son of a United States senator, a slam-dunk ransom. McCabe didn't have his wallet with him, rarely carried it unless he was traveling and needed ID. He'd left it at school so there was no way they could identify him. All they knew, he was Charles Tallenger III. Eventually they'd find out he was the wrong guy. They'd call the school and Mr Rady would check and see that Chip was in Sicily, call his cell phone and that would be that. They'd realize McCabe wasn't who they thought he was and let him go.

Hours later he heard keys rattle and a door open upstairs. Then he heard someone coming down and saw him appear, first his feet and legs and then the rest of him. It was the big guy, the nose guard from Villa Borghese, carrying a tray like he wasn't used to it, taking small steps so he wouldn't tip the wine bottle over. He still wore the blue-and-white bandana over his face like an outlaw waiter. He came over, stood in front of McCabe, fingers thick as sausages, holding the tray that had olive branches painted on it.

"*Mangia*," he said.

McCabe took the tray, staring at the plate of salami, bread and cheese, and put it on the mattress next to him. The big man picked up the wine bottle, filled a stemmed glass about halfway and handed it to McCabe. He took the wine bottle and the other glass and sat in the chair. He drank wine, lifting the bandana to bring the glass to his mouth.

McCabe folded a piece of salami in half and put it in his mouth and drank some wine while he was chewing. He ate some cheese, broke off a piece of bread and washed it down with more wine.

McCabe said, "Where are we?"

He looked at him but didn't answer, poured another glass of wine. Drank that and filled the glass again. When the wine was gone he put the bottle and glass on the brick floor. Closed his eyes, leaned back and a few minutes later he was snoring, big chest rising and falling, big body dwarfing the chair, making it look like it was designed for a little kid.

He'd been asleep for a few minutes when McCabe got up and gathered the chain, trying not to make noise. He was watching the big man's face, not paying attention, and kicked the wine bottle over, rolling on the brick floor, making a racket. McCabe picked it up and stood frozen next to him, holding his breath, expecting him to wake up and hoping he wouldn't. Now he heard a voice calling from upstairs.

"Noto . . ."

McCabe was squatting next to him, staring at the ring of keys on his belt. He heard footsteps on the stairs. Someone came partway down and stopped.

"Noto, you down there? What are you doing?"

"I tell him I have one of his students," Mazara said. He took out a pack of Marlboro reds and lit one, blowing smoke across the table.

Angela sipped cappuccino and wiped foam from her upper lip with a napkin. "What did he say?"

"'Who are you?'" Roberto said.

"You can't criticize him for that, uh?"

"I say, 'Signor Rady, it does not matter who I am, it is who I have.'"

"That's a good line," Angela said.

"He say, 'What is this about?' I say, 'It's about a kidnapping.'"

Angela said, "Is he stupid? What did he think it was?"

"He must be. He say, 'Who do you have?' I say, 'Chip Tallenger.' He say, 'How do I know you have him?' 'I tell you I do. Check around. Do you see him? No, because he is not there.'"

"What did the man say?"

"You will not believe this. He say, 'Call back in twenty minutes.'"

Angela said, "Come on, he did not."

"I say, 'Listen, I am the one give the orders. You have twenty-four hours to get this money, half a million euro. Do you understand?' He say, 'That's 650,000 dollars.'" Mazara took a long drag on the cigarette, blowing out smoke. "He say, 'What if we need more time?'"

"Did you tell him there is no more time?"

"Yes, of course."

They were sitting at a table at a *tavola calda* in Orvieto, Angela sipping cappuccino, Mazara smoking.

Angela said, "Did he understand? I do not have much confidence in this Signor Rady. Is there someone else?"

"It will be okay. Signor Rady will call the father and the

father will know what to do."

"Did you tell him Signor Tallenger's life is in danger? Does he understand what will happen if the ransom is not paid? Did you impress that upon him?"

Roberto nodded. "I made sure to tell him."

Angela said, "We better go, uh?"

"What is the hurry? He is not going anywhere."

Angela was thinking about the American. She was expecting him to be different, this student from a wealthy family, the son of a well-known American politician, a senator, an important man. The senator was profiled in *Corriere della sera* as a self-made multi-millionaire living in Greenwich, Connecticut, one of the wealthiest cities in the United States. The one she met didn't seem to fit this background – his attitude, his clothes.

Pulling the thief off the motorcycle was the first indication. That was unexpected, but made it all work. Her job was to get his attention and hope he wanted to meet her. The thieves had made it much easier. But what really surprised her was how tough he was, fighting four of them. It was lucky Mazara hit him when he did or Chip Tallenger would have gotten away for sure.

She wondered what might have happened if they had met under different circumstances. There was something about him.

McCabe unlocked the handcuffs and placed them on the floor, trying not to make any noise. The big man was asleep, snoring. He went up the stairs, stopped and listened. He turned the handle, opened the door a crack and looked down a hall into the house. He smelled onions cooking. Went through the door, moving to his left and looked into the kitchen. There was a skillet on the stovetop, the smell of pancetta and onions filling the room. There was a cigarette burning in an ashtray.

A voice said, "What are you doing in there? You are worse than a woman."

He came in the kitchen now, the stocky guy with red hair from the holding cell, picked up his cigarette, took a drag and put it down. He wore a shoulder holster over a white tank top. He moved toward the doorway and yelled, "Noto . . ." And to himself he said, "Where is he?"

McCabe crept down the hall and went out the front door and took off, running.

Angela had an odd feeling as they got in the car and called Sisto at the house. She listened and said, "Where is he?" She listened. "What do you mean you don't know? Find him." She flipped the phone closed and said, "The American has disappeared."

Mazara floored the Lancia. She watched the speedometer climbing – 80, 100, 120, 140, 160 – flying now on the two-lane country road, heading south out of Orvieto, six kilometers to the farm.

Mazara said, "He is chained to a post. How can he disappear?"

"Why are you asking me? They are your friends," Angela said.

They were a street gang when she met Mazara at the Scene, a disco in Rome, a year earlier. After she got to know him he told her he was an *'ndrina*.

Angela said, "What is that?"

Mazara said, "'Ndrangheta."

She had heard of them, the Calabrian Mafia. "What are you doing in Rome?"

Mazara said, "I was born in Calabria, but my family moved here when I was a boy."

She said, "What do you do?"

He said, "A little of everything: kidnapping, extortion, guns, drugs."

He was good-looking and fun to be with. Mazara had dropped out of the Lyceum school and formed a gang with some friends. But they were no more 'Ndrangheta than she was. All of them except for Mazara were born in villages outside Rome.

Angela dated him, but quietly. If her father found out she was seeing a Calabrian he would have disowned her or worse. She joined the gang and took a twenty per cent cut of everything she was involved in. Mazara had suggested they kidnap the American after reading the article in *Il Messaggero*, Mazara telling her he knew him. He had played basketball against him in Rebibbia. It looked like easy money.

Up ahead she could see something blocking the road. "What is that?"

"Sheep," Mazara said.

He hit the brakes hard, tires squealing, the back end of the Lancia fishtailing, coming to a stop. Sheep were crossing the road, twenty-five, thirty, at least. Mazara honked the horn, leaned on it, but the sheep just stared at them, not moving.

Angela said, "We better try something else and do it fast."

She reached down under the seat and brought out her Beretta. She raised her arm out the window, aimed at the sky and pulled the trigger. The sheep took off, scattering in all directions, clearing the road enough so they could get by. Mazara put the car in gear and floored it. They passed a truck going the other way and then a car, lettuce fields on both sides of the road. She could see the farmhouse now, and coming toward them, the figure of a man running, it looked like the American, going full speed, the blue van coming fast behind him.

McCabe could hear a truck coming behind him. Turned and saw a big diesel semi, waved his arms and it blew by him. He glanced back at the farmhouse, saw the big man and the two others come out of the house, scanning the flat fields. One of them spotted him and pointed. They ran and got in the van. A car was approaching from the opposite direction. He waved his arms and it started to slow down, a red Lancia pulling up next to him, Angela pointing a gun at him from the front passenger seat.

"Where you going?" she said.

"Back to Rome."

"What's the matter? You don't like it here?"

"Not so much."

"I think you better stay where you are, don't move."

Mazara got out from behind the wheel and came around the car toward him. The girl got out too, holding the gun on him, standing a few feet away. The blue van pulled up behind the Lancia. The big man and the two others got out and came toward him. He could see all the faces of the kidnappers now. "How much you asking for me?'

The girl said, "What difference does it make?"

"Believe me, it does," McCabe said. "I think we have a

misunderstanding. You think I'm someone I'm not."

Mazara said, "We will go back and talk about it."

McCabe said, "What's wrong with right here? This is a good place to talk."

"We can make it difficult," Mazara said. "Or we can make it easy. How do you want it, uh?"

"First, I've got to ask you something," McCabe said. "Who you think is going to pay to get me back?"

The girl said, "Your rich father."

McCabe said, "I don't have a rich father."

"Then you have a problem," the girl said.

"No," McCabe said. "I think you do."

Eight

"Signor Tallenger, we do not know who kidnap your son," Captain Arturo Ferarra said. "Most of the kidnaps, eighty per cent, are from gangs hired by the Mafia. The other twenty per cent are political, which clearly this is not. You have heard of the Cosa Nostra, the Sicilian Mafia? The Sicilians are in Rome for many years. They can be responsible. But more likely, I believe, is another organization. Do you know of the Camorra?"

"No, I don't think so," Tallenger said.

He was wearing a blue sport jacket, and a white shirt but no tie. They were in a conference room at police headquarters. The man from the university, Signor Rady, was sitting across the long table next to Signor Tallenger, perspiring as if it were his profession. The armpits of his yellow golf shirt were dark with sweat, and his face was slick with it, Signor Rady blotting his forehead with a handkerchief.

"Camorra is the Neapolitan Mafia, the Mafia of Napoli, and the surrounding area, Campania." He took his pipe and tobacco out of his shirt pocket. The pipe was a full bent Brebbia. He filled the bowl with Cyprian Latakia and lit it, blowing incense-like smoke into the air.

"That's 150 miles south of here on the Mediterranean," Signor Rady said.

Signor Tallenger ignored him.

Arturo took the pipe out of his mouth and said, "The

Camorra began after the Second World War. They smuggle weapons and cigarettes. Over the years they expand into other type of crime: drug trafficking, prostitution, kidnapping. The suburbs of Naples are ruled by the Camorra. Children sell heroin and cocaine in the streets."

Signor Rady said, "So you're saying they've moved to Rome?"

"Let him tell us," Signor Tallenger said, an angry tone in his voice.

"They have been in Rome for many years," Arturo said. "They are all over Italy and Europe. The Camorra is a possibility, but more likely, I believe, is a faction of 'Ndrangheta."

"What's that?" Signor Rady said, as if Arturo was speaking only to him.

"An-Dran-Ged-Ah," Arturo said it slowly, accentuating each part of the word.

"Never heard of it," Signor Rady said, interrupting again.

Arturo could see Signor Tallenger give him a serious look. This man Rady was very annoying. "'Ndrangheta is a criminal organization from Calabria, located in the toe of the Italian boot. More powerful even than the Sicilian Mafia, generating thirty billion euro every year. And until 1980 their principal business was kidnapping."

Signor Tallenger said, "You're telling us there are three major criminal organizations in southern Italy?"

"Four, if you include Sacra Corona Unita in Apulia."

"You say it as if you're proud," Signor Rady said.

Pride had nothing to do with it. They misunderstood him. It was complicated. Arturo was trying to give them perspective. "I tell you so you will understand the situation, what we are dealing with."

"I'd say you've got a serious problem," Signor Tallenger said, "I understand that much. What I don't see is what this has to do with my son."

It had everything to do with his son, Arturo was thinking. But if the man did not want to listen there was no point in telling him again. He remembered the son sitting in this same room the night he was arrested, his arrogance, acting as if he was better than everyone, as though he deserved special treatment after stealing a man's taxi, his livelihood. Arturo had had to walk out of the room he was so angry, walk out or he might have done something he would later regret. He puffed on the cool-smoking Latakia, blowing smoke down the table away from the Americans.

Signor Rady said, "I'd like to know what you've done to find Chip Tallenger?"

Arturo ignored him. He took the pipe out of his mouth and held the bowl in his hand. "We send the photograph of young Signor Tallenger to departments in the regions and provinces around Rome. We have alert the Raggruppamento Operativo Speciale and Gruppo di Intervento Speciale, the elite forces of the carabinieri fighting organized crime. We give the photograph to Polizia di Stato and our contacts on the street. That is what we have done."

Signor Tallenger said, "What per cent of kidnap victims make it home alive?"

Arturo knew the answer, less than fifty, but he said, "I do not recall." Nor did he tell the man most victims were found strangled or shot to death.

Signor Tallenger said, "The odds aren't very good, are they?"

Arturo took the pipe out of his mouth and shook his head.

Signor Tallenger said, "What do we do now?"

"You withdraw the money and we wait to hear from them," Arturo said. "Are you a religious man?"

Signor Tallenger glanced at Arturo, his expression giving nothing away.

"I suggest you pray to God," Arturo said. "It is in his hands now."

~

Arturo listened to the distorted voice of the kidnapper, the voice slow and deep, the conversation recorded earlier on Signor Rady's telephone.

"Signor Tallenger, are you there?"

"I'm here."

"Do you have the money?"

"I have the money. Do you have my son?"

He had been instructed to buy a white Adidas soccer bag and put the money in it.

"Yes," Signor Tallenger said, "now I want to speak to Chip."

"He is not with me," the kidnapper said, "but if you do as I say, you will speak to him tonight or sooner."

Signor Tallenger said, "How do I get the money to you?"

"You get on a bus, and I tell you where to go and what to do. Remember this – we are watching you, but you never know when or where. If we see police, say goodbye to your son. Do you understand?"

"The police aren't involved," Signor Tallenger said. "You won't see anyone."

"Now you better go," the kidnapper said. "The bus is coming in ten minutes."

Signor Tallenger told Arturo he did not want any police involvement.

"We'll do it their way," he'd said. "I don't want to take any chances."

This was high-profile. Arturo understood the concerns of the senator, but his duty was to protect this man, and engineer the safe return of his son. He did not tell him he had assigned two detectives, Grossi, a man, dressed as a tourist, with maps and a camera, and Pirlo, a woman, dressed as a nun, to go with him, the detectives standing near him but not too near at the bus stop on Via Trionfale.

Arturo and Luciano, a young detective named after the great tenor, were watching them from his car parked on the street. He looked in the rearview mirror and saw the 913 bus approaching. It passed them and stopped. He saw people get off. He saw Signor Tallenger with the heavy athletic bag, and the two detectives, get on.

The bus was pulling out, picking up speed. Arturo was following, but keeping a safe distance. There was a GPS tracking chip sewn in the bottom of the soccer bag. He could see it, a red icon on his laptop, the screen displaying a map of Rome.

The bus stopped at St Peter's Basilica. Arturo was watching Signor Tallenger emerge and walk to Piazza San Pietro. He was standing in the middle of the immense square, the white soccer bag hanging from his right shoulder, as if he was waiting for the team to arrive, the bag looking out of place on a man his age, the senator long past his playing days, glancing in different directions.

Arturo was parked behind the taxi queue at the east end of the square on Via della Conciliazione. He watched Grossi and Pirlo walking in opposite directions, disappearing behind columns in the colonnade. He glanced at Luciano next to him in the front seat and said, "How long have you been engaged?"

"Four years."

"Four years? How do you do it?"

"It's not me. It's her. I want to get married, Carmen has a career, her own apartment."

"You don't live together?"

"A few days a week." Luciano grinned. "It's not bad, I have to tell you. She has her space, I have mine."

Arturo knew he was old-fashioned, but this was crazy.

Luciano said, "It might be the new model for a modern relationship."

Arturo was going to tell Luciano he was out of his mind. If you have a disagreement, how do you work it out if you both have your own apartment? He watched Signor Tallenger take out his mobile phone and hold it up to his ear, listening and then moving, running awkwardly with the heavy bag.

Instead of proceeding east out of Piazza San Pietro toward the open street, he went south through the colonnade. Pirlo radioed him and said Signor Tallenger got in a taxi. He glanced at the map on his laptop: the red icon was moving south toward the river. Grossi and Pirlo were running to the car. They opened the doors and got in the rear seat.

"Go straight and take a right on Via Pio X," Arturo told Luciano.

They were waiting to turn when the taxi passed them, Signor Tallenger in the rear seat, clearly visible. They followed, took the bridge over the Tiber and drove along the river, giving the taxi plenty of room. Arturo was thinking he should radio backup and tell them what was happening. The taxi was going left now, slowing down and stopping at the Pantheon.

They parked on the street across from Replay, a clothing store. It was interesting to watch Signor Tallenger step out of the Fiat with the heavy bag, the weight of it pulling him to one side. The kidnappers had this rich, powerful man running around the city and he was clearly not used to this. He was standing with his back to the Pantheon, standing out among the tourists posing in front of the famous church, or was it a temple? Signor Tallenger, the only person not staring at it, smiling, pointing, admiring it. His body language saying he was waiting for something to happen.

A few minutes later Signor Tallenger reached into his jacket pocket and took out his cell phone and brought it to his ear. He listened for several seconds and then he was moving again, running, or trying to, the bag weighing him down. He crossed the square, Arturo picturing the maze of streets behind the Pantheon, narrow and congested, difficult to follow in an automobile. He sent Grossi and Pirlo after the senator. Then he radioed his backup units, explaining what was happening. He had two cars, four Gruppo di Intervento Speciale, GIS, in each. One car was standing by at Palazzo Ruspoli, the second on Via Nazionale east of the Forum.

Arturo watched the red icon wind slowly around to Via del Corso and stop, not moving for several minutes and then resuming, going faster now, heading toward the Piazza Venezia. Pirlo checked in and told him Signor Tallenger had gotten on a bus.

"What number?"

"Twenty-three."

Arturo said, "Where is it going?"

"I called transit dispatch, a man named Fortuna said Via Labicana," Pirlo said. "East of the Colosseum."

Arturo glanced at Luciano. "What is on Via Labicana?"

"I don't know."

They turned right on Via del Corso and they drove past Piazza Venezia and the Wedding Cake and the Forum, the red icon moving southeast. Arturo could see the green 23 bus a few car lengths ahead. The bus slowed and stopped when it got to the Colosseum. He saw Signor Tallenger get off and move to a taxi and get in.

The taxi drove around the Colosseum, turned right on Via Claudia and right again on a narrow street with a church straight ahead.

"What is this place?" Luciano said.

Arturo glanced at him and said, "Santi Giovanni e Paolo, a church and monastery."

The taxi stopped in the piazza in front of the church. Signor Tallenger emerged with the soccer bag over his shoulder.

"The second church," Luciano said.

"The third if you count the Pantheon. It is a church or a temple? I suppose that depends on what you believe."

"It was built as a temple and used as a Catholic church." He paused.

"Maybe the kidnappers are priests," Luciano said, his eyes smiling again.

"They're robbing tourists because the Vatican has run out of money," Arturo said, taking it to another level of absurdity.

"The Vatican has more money than the Italian government," Luciano said.

They watched Signor Tallenger enter the church and watched the taxi drive off.

"Captain, is this going to be another false alarm?"

"I wish I could tell you." All he knew was the ransom would eventually exchange hands and he hoped he would be there to arrest the kidnappers. But as they entered the church, it occurred to Arturo that yes, they had followed the senator to two other churches, but this was the first time he had actually entered one of them, so he believed this was where the exchange would take place.

Nine

They crossed the small piazza lined with palm trees in terracotta planters. Arturo glanced at the bell tower that was Romanesque, and the front of the church that was medieval. He walked between two lions guarding the entrance, dipped his fingers in the holy water font, and made the sign of the cross. The interior was narrow and not very deep from front to back, maybe fifty meters, a series of columns left and right, extending the length of the nave, forming a semi-circle where it met the altar. It was a well-preserved gem, with mustard-color walls that had a marble pattern, trimmed in dark green and brown.

He looked down the main floor for Signor Tallenger. It was dark and difficult to see. There were a few tourists moving around, but no one carrying a white soccer bag. He was looking up at the engaged columns with jutting pilasters. Words remembered from an art history class taken at the university thirty years before. It was difficult to admit it had been that long. But, it was true. Arturo was going to be fifty-one in March. Fifty-one! Remembering his father, a laborer at that age, used up and on the decline, his life almost over.

He moved along the transept to the right, glancing through the columns, trying to find Signor Tallenger. Luciano went to the left and they would meet near the main altar.

Arturo had gone almost as far as the altar before he saw him, the man standing in the shadow of a column as Arturo came up behind him, the shape of the soccer bag unmistakable. Signor Tallenger seemed to be waiting for a tourist group that was huddled together, looking up at the ceiling of the nave. When they finally moved away, continuing their tour, Signor Tallenger approached the altar and placed the white bag somewhere on the floor next to it, and walked down the main aisle toward the front of the church.

Arturo looked up over the altar at the shafts of light angling in from the clerestory windows, and he had a feeling that something was wrong. That the money had already exchanged hands. In his mind, he saw Tallenger meeting a kidnapper on the 23 bus and discreetly transferring the money into another identical bag. The notion actually seeming intelligent and likely to be true.

Arturo stood inside the transept, using a column for cover. He saw a monk appear behind the altar, hands in prayer, genuflecting before the crucifix. He had seen monks in their simple brown tunics outside the church and knew there was a monastery next door. The monk made the sign of the cross. He lighted candles on the altar, a dozen of them, taking his time. He did not seem to notice the soccer bag that was clearly out of place in the house of God.

The monk lighted a few more candles and came back to the altar. Now he seemed to focus on the soccer bag, bending his legs, genuflecting, and disappearing from view. Arturo hesitated for a minute, thinking the monk was still on his knees, praying, but then he saw him reappear with the bag, moving behind the altar. The monk moved to the rear wall and disappeared again. Arturo radioed Luciano, "Did you see him, the monk? Let's go."

They were sitting outside at a café in Campo di Fiori, the market bustling with activity, women hassling vendors over the price of parsley and basil and tomatoes, everyone wanting a bargain.

"You don't look like a priest," Angela said, looking at his hair pulled back in a rakish ponytail. "Priests don't have hair like that. You'll call too much attention to yourself. We should have Sisto do it. He looks desperate enough."

Mazara said, "You think priests look desperate?" He drank espresso, thinking he needed some extra energy for what he was about to do.

"The ones who know they do not have the calling," Angela said.

Mazara said, "How do you know about priests?" He lighted a cigarette.

"I have a cousin who was ordained and lives there at the monastery," Angela said. "He tells me what they talk about." She picked up her cup, sipped cappuccino.

"I will use the hood," Mazara said. "Do you feel better now?" He brought the cigarette to his mouth, inhaled and blew out the smoke. "Did your cousin tell you how to get into the monastery?"

"I used to visit him," Angela said. "He is a Passionist."

"What is that?"

"A Catholic religious order founded by St Paul of the Cross. Its real name is the Congregation of Discalced Clerks of the Most Holy Cross and Passion of Our Lord Jesus Christ."

Mazara gave her a broad smile. "Did you make this up?"

"No," Angela said. "It happens to be true. Only they are not a full order, but a congregation. Founded to teach people how to pray. I think you could use some help in that area."

"What is there to teach? You want to pray, you pray."

"What do you know about it?"

"Praying? Not very much any more," Mazara said.

Angela lit a cigarette.

"You said women are allowed in the monastery?"

"If you are related," Angela said.

"Or if you are a prostitute," Mazara said.

"Why are you so negative about priests?" She pulled her sunglasses down and looked at him.

"You would understand if one tried to molest you."

Angela said, "This really happened?"

"The priest from our village invited me to his office in the rectory," Mazara said. "It was a great honor. He told me to sit on his lap and I felt something hard poking into me. He said, 'Do you know what that is?'"

Angela said, "How old were you?"

"Eleven," Mazara said. "Old enough to know better."

"What did you say?"

He gave her a questioning look. "What do you think?"

Angela said, "What did the priest say?"

"It was the staff of God, and he wanted me to hold it."

"What did you do?"

"I ran," Mazara said.

"I'm sure it was shocking," Angela said, "but I have to ask you – can you do this? Because if you are not sure, I will dress like a nun and pick up the money."

He said, "I like to see that. You would be a sexy nun."

She said, "Let's go over it again."

"You sound like your father. You have to be in control."

She had to be careful what she said or he felt threatened. "I'm being cautious," Angela said. "Are you sure you know what to do?"

He gave her a hard look. "That's enough."

She dropped him off on Clivo di Scauro, and he walked up the hill to the monastery next to the church. He felt like a fool wearing the coarse brown robe with the hood pulled over his head and a rope belt – like he was going to a costume party. The robe was made out of wool and it was hot and itched.

They had discussed the plan a dozen times. He would enter the monastery and walk through to the rectory and enter the church from the altar side. Angela told him if he saw anyone to press his hands together in prayer, close his eyes and pretend he was praying. She also told him some monks took the vow of silence. At that moment he wished she had taken a vow of silence – just close her mouth, stop talking and let him do it.

He walked through to the sacristy, entering the church behind the main altar. He turned and genuflected, making the sign of the cross the way he had been taught as a schoolboy – so long ago he barely remembered the words to the prayers and the ritual of the mass.

He looked down the main aisle into the darkness of the church, past the chairs set up for evening service. He expected to see a brigade of carabinieri, but instead he saw tourists scattered around the front of church, staring up at the ceiling the way he once had, studying the murals depicting the lives of apostles and saints, what else? He approached the altar from behind. The soccer bag was on the tile floor where Signor Tallenger had placed it. He pretended not to notice, taking care of his pre-mass duties, lighting candles and trying to stay calm, relaxed.

Now he pressed his hands together in prayer, picked up the bag and moved to the back wall of the nave. There was a door. He opened it and walked down a staircase leading to the passages under the church. It was cool and dark. He turned on the flashlight and saw ancient rooms of the house of worship the church was built on.

Mazara put the bag down and pulled the robe over his head, happy to remove it, the coarse fabric itching him like crazy. Above him he heard voices and the sound of footsteps coming down the stairs. He picked up the bag, fit the strap over his shoulder and started running down a narrow passageway that was cut through the soft tufa rock. He imagined the graves of martyrs filling the walls. It was cool and smelled like the woods on a wet day, like soil, the air musty and heavy, difficult to breathe. He heard voices behind him but he did not stop to look.

Arturo and Luciano followed the monk down the stairs into the darkness under the church, Arturo using his silver Zippo for illumination. He felt foolish. What was he going to do – chase the kidnapper through the *scavi* with a lighter? He stepped on something and almost tripped. He held the lighter down and saw the monk's robe on the brick floor. He tried to radio his backup units, but could not make contact through the thick stone foundation of the church.

He went back up and moved through the church, running outside. There was an old man sweeping debris near the entrance to the church. Arturo identified himself and asked if the man knew where the tunnels under the church led.

The man pointed at a green gate that resembled a stable door.

"Come this way, I will show you."

Arturo and Luciano followed him. The man unlocked the gate to reveal ancient ruins, large Roman-style arches that wrapped around the ceiling and extended down fifteen feet under the foundation of the church. There were underground columns, and two bricked passageways that appeared to continue for some distance. There were also crushed pieces of statues against the underground wall. The scene reminded Arturo of an architectural dig. He fixed his attention on the man and said, "How far do the tunnels go?"

"Two hundred meters," the man said.

"Two hundred meters?" Arturo scratched his head. "What is on the other side?" he said, pointing in the direction of the Colosseum.

The man said. "Ruins, I think, but I do not know for sure."

Arturo thanked him and ran to the car for his laptop, breathing hard as he sat in the front passenger seat. Luciano was standing at the edge of the square talking to Signor Tallenger. He opened the laptop and put his cursor on the map and clicked. The red icon did not appear. He clicked again and nothing happened, and it occurred to him that GPS probably could not pick up the sensor underground. The kidnappers, who Arturo assumed were a ragtag "'Ndrangheta gang, had surprised him. They were more organized and better prepared than he had imagined. It was almost as if they knew where the police were, and knew a sensor was in the bag.

Luciano opened the door and sat in the front passenger seat. "Where is Signor Tallenger?"

"I told him to go back to his hotel and we would contact him when it was over." He paused. "Do you see the kidnapper?'

Arturo was going to tell him, no. But he glanced down at his computer screen and saw the red icon appear, moving toward the Colosseum. Then they were too, Luciano taking charge, speeding down Clivo di Scauro under the five arches that had once been part of an aqueduct that brought water to the ancient Romans. He turned right on Viale del Parco del Celio, the Colosseum looming in front of them now. Arturo glanced over his shoulder and saw the backup units with heavily armed GIS behind them. The red icon stopped. Arturo's eyes were fixed on the computer screen. Then it was moving again, and moving fast along Foro Romano.

Siesta was over, traffic was heavy. Arturo called headquarters for patrol units, giving their co-ordinates, and then felt foolish when the dispatcher asked the make and color of the vehicle they were chasing, and Arturo realized it would be difficult to find them in the city.

Ten minutes later they were following the red icon on the autostrada heading for Fiumicino, the airport. The thief was probably catching a plane, leaving the country. But then the icon turned, going north now toward Civitavecchia. Luciano was passing cars, and they came up behind a stake truck. The icon was flashing. Arturo radioed the backup units. He told one unit to get ahead of the truck and slow it down. He told the other to position itself in the lane to the left of the truck and they would have it surrounded on three sides. The only escape was going off-road into a field.

When the backup units were in position, Luciano turned on the flashers and siren. The truck pulled over on the side of the road. Eight GIS surrounding the truck, aiming HK MP5 machine guns at the driver, an old man with dark wrinkled skin.

Arturo saw cars slowing down, people curious, wondering what was happening – all the police – all this firepower. He found the white soccer bag in a wooden crate in the open bed of the truck, the inside of the crate stained red from the fruit it had carried. He reached in and brought the bag out. It was empty. Luciano told the old man to get out of the truck and he did and started to run. Eight guns pointed at him and he tried to get away. Luciano caught him and the GIS teams came closer, aiming their automatic weapons, forming a tight circle around him. Arturo held up the soccer bag. "Is this yours?" he said.

The old man shook his head. "I have not seen it before."

Arturo believed him. The man was afraid. Who wouldn't be? All these guns aimed at him as if he were a wanted criminal, a fugitive. He thought they were overdoing it a little, and told the men to lower their weapons and disperse. He did not consider this bent, wrinkled old prune much of a threat. Arturo said, "Where are you coming from?"

"Campo di Fiori, the market," the old man said. "I am a farmer. I grow vegetables and fruit."

He had the hands of a laborer, fingers permanently stained from the soil, fingernails caked with dirt. Arturo said, "Why did you try to get away?"

"I have no driving license," the man said.

"You lost it?"

"Never had it."

"How long have you been driving?"

"Since I was thirteen years old."

Arturo took out his pipe and tobacco and filled the bowl and lighted it, blowing out smoke that had a spicy aroma. "You can go," he said to the old man.

Luciano said, "Captain, can I talk to you?"

They stepped a few feet away from the truck.

Luciano said, "You are not going to bring him in?"

Arturo said, "For what reason?"

Luciano said, "Maybe he knows something."

Arturo said, "Did you look at him?"

The old man drove away. Arturo and Luciano went to their car and got in.

Arturo could now see how the kidnappers were able to escape. He imagined the monk emerging from the tunnel, walking down to Viale del Parco del Celio where an automobile picked him up. They emptied the money and threw the soccer bag on the truck. The only question: if the farmer was at Campo di Fiore, where did the kidnappers cross paths with the truck? It had to be on Corso Vittorio Emanuel as the farmer was leaving the market. He could see the truck stopped at a traffic light and one of the kidnappers throwing the soccer bag on the back of it.

Luciano said, "Captain, what do we do now?"

"Hope they release the American, and hope he saw something, or knows something." Arturo said, although based on statistics, the odds were not good.

It was dark. The streets of Rome were deserted. She heard the *bang*. It sounded like a pistol firing. Psuz came around the side of the van with the Beretta in his hand. She saw the American lying on the sidewalk, Victor Emmanuel rising up behind him. She put the Lancia in gear and pulled away from the curb, sorry for him, but relieved it was over.

Ten

Ray expected to see Sharon sitting at the kitchen table when he came in, watching Oprah on the small TV on the counter, or reading the *Free Press*. He rolled his suitcase across the wood floor through the dining room, down a hallway into their bedroom. She wasn't in there either. He bet she was at Costco or getting her hair done. She had to have her hair colored more often to get rid of the dark roots after going blonde. He didn't know why she did it. What would possess a woman to change her natural hair color at age thirty-eight? He wasn't sure if he liked it or not. He'd only seen it once. Now he'd have a chance to get used to it, that and a lot of other things.

He went to the kitchen and got a beer and went back to the bedroom and put his clothes away, hung up his suits, put trees in his black dress shoes, threw his dirty clothes in the laundry hamper. Ray had his own closet and Sharon had hers. His was neat and orderly like his life with the Service, and hers was a mess.

He carried his empty suitcase through the living room. He was going to take it upstairs to the attic. They lived in a bungalow in Beverly Hills. He stopped and put the suitcase on the floor in the front hall. There was a pile of mail, days' worth on the carpet, shoved through the slot in the door by the mailman. He got on his knees and scooped up the envelopes and magazines and took them into the kitchen.

He sat at the table shuffling through the mail. There were bills from US Bank Visa, DTE Energy, Honda, Verizon Wireless, Green Trees Lawn Care and half a dozen more including a letter from Pat, Sharon's sister in New Jersey. He checked the postmark on each envelope, a couple of them going back to October 5th, three days earlier.

Ray was trying to remember the last time he talked to Sharon and thought it was October 1st, a few days before he was dismissed from the Service. He was going to call and tell Sharon but decided to just show up and surprise her.

He went through her magazines: *People*, *Rolling Stone*, *Vibe*, *Scene* and *Murder Dog*. Sharon told him she had to read them to stay current with the music scene.

He said, "*Murder Dog*?"

She said, "Where else are you going to learn about Snap and Crunk and Hyphy?"

He said, "What the hell're you talking about." The words sounding like what you heard when you ate cereal.

She said, "Current trends in music, dawg. It's time to broaden your musical horizons. Take a break from the old stuff."

She was talking about what he liked, Marshall Tucker and Hank Williams Junior and Neil Young. She said, "How'd a guy from Motown get turned on by country in the first place."

He thought of it as rock not country.

She said, "You want to get contemporary? Check out the Ying Yang Twinz and Soulja Boy." She said it serious and then broke into a big grin.

He said, "Yeah, fix me up, then who knows, I may sign up for breakdancing lessons."

"You're about twenty years too late."

Ray glanced at the answering machine and saw the orange message light blinking. He hadn't noticed it before. He got up and looked. There were eleven messages. He pushed the play button and listened to all of them, checking the date and time of each call.

DeAnn, Sharon's boss, said, "When are you planning to come back? I have to tell our clients something."

Lisa from Dr Lambrecht's office was confirming an appointment. Barry from Balboa Capital had to talk to Ray immediately about a home-run stock opportunity.

Pat, Sharon's sister, said, "You're being very mysterious. Is this a vacation? Is Ray going with you?"

The next one was from Sharon's mother, Annette. "I got your email. Where are you going? Is it a business trip?"

Ronni Keating from SKBK Sotheby's was wondering if they were interested in selling their house. She had a potential buyer.

A TruGreen salesman started his pitch and Ray hit the skip button.

He heard a man's voice say, "Hey, babe, you there? Call me."

Ray didn't recognize the voice. He played it back and wrote down the number, a 586 area code, which meant it came from somewhere on the east side.

According to the dates on the answering machine, Sharon hadn't checked the messages for three days. And that was unusual, she'd get up from the dinner table when the phone rang just to see if she was missing an important call.

Ray tried Sharon's cell number. It went right to voice mail: "This is Sharon, please leave a message and I'll get back to you as soon as I can."

He went into the bedroom and looked around. The bed

was made, six pillows, two rows of three lined up across the headboard. Her reading glasses were on the table on her side of the bed. He checked her closet, scanned her clothes, shoes and purses. The shelves were full. Nothing seemed to be missing. Not that he could tell with any certainty if anything was. He went in the bathroom and saw her toothbrush on the counter in a ceramic cup, makeup brushes next to it in a clay bowl. No woman would leave town without her makeup. He knew that much.

He went out to the garage and opened the side door and looked in. Her car, a silver Honda Accord, was gone. He went back in the kitchen, opened the Verizon bill, checking the list of phone numbers. Thirty calls, he counted them, were to a number with a 586 area code in Harrison Township. It was different than the one he'd copied from the answering machine.

He called Jim Teegarden, an old friend who was still with the Service, the Office of Protective Research, OPR, in downtown Detroit. Teeg and his colleagues gathered intelligence about individuals or groups who might pose a threat to the president, vice president or any other high-level protectee. Their paths had crossed on a number of occasions over the years when Ray was on protective detail.

Teeg was a devout Catholic, and one night over drinks he told Ray his surname was sacrilegious. There's only one Pope and he's in Rome. I think you should change your name to Cardinal or Bishop. He said it with such conviction Ray thought he was serious until Teeg started laughing.

Ray said, "You Catholics sure have a wicked sense of humor, don't you?"

~

"I'm sorry to hear about what happened," Teegarden said.

Ray said, "Don't be. It's a blessing in disguise. I'd had enough."

"Why didn't you stay on, take a job with uniform?"

"Wear one of those fancy outfits, and guard a foreign embassy, you think that sounds like me?"

"You always did have an interesting way of looking at things," Teegarden said. "What's Sharon think, having you home all the time now?"

"Are you kidding? She loves it," Ray said. "Hey, I'm hoping you can help me out with something. Some guy's been calling Sharon, stalking her. I've got the phone number but I need the name and address."

"Why don't you call the police?"

"You know how it works," Ray said. "They won't do anything till a crime's been committed. I'd rather not wait that long."

"All right. What's the number?"

Ray said, "There are two."

Eleven

Kathy Keating, a cute blonde from Chicago he barely knew, said, "Are you all right?" Looking concerned. Like he had inoperable cancer. She was standing at the front desk, talking to Canzio. He was sitting in a chair behind the desk in the school lobby. Canzio was about five six, a Roman with a Caesar haircut and long sideburns, Chip thought he looked like an extra in a spaghetti western.

"We're so glad you're safe," said Beth, a pale dark-haired goth from Boston he'd seen around the BU campus. She was shuffling through her mail.

Chip glanced at Brianna. "What's going on?"

Brianna shrugged and shook her head. Trish walked through the lobby and didn't say anything to anyone, still angry McCabe didn't go with them.

"Dude, what's good?" said Cody Gorman, a six-foot-four surfer from Huntington Beach, California. "Where you been?"

"Messina," Chip said.

"Bitchin'," Cody said. "Catch any sick waves, or was it mush?"

"Mushburger, dude," Chip said, using one of the five words of surfer slang Cody had taught him.

Canzio stood up and said, "Signor Chip, I am so glad to see you. Are you all right? I must notify Signor Rady at once."

He picked up the phone, punched in a number.

"Signor Tallenger has return." He listened. "Young Signor Tallenger. *Si*, just now."

He hung up the phone, glanced up at Chip.

"Signor Rady say to tell you he will be right here."

"For what?" Chip said. What was going on?

Canzio said, "To see you. Are you hurt?"

"Why would I be hurt?" It was really getting crazy.

Canzio said, "Do you need medical attention?"

"No, I need my mail."

Canzio said, "Yes, of course." He turned and took three envelopes out of Chip's mail slot and handed them to him.

Frank Rady appeared now, entering the lobby, walking fast, coming toward him.

"I called your father. He's on his way. We never gave up hope."

"We went to Messina," Chip said. "Spent the weekend on the beach."

His dad, Mr Rady and the Rome cop, Captain Ferrara, all had their eyes glued to him, staring with somber expressions. They were sitting at a small round table in Rady's office, and Chip felt claustrophobic. He moved his chair back to give himself more room.

Rady said, "Why didn't you sign out? You know it's mandatory, school policy."

He was trying to deflect any blame, cover his ass.

"I did," Chip said.

"What're you talking about?" his dad said. He was wearing a crisp white dress shirt with his initials, CET, Charles Erickson Tallenger, on the right cuff, as always. Erickson was Chip's grandmother's maiden name.

"When students leave campus for an extended period of time – weekends included – they're supposed to fill out a form and give it to whoever's at the front desk," Frank Rady said. "So we know where our students are going, where they're at."

"I gave it to Franco," Chip said. "Thursday through Sunday – Messina, Sicily."

"We have no record of it," Rady said.

There was no record because Chip forgot to do it. His word against Franco's. Who were they going to believe?

"We tried your cell phone," his dad said.

"I misplaced it," Chip said.

"You misplaced it, or lost it? What's that, the third one this year?"

There was his dad on his case, giving him a hard time as usual. He decided not to tell him he dove off a cliff into the Mediterranean and the phone was in his pocket and he didn't realize it. That would've sounded even dumber.

Now Captain Ferrara, who hadn't spoken, said, "If they did not kidnap young Signor Tallenger, who do they have?" He stared at Chip when he said it.

"I don't know," Chip said.

"Maybe they didn't kidnap anyone," his dad said. "They tell us they've got Chip and we don't know where he is, can't reach him so we believe it."

'I was just thinking," Chip said. "It could be McCabe."

His dad looked at him now, waiting for an explanation.

"He was supposed to go with us," Chip said, "and never showed."

"Find out if McCabe's here," his dad said to Rady. "That shouldn't be too difficult, should it?"

Rady got up and walked out the room.

"What do you think?" his dad said to Captain Ferrara.

"They have someone. They are not bluffing. But if the school did not know your son's travel plan, how would the kidnappers?"

Fifteen minutes later Frank Rady came back in the room and said McCabe had missed his Italian class Thursday evening. He hadn't checked out and hadn't picked up his mail since Wednesday. No one working the front desk could remember seeing him for a few days.

It wasn't conclusive, but it didn't look good, either.

"Captain, what do you suggest we do?"

"There is nothing we can do. We wait and see."

Twelve

McCabe thought they were going to kill him. He had seen all their faces, could identify them. Why take a chance? But if that was their intention, they'd have done it at the farmhouse, out in the country where no one was around.

He was in the back of the blue van, blindfolded, hands cuffed behind his back, sitting on the metal floor against the side wall, trying to keep his balance. There were two of them in front, talking about what they were going to do with their share of the money. McCabe recognized the big man's voice, the big man saying he was going to buy a car, a Toyota.

The one he was talking to said, "How are you going to fit in it?"

The big man said, "*Vaffanculo.*"

McCabe was trying to figure out how long they'd been on the road – thirty, forty minutes – when the van slowed down and stopped. He heard the rear doors open and he was lifted out and dropped on concrete. The van doors closed. The handcuffs were unlocked and removed. He heard a pistol shot, body tightening, bracing for impact, and realized it was the van backfiring as it drove off. He untied the blindfold. He was lying on the sidewalk in front of Victor Emmanuel.

It was dark and quiet, the streets deserted. McCabe didn't have any money for a bus or a taxi, or even a phone call, so he walked through the city and up Monte Mario, one of the seven hills, to Loyola, had to be six miles.

He went in the lobby expecting to see Franco behind the front desk, but no one was there. He went upstairs to the second floor and down to 217, the room he shared with Chip. It was 4:05 a.m., Monday morning. He sat on his bed, too tired to take his clothes off, and laid back, head on the pillow, body aching and let out a breath. The side of his face was swollen where the big man had hit him, paying him back, but he felt lucky, fortunate to be there. He still couldn't figure out why they let him go. But he wasn't complaining.

Chip was in his bed ten feet across the room from him. Chip sat up, leaned over and turned on his desk light.

McCabe said, "Turn that goddamn thing off."

Chip got up and crossed the room, standing over him in his underwear.

"What'd they do to you, Spartacus?"

McCabe said, "What's it look like?"

"You got your ass kicked," Chip said.

"That sounds about right," McCabe said.

"They thought you were me, didn't they?"

Chip moved back and sat on his bed, legs over the side, feet on the floor.

McCabe said, "How much was the ransom?"

"Half a million euros."

"Who paid it?"

"The senator."

McCabe closed his eyes. That was the last thing he heard him say.

~

The next morning there was a note on the floor, pushed under the door, telling McCabe to contact Mr Frank Rady immediately. He took a shower and went to Rady's office. The door was open. Rady was sitting at his desk and looked up when he walked in.

"What I don't understand, McCabe, is why you didn't come and see me when you got back."

He couldn't win with this guy. He'd been kidnapped and beat up and Frank Rady acted like it was his fault. "It was the middle of the night. I was tired. There was nothing you could've done till morning."

"That's up to me," Rady said. "Not you. How'd you get past the front desk without Franco seeing you?"

"He wasn't there. What difference does it make?"

"You let me worry about that," Rady said, staring at him. "Looks like you pissed off the wrong people." He seemed pleased all of a sudden, flashed a grin. "Somebody tagged you good, huh?"

McCabe didn't say anything.

"Change your clothes, put on a nice shirt. We're going to go downtown, talk to Captain Ferrara with the carabinieri. I think you know him."

McCabe looked around the room. It was the same one he and Chip had been taken to the night they were arrested. He remembered the light-green walls, and the clock that made time creep by, and the line gouged in the tabletop that looked like it was made by a key or a belt buckle. McCabe could relate. Being in this room put you on edge.

"Tell me what happen," Captain Ferrara said, taking the pipe out of his mouth.

McCabe liked the sweet smell of the tobacco. The captain sat next to Frank Rady, across the long table from him. "I was walking through Villa Borghese and four guys jumped me."

Captain Ferrara said, "You were alone?"

"Yes," McCabe said.

Ferrara said, "What were you doing in Villa Borghese?"

"Looking at the Bernini sculpture in the gallery." McCabe paused. "And four guys came through the trees and took me down."

"When this was happening," Captain Ferrara said, "what were you thinking? Why did they come after you?"

McCabe said, "I had no idea at the time. But later, I figured they'd seen the article in the newspaper and thought I was Chip."

Captain Ferrara said, "What did they say to you?"

"Nothing. They kept me chained in the cellar of a farmhouse somewhere outside Rome."

"And you told them you are not Chip Tallenger," Ferrara said.

"I did."

"Why not prove it, show them your ID," Rady said.

McCabe said, "I left my wallet at school."

"Nice going," Rady said. "That wasn't very smart, was it?"

"It wouldn't have mattered," McCabe said. "They were going to demand the ransom no matter who they had."

"You can identify the kidnappers?" Ferrara said.

"They wore bandanas over their faces," McCabe said, "like western bandits, and I was blindfolded part of the time, but I saw two of them. They thought I was sleeping and came down to the cellar to check on me."

Frank Rady, with his big white freckled arms on the table, said, "Were they Eye-talian?"

McCabe frowned. "Yeah, they were Italian." What did he think they were?

"Don't get smart, McCabe," he said. "We're trying to help you here."

Captain Ferrara opened the laptop that was on the table in front of him. It was a Dell.

"You look at this," he said. "I believe you will see the ones who kidnap you."

He turned the laptop screen toward McCabe and slid it over to him.

Rady said, "Who's he looking at?"

"The criminals, the known offenders," Ferrara said. "Many are in a gang. They work for the Camorra, 'Ndrangheta, or the Sicilian Mafia."

McCabe studied the first screen, three rows of headshots.

"If you recognize one of them," the captain said, "click on the image to make it larger, fill the screen."

McCabe went through half a dozen screens, scanning rows of faces and saw the big guy, no mistake about it, same heavy beard, thick neck and double chin. He clicked on his face, Luigi Bagnasco, it said under the photo. McCabe remembered them calling him Noto. He clicked through ten more faces and saw the stocky guy with red hair, Sisto Bardi, remembering him from the newspaper article, one of the men who had escaped. He kept going and hit the jackpot, saw Mazara. He put the cursor on him and clicked, his face looking younger, thinner, filling the screen. Roberto Mazara.

It was interesting to think about the name fitting him. Yeah, he could see it: Bob Mazara, trying it out. Captain Ferrara studying his face as he studied the computer screen.

"You recognize one of them?" the captain said.

McCabe shook his head. "I don't think so."

"You are sure?" the captain said.

"Yeah," McCabe said.

He scanned through the rest of the faces, stopping on the last one. "That's it," McCabe said. "I don't see any of them, but this guy reminds me of De Niro in *Goodfellas*." He turned the screen toward Captain Ferrara and slid the laptop over to him.

"*Quei bravi ragazzi*," Ferrara said.

McCabe said, "That's the translation for *Goodfellas*, huh? You like him?"

"*Raging Bull*, *Taxi Driver*, *la sfida*, I see them all."

McCabe said, "What's *la sfida*?"

"*Hot*, I think it is called."

"You mean *Heat*," McCabe said.

"Yes, *Heat*. I love the cinema."

"If he doesn't see them here," Rady said to the captain, "who do you think they are?"

"It is difficult to say. They could be a new gang we do not know," Captain Ferrara said. "Unfortunately, Signor Rady, there is nothing more we can do until they spend the money. We record the serial numbers of the euro notes."

~

McCabe watched a pigeon circle around the Fountain of the Four Rivers, land on the obelisk and fly off. A waiter approached the table with a tray of drinks. He said, "*Due birre, uno cappuccino,*" and put stemmed glasses of Moretti in front of McCabe and Chip and the cappuccino in front of Senator Tallenger. He said, "*Va bene,*" and walked away. They were at a café in Piazza Navona.

Senator Tallenger said, "McCabe, I know you're angry, but do me a favor, will you? Let it go. There's nothing you can do."

"You're lucky to be here," Chip said.

"He's right," the senator said. "I looked into it, found out more than half of the kidnap victims never make it home. They find them shot to death or strangled." He paused. "McCabe, am I getting through to you?"

Yeah, he heard him. But he was thinking of a way to get the money back. To do it he had to find the girl.

Thirteen

Mazara was thinking about the last time he came here. Don Gennaro was studying a painting on one of the walls in his office, a room that had to be twenty meters one way and thirty the other way. The don turned and looked at him and said, "Do you know what this is?"

It did not seem complicated. It was a painting so that is what Mazara said, and the don looked at him like he was a moron.

"Do you know Bronzino?"

The man made him nervous. Who was this Bronzino? The name was vaguely familiar. "I think he played goalie for Lombardy. Is that right?"

Don Gennaro said, "He was the court painter for Cosimo de Medici."

Mazara said, "Who?" He stared at the painting on the wall, naked people running around. It looked like a fun party. "What are they doing?" It looked like an orgy.

"It is an allegory," Don Gennaro said. "Do you understand?"

Mazara had no idea what he was talking about and decided not to say anything else.

Don Gennaro said to Mauro, "Give him the money and get him out of here."

That time the don had hired him to steal a painting from a villa near Florence. The don saying the owner had stolen it from the Uffizi. The Uffizi? Did he mean the museum?

This time the don was having lunch on the veranda with someone he had never seen before. They were drinking wine and talking. He could see the bodyguards at the edge of the olive grove. They were alert, but keeping their distance, the grove extending behind them as far as he could see. The bodyguards wore berets and had shotguns on straps slung over their shoulders like Sicilian peasants.

Mauro, the don's secondo, had met him at the front door, searched him for weapons, and looked in the paper bag he was carrying that contained money, the don's share of the ransom. Mauro was a weird, quiet Sicilian, wiry, with dark skin, almost as dark as a Tunisian. Mazara had been escorted out to the veranda that was made of stone and built on two levels, wrapping around the back of the villa. There was a swimming pool at one end. There was a wicker couch and chairs and a low table with a glass top in the middle of the veranda and a long table at the far end under a wrought-iron pergola that was covered with vines. He admired the house and the grounds, thinking, this son of a peasant, who did not finish his fifth year of school, had done well for himself. Roberto stood only five feet from the man's table now, Don Gennaro ignoring him, making him stand there like a servant. They were eating roast chicken and fried potatoes, washing it down with a chilled bottle of Terre di Tufi. He recognized the tiny label. Seeing the food was making him hungry. When he finished here Mazara would drive back to Rome, pick up Angela and celebrate.

The don finally looked up at him and said, "Why are you here, interrupting my lunch?"

"I bring your share of the money," Roberto said. "The ransom."

The don said, "Oh, the ransom."

Of course, the ransom, what did he think it was?

The don said, "Do I have to count it?"

Roberto said, "If you prefer."

"No," the don said. "Do I have to count it?"

The man sitting at the table next to the don said, "Unk, want me to count it?" He was American.

The don ignored him, staring at Roberto, and Roberto froze. He did not know what to say, the don was keeping him off balance, making him nervous. What was this about?

The don picked up his glass and sipped the white. He leveled his gaze on Mazara and said, "Is it all there?"

"Yes, of course." He could feel beads of sweat sliding down his face. He raised his arm and wiped his forehead with his shirt sleeve.

The don said, "Are you sure?"

Mazara's mouth was dry. He wished he had a glass of cold white wine. "Yes, I am sure." The man was acting strange.

The don handed the bag of money to Mauro and Mauro went back into the villa. He told him to wait, to go sit until he finished his lunch and Mauro had counted the money.

He walked over and sat on the stone wall that separated the upper and lower levels of the veranda, sun beating down on him. He did not expect to be treated this way. He thought the don would accept the money and thank him. He watched a woman in a bikini rise from the lounge chair where she was laying in the sun, move to the pool, and dip her toe in the water. She had long dark hair and a beautiful body. If you had the don's money you would have a girl like her around to look at, maybe several.

Mazara watched her step down into the shallow end of the pool and disappear. It was hot for October and the water looked cool and refreshing, better now with the woman in it. He wondered what the don would say if he stood up and jumped in. That was what he wanted to do. Take off his clothes and swim under water, looking at the girl.

Mazara sat on the wall, and fifteen minutes later Mauro came out of the villa with the paper bag. Why did it take so long to count €60,000? He handed it to the don, whispering something to him and the don saying something back.

Now Mauro called to him. He got up and walked back to the table. They were finished with their meal, Mazara looking at chicken bones on their plates.

Don Gennaro said, "What is this?"

Mazara was confused. "Your share."

"I don't think so," he said. His face was serious as always.

Mazara was nervous. "I do not understand."

The don stared at him.

"It is from the money we collected." He could feel his stomach churning, all of them watching him.

"Why do you insult me?" the don said. His eyes stabbing him like daggers.

"What do you mean?" Mazara said.

"It is not enough," the don said.

"It is what we agreed – thirty per cent." Mazara resented that he had to pay this Sicilian anything at all and refused to give him the full amount.

The don said, "Of what?"

"The money." Roberto could feel sweat running down his face.

"Either you don't know how to calculate percentages," the don said, "or you are trying to cheat me. Tell me, which one is it?"

Was he bluffing? Did he know how much the ransom was, how much they collected? How could he possibly know?

The don said, "How much is in the bag?"

Trying to confuse him again. He knew how much was in the bag. Mazara said, "Sixty thousand."

"How much was the ransom?" he said, raising his voicc. If you saw him on the street, you would think he was a quiet, easy-going old man, but he was nothing like that.

Now Mazara was in trouble. Trying to get his brain to figure out what €60,000 was thirty per cent of. He had failed algebra and dropped out the Lyceum at the beginning of his second year. He did not try to figure it out earlier because he believed the man would accept the money, €60,000 and thank him, Jesus, shake his hand. He had no idea how to figure it out. He said, "What do you think it should be?"

The don said, "I think it should be thirty per cent." He pointed to the bag. "I am going to keep this, I want you to come back with the rest of the money you owe me."

Mazara was thinking, no wonder this old man controlled eighty per cent of the crime in Rome. He was smart and he was tough.

"I give you two days to bring the money," the don said. "And if you do not come back, we will be looking for you."

The American turned to the don and said, "Want me to go with him, Unk?"

"I want you to stay out of it," the don said. "This does not concern you." His voice measured, even.

The American said, "Show you how you how we do it in the Motor City."

Don Gennaro ignored him.

The American looked at him and said, "Hey, what's your name?"

"Roberto Mazara."

"Roberto Mazara, huh? Listen, you're not back here day after tomorrow, I'm coming after you myself."

Mazara grinned. It slipped out. He knew it was the wrong thing to do and regretted it. But couldn't help himself. It just happened.

The American got up. He was a big man. Forty pounds heavier than him, at least.

He said, "You think this is funny?"

He seemed like he was acting, overdoing the part like an amateur. Mazara said, "I don't know what you mean."

"You're giving me that little smartass grin," the American said. "Aren't you? Fucking with me."

"I think you are mistaken," Mazara said. He fixed his attention on Don Gennaro now. "I will bring you the money." What else was he going to say?

Fourteen

Uncle Carlo had hugged Joey when he got there, the man sitting in the main room of the villa he used as an office, wood beams in the ceiling, real ones, holding up the roof, nothing like the fake, distressed beams in his house, built in 2005 by Pulte. His uncle had statues and sculptures, too, and paintings on walls that were stucco, the real thing.

Uncle Carlo, who Joey had called Unk since he was a little kid when he couldn't pronounce uncle, told him the villa was built in the fifteenth century by an Italian nobleman. Fifteenth century was the 1600s, right? Joey said to himself. He didn't want to look like a dumbass. The villa was so famous, it even had a name: Santa Maria.

Uncle Carlo, based on what Joey saw, didn't look like the tough guy in charge of the Roman Mafia. He was listening to opera when Joey came in the room, his Unk leaning back in a chair behind his desk, eyes closed, the fruitcake moving his arms and hands like he was conducting the orchestra, really getting into it.

After hugging Joey and saying hello and asking about his sister, Joey's mother, and his flight over, his uncle said, "Listen."

He extended his arms, index fingers pointing at opposite side of the room where the sound was coming from.

"You know this?" he said.

Joey's parents listened to this shit too. "It's an opera." He was sure of that, but no idea which one.

"*Rigoletto*," his Unk said. "Act two. The Duke has returned to find Rigoletto's house empty, and is angry that his newest love is taken away from him, but the courtiers gleefully tell him of their trick."

His uncle was talking like he believed it, like it was a true story. Joey wanted to say, are you fucking kidding me? He wished the old boy would put Sinatra on and offer him a Grey Goose Martini straight up, with four queen-size olives, let him relax after ten hours in coach, back of the fucking plane, packed in a tight row like being on a slave ship.

"And the Duke," Carlo said, "learning they bring Gilda to the palace, rushes to be with her."

Joey was thinking, come on Unk, give it a fucking rest, okay? Jesus Christ.

Then, like he was reading Joey's mind, he said, "*Mi dispiace*, Giuseppe. You must be tired from your journey."

Fucking-A right he was tired.

"Mauro will take you up to your room. We meet for lunch on the veranda in an hour. Is enough time?"

"Sure," Joey said. That was more like it. Christ, invite him in, show a little family hospitality.

Mauro was a quiet, skinny little guy looked like he weighed about 120, with skin so dark, at first, Joey thought he was a jig, but he had the features of a white guy. Like somebody had taken brown shoe polish and covered his face. He had picked Joey up at the airport, waiting outside customs, holding up a little sign said SIGNOR BITONTE, Joey's fake name, his alias. On the way to the villa Mauro didn't say anything, not a fucking word for three and a half hours.

Now he carried Joey's suitcases up a winding staircase to his room that had a wood floor and a bed that had posts and some kind of fabric over it, looked like a girl's bed. Mauro put the suitcases on the floor and started to walk out of the room.

Joey said, "Hey, Mauro, wait, I've got a tip for you."

Mauro stopped and turned.

Joey said, "Never feed a Canadian," grinning, fucking with the skinny little guy.

Mauro looked at him but didn't react and walked out of the room.

Joey looked out the leaded glass windows, saw a good-looking babe sunning herself topless by the pool, nice taters and they looked real. Joey thinking he was going to like it here. He didn't have a choice. His father said he'd have to stay away for a while, see how it all played out.

His father had made the decision, told Joey he'd fucked up and there was nothing any of their people could do for him. He had to leave the country, move to Italy, stay with his uncle until it blew over. Joey's dad was Vito Corrado's under-boss.

Joey understood the situation, knew this business with Sharon – when and if it became known – would reflect poorly on his father, embarrass him and jeopardize his standing in the family. Getting rid of Joey would be seen as proactive, Joe P. handling the situation, taking care of it, protecting the family even at the expense of his son.

Joey told his dad what happened with Sharon.

His dad said, "What's the matter with you? All the girls in the city, you pick her?"

Joey had asked himself the same question, but he didn't

pick her. "We met, started going out, she said she was separated, getting a divorce."

"You got to check the people you go out with."

Like his father knew anything about dating. Joe P. had gotten married to his mother in a Sicilian village forty-five years earlier. He doubted his dad had ever had a date in his life. Joey remembered his expression when he told him what happened, the old man's dark eyes sunken behind the thick lenses of his glasses, black horn-rims – Jesus Christ, looking at Joey like he was a little kid.

"You know how this is going to make me look?"

Yeah, he knew. That's what this was all about.

"You think we want a federal agent snooping around, sticking his nose in our business?"

He didn't want it either, but what could he do now? Nothing. So the solution was to get rid of Joey. He didn't tell his father he and Sharon had had phone conversations for five weeks and sent emails back and forth to each other. He doubted his father knew what email was. There were also phone records and sooner or later Sharon's husband was going to figure it out and come looking.

That's why he'd cleaned out the house, packed everything in boxes and had Anthony take it all to a storage place. The husband came calling, Joey wouldn't be there. And nobody but his old man knew where he was.

He'd never fallen for a girl as hard and fast as he did for Sharon. He was sure she was the one. Asked her to marry him and she said, I've got to tell you something. He remembered what she said like there was a tape recorder in his head.

"I can't marry you 'cause I'm already married. I should've

told you. I'm sorry. I care about you. I really do."

He was head over fucking heels, and she said she cared about him. By the way she acted, he thought it was mutual that she was into it as much as he was. How could he have been so wrong? Joey had said, "You're married? What're you doing going out to bars?" Joey believed that married women should be faithful at all times. There were rules you followed and lived by.

Sharon had said, "I'm lonely."

Joey said, "You're lonely, huh? How many of us have there been?"

Sharon said, "Listen to me, I'm crazy about you. I really am."

That sounded a little better. If she was putting him on she was pretty goddamn good. Joey said, "If you're not happy, why don't you get a divorce?" He felt bad for her locked in a fucked-up marriage.

"I'm afraid of him," Sharon said.

Joey said, "You've got nothing to worry about, I'll protect you." He grinned, thinking he'd have a talk with the guy, tell him the way it was, the way it was going to be. He sipped his champagne, picturing the husband, a balding, out-of-shape suburban executive wearing a coat and tie. This was before Joey found out who the guy was.

Sharon looked out at the lake. He could tell she was worried. "What's your husband do, he's out of town all the time?"

"Works for the government," Sharon said.

"For the government?"

"Uh-huh."

"Don't tell me he's with the IRS." You didn't want them on your ass. They could make your life miserable.

Sharon said, "He's not."

Joey was curious now. "What's he do?"

She held up the champagne flute. "Can I have some more?"

Joey grabbed the neck of the champagne bottle and pulled it out of the cooler. He said, "Come on. What's the big deal?"

"He's a special agent in the Secret Service."

Joey stood there, mouth open, staring at her, unable to move or talk, like her words had Tasered him. When he could, he said, "Tell me you making this up?" But he knew she wasn't.

Fifteen

Dr Mencuccini said, "Impressive, isn't it?"

She gazed out across the lower level of the Colosseum, students packed in a tight group in front of her.

"Fifty thousand Romans could enter and be in their seats in ten minutes. Can you imagine that happening in a modern stadium?"

McCabe wondered if he paid more attention to Dr Mencuccini than his other teachers because she was good-looking. She reminded him of an aging starlet, early forties, with a small knockout body and dark hair. She had her own style, wore scarves and coats over her shoulders, and designer sunglasses.

Chip standing behind him said, "'All gladiators up to the training area at once,'" in a theatrical Brit voice.

The students around him could hear but not the teacher.

Dr Mencuccini said, "The concrete core – with its miles of corridors and stairways – was a masterpiece of engineering."

Chip said, "'What sort of man is this leader of the slaves?' 'I don't know. I think they call him Spartacus.'"

McCabe could see students next to him smiling.

Dr Mencuccini fixed her gaze on him and said, "Signor McCabe, do you have something to add?"

McCabe said, "I didn't say anything."

"With your cuts and bruises, you look like a gladiator who

fought here," Dr Mencuccini said.

Behind him, Chip said, "'Get back. I tell you, he's an expert with a Thracian sword.'"

Students around Chip were laughing now.

Dr Mencuccini said, "Signor Tallenger, do you want to come up here and entertain us?"

"*Mi dispiace, Dottore,*" Chip said.

"*Prego,*" Dr Mencuccini said. "Do you mind if I continue?"

"*Per favore,*" Chip said.

She said, "To celebrate the thousandth birthday of Rome, gladiators slaughtered thirty-two elephants, ten tigers, sixty lions, ten giraffes, forty wild horses, ten hippopotamuses and twenty Etruscans. It all happened right here." She paused and continued. "Condemned criminals – and occasionally Christians – were stripped naked and thrown to the lions. The violence of ancient Rome has troubled scholars for centuries. Were the Romans exceptionally bloodthirsty?" She scanned the students in front of her. "Signor Tallenger?"

Chip said, "I defer to my learned colleague, Signor McCabe."

"Signor McCabe?"

"It was violence at a distance," McCabe said. "Safe and controlled. Like a boxing match, or a violent movie." He was aware of students around him, watching him.

"*Molto bene,*" Dr Mencuccini said.

"'Spartacus, you know things that can't be taught,'" Chip said. "'Why a star falls and a bird doesn't. Where the sun goes at night. Why the moon changes shape . . . where the wind comes from.'"

Dr Mencuccini, amused herself now, said, "I don't recognize the lines. What is that from?"

"*Spartacus*," Chip said. "Appropriate, don't you think?"

"Yes. And I think that's enough for today. I will see you all Thursday at Campidoglio. *Ciao*."

They walked out of the Colosseum, Chip and McCabe, and stood there surrounded by tour groups and students. It was four o'clock, classes over for the day.

Chip said, "Let's get a beer."

McCabe said, "I can't. I've got to go back to the police station, meet Captain Ferrara. More photos he wants me to see."

"Call me when you're finished," Chip said.

McCabe walked along Via dei Fori Imperiali, the Roman Forum to his left below street level. He passed the Basilica of Constantine and Maxentius and the Temple of Antoninus and Faustina and the Forum of Caesar.

At Piazza Venezia he thought about taking a cab, but decided against it and walked down Via del Corso to the Condotti area, trying to find the *enoteca* Angela had taken him to.

He thought it was on the corner where Della Croce met Via Bocca di Leone. He went there looking at the back-alley intersection, remembered the bar, remembered sitting at a sidewalk table across from Angela, thinking how lucky he was and trying to make the most of it. He went inside, scanned the people sitting at the bar, didn't see a good-looking girl with streaks in her hair, and went back out. He tried to remember which way they'd gone when they left the *enoteca*, but he hadn't been paying much attention, his main focus was on Angela that afternoon.

He walked to Via Mario de' Fiore, took a left and then a right on Via delle Carrozze. He thought it was on the corner.

Remembered the red awnings and the rows of round tables set up outside, and the waiters in white sport coats with gold trim.

He sat at a table and ordered a beer and watched people go by. He saw Angela's friend, Enzo, come out of the restaurant with a tray of drinks and serve four well-dressed, middle-aged women. He came toward McCabe's table, carrying the tray under his arm.

McCabe said, "Enzo, how're you doing? I'm a friend of Angela's. We were supposed to meet here." He said it one guy to another. The waiter stopped and looked at him. It was obvious he didn't recognize McCabe or have a clue who he was.

"Have you phone her?" Enzo said.

"I've tried for over an hour," McCabe said. "I think she's talking to someone."

"Women," Enzo said. He turned his hand sideways, opening and closing his thumb and fingers, making a mouth.

McCabe nodded. Now they had a common bond, men waiting for women to stop talking, get off the phone. Like it was a problem all men had to deal with. "You know where she lives?"

"Near the Colosseum," Enzo said.

McCabe said, "What direction?"

"Via Cavour?" Enzo said.

McCabe knew where Via Cavour was. It ran northwest from Via dei Fori Imperiali. It wasn't much to go on, but it was a start.

McCabe had seen a Budget car rental office on Via del Corso. He walked there from the restaurant, ten blocks, and rented a blue Fiat Stilo with a credit card, a Visa, his dad told him to use only in an emergency, as a last resort. He thought what he was about to do qualified. The car cost €43 a day. Not knowing how long he'd need it, he rented it for a week.

He took a left on Via del Corso and drove straight down toward the Colosseum. He'd never driven in Rome, and it took him a few minutes to get used to it, cars and motorbikes flying by him like he was in slow motion. By the time he got to Piazza Venezia he was keeping up with traffic, feeling confident behind the wheel, his Detroit rush-hour instincts coming back.

It was 6:07 when he took a left on Via Cavour, cruising the streets to the south, Via Frangipane, Via delle Carine and Via degli Annibaldi, catching glimpses of the Colosseum in the distance. Traffic was heavy and it was difficult to take his eyes off the road for more than a couple seconds at a time. It was a residential neighborhood, beautiful old apartment buildings, restaurants and shops lining the streets on both sides. He was looking for a red Lancia and a dark-haired girl with blonde streaks in her hair, which described half the women he saw. He didn't even know if the car was hers, but that's all he had to go on – not knowing her last name or anything else about her except she had an uncle who lived in Detroit.

Now he tried the neighborhood north of Cavour, taking Via della Madonna dei Monti past the Hotel Forum and Birra Moretti. There were more bars and cafés. This area looked familiar. He'd been to Birra Moretti, an Italian beer hall, one night with Chip and a group of students, drinking beer out of glass boots. There was a café he passed next to Hotel Duca di Alba that also looked familiar.

He'd been driving around for an hour and twenty minutes. He was thinking about giving up, thinking that what he was doing was insane. He wasn't going to find this girl and if he did, what was he going to do with her? He pulled over and parked on the street, considered taking the car back, cut his losses.

There was a map of Rome in the console between the seats, courtesy of Budget. He took it out and unfolded it. He found his approximate location, traced a line where he'd been down Via Cavour and the neighborhoods north and south. To the west was Via del Corso and Piazza Venezia. There was another neighborhood to the east he hadn't been to yet. He glanced in the rearview mirror and when the traffic was clear in both directions he made a U-turn. He drove a couple blocks and it turned into Via Leonina. Nothing.

He drove back the way he had come. If she had a view of the Colosseum, her apartment had to be closer to it. He passed the tunnel that led to San Pietro in Vincoli, a little piazza tucked back behind the buildings lining the east side of Via Cavour. He parked and ran across the street and went up the steps and through the tunnel.

The square was surrounded by buildings, and had a parking lot in the center that was filled with motorcycles, hundreds of them, and cars. He walked past the university building, students standing in groups on the steps in front, talking, and a vendor truck that said BIBITE, GELATI, COLD DRINKS on a brown awning that ran along the side.

He walked down the street to Bar del Mose and went in and had a quick espresso. He came out, and went left and saw the Colosseum. He walked down Via della Polveriera and saw a red Lancia parked across the street from an umber-colored apartment building. He looked in the driver's side window. It had tan leather seats, and the front left fender was dented. He pictured it on the road that day when they caught him trying to get away. It was definitely the car.

The number of the building next to it was 44. It had a decorative black wrought-iron door with glass panels. He checked the directory, two rows of names on a brass plate: *Di Nello, Gabriel, M. Puraro, L. Terrachina, Sacelli, Liquori, Soave, J. Fabiano, G. Migliorelli, and P. Confalone.*

He walked back around the block, across San Pietro in Vincoli, went back through the tunnel to his car. He drove west and took a left near the Roman Forum. The Colosseum was straight ahead. He drove past it and took another left on tree-lined Via delle Terme di Tito. There was a park, deserted now, set back behind a fence. He drove around the block and parked next to a green city trash bin twenty yards behind the Lancia. He had a good angle on the car and the apartment building. He put the window down and turned off the engine and waited. It was 7:19 p.m., almost dark.

At 8:45, he saw a woman appear down the street, coming toward him. Even from thirty yards he knew it was Angela. He could tell by the way she walked, the way she carried herself, looking good in dark slacks, a white blouse and a black leather jacket, dressed nice, going out for the evening.

He was thinking about what Captain Ferrara had said, profiling the street gang that grabbed him, contrasting that with the expensive car and upscale neighborhood Angela was living in, and it didn't fit. What was this well-heeled girl, with an apartment near the Colosseum, doing with a Roman street gang?

As she came toward him, McCabe wondered if she shared the apartment with Mazara. Of the gang members he'd be the obvious choice. Or did she live by herself? He saw the

Lancia's front parking lights flash as she pressed the remote, and saw her open the door and get in behind the wheel. She started the car, put the lights on and pulled out. McCabe stayed close, following her across town to a restaurant near the Trevi Fountain called Al Moro. He'd read about it, a place that catered to wealthy Romans and tourists. He watched her park, and saw her walk in the restaurant. Saw the maître'd kiss her on both cheeks.

McCabe figured he had some time and drove back through the city, over the river and up Monte Mario to school. Chip was standing at the sink brushing his teeth when McCabe came in the room, Chip barefoot in a pair of sweatpants and a tee-shirt. McCabe moved past him and went to his dresser, opening drawers, pulling out clothes – a pair of Levis and a couple of tee-shirts and a blue long-sleeved work shirt. He folded the clothes in a pile on his bed. He could see Chip looking in the mirror, watching him.

Chip turned away from the sink and came toward him, still brushing his teeth. He took the toothbrush out of his mouth.

"What're you doing?"

"Taking some time off."

Chip went back to the sink, spit out the toothpaste and said, "What does that mean?"

He had been hoping Chip wouldn't be there so he wouldn't have to explain himself, answer any questions. Just get his things and go. He put the clothes in his backpack. He opened his desk drawer and grabbed his Swiss Army knife and sunglasses and threw them in too.

Chip walked over and sat on his bed. "Rady's looking for you."

"I know," McCabe said. There was a note in his mailbox that said to see him ASAP. He showed it to Chip then crumpled it into a ball and threw it at the wastebasket next to his desk, nailing a ten-footer. McCabe went to the sink and got his toothbrush and shaving kit, and came back and put them in his backpack.

"You leave," Chip said, "he's going to take your scholarship."

McCabe said. "Got some money I can borrow?"

Chip got up and went to his desk and picked up his wallet, opened it and took out a wad of euros. "How much you need?"

"All of it."

He gave the money to McCabe, and McCabe folded the bills in half and put them in the front pocket of his Levis. "I'll pay you back."

"I'm worried about you, Spartacus," Chip said. "You're wigging big time. What the hell're you doing?"

McCabe picked up the backpack and slipped his arms through the straps. He said, "Take it easy," and walked out of the room.

In the lobby, he was surprised to see Franco behind the desk. Canzio had been there when he walked through twenty minutes earlier. McCabe said, "Yo, Franco, what's up?"

Franco said, "McCabe, listen, Signor Rady is looking for you and he is very angry."

McCabe had missed his Italian class again, and that's what Rady wanted to talk to him about. Rady appeared now, coming from the administrative wing, his pale white face almost as red as his flat-top.

"McCabe, in my office, now," he said, raising his voice.

McCabe said, "I'm kind of busy."

Rady said, "I don't think I heard you right."

He moved toward the door.

Rady said, "I'm warning you, McCabe, walk out of here, you're through."

McCabe could see Franco waiting to see what he was going to do. He pushed the door open and went out. The Fiat was parked in the circular drive. He got in it and drove to a hardware store on Via Trionfale and bought a roll of duct tape, fifty feet of rope and a green plastic tarp. He drove back toward school and stopped at Pietro's. He went in. It was packed at 9:00, Pietro working the room, shaking hands, talking to people. McCabe waited till Pietro was alone and made his move.

"McCabe, you here for dinner?"

"Can I talk to you for a minute?"

McCabe drove back to Al Moro and saw the red Lancia still there where Angela had left it. He pulled up and parked on the narrow street thirty feet from the front door of the restaurant, two cars behind the Lancia, and waited. It was 10:06 p.m.

He was tired, closed his eyes. Just for a couple minutes, he told himself. Next thing he knew it was 11:25. He heard voices and footsteps on the cobblestone street. He looked through the windshield and saw Angela walking with a well-dressed grey-haired guy, mid-sixties. There were two men walking behind them. He couldn't tell if they were all together or not.

Angela and the old dude stopped next to a Mercedes sedan. McCabe's side window was down, and he could hear them arguing in Italian. When the two men caught up to them they stopped talking and stared at each other. One of them, a heavyset guy, said, “See you tomorrow, Cuz.”

He was an American, no mistake about it.

Angela said, “What time you want to start?”

The heavyset guy said, “I’m up early.”

“I’ll see you at ten,” Angela said.

No you won’t, McCabe was thinking.

Sixteen

Teegarden called Ray back the next day and said, "The one in Harrison Township's registered to a Joseph Palermo. Know who he is?"

"Should I?"

"Swinging Joey. He's a mob lieutenant that works for the Corrodos. Know how he got his name?"

"He likes to dance?"

"He likes to bust heads open with a baseball bat. Second number's registered to Venice Motors on Van Dyke in Warren," Teeg said.

"You see Joey's name connected to the car lot?"

"I don't see his name, but I see him all over it. They hide gambling profits in the business books and accept cars as payment for debts. Let's say you borrow money, you can't pay it back. Joey shows up with his Louisville Slugger and takes your car. That's how I think it works. What I don't see is why a guy like Joey is bothering Sharon."

"That's the big mystery, isn't it?"

"What's Sharon say?"

"She met him at a club after a concert," Ray said, "couldn't remember his name."

"Sounds a little odd," Teeg said.

It did to Ray, too, but that was the best he could come up with on short notice.

Teegarden gave him the address of the guy's house in Harrison Township and the car lot on Van Dyke, said good luck and hung up.

Ray went to the used car lot first. He found Venice Motors just south of Twelve Mile on Van Dyke Road after passing every fast-food restaurant he'd ever heard of. He pulled in the lot, parked and walked in the showroom that didn't have any cars in it. There were two big dark-haired guys eating dinner, white paper napkins tucked into the necks of their shirts. They were sitting across a desk from each other, rolling their forks through spaghetti with red sauce, using a spoon to balance the load. They were eating and washing it down with red wine they drank out of plastic cups. Neither seemed interested in waiting on a customer.

"What can we do you for?" one of them said.

He had curly hair that looked like a perm. He nodded at the guy sitting across from him, got up and pulled the napkin out of his shirt and wiped his mouth.

"How you doing? I'm Anthony. Looking for something in particular? I got a Caddy STS that's so clean, 2,500 original miles, I'd sell it to my own mother, but she don't need a car."

He grinned, showing food in his teeth, probably thinking that was clever. He was a big dude, six two, baggy island shirt hanging out over black pants and thin-soled loafers with tassels.

Ray said, "Seen Joey around?"

Anthony said, "Joey who?"

"Joey Palermo," Ray said. "Swinging Joey."

The guy at the desk still eating his dinner said, "Never heard of him."

"That's strange," Ray said, "because we agreed to meet here. I owe him some money. But you've never heard of him, huh?"

The guy at the desk got up now, still chewing, pulled the napkin out of his shirt and laid it on the desktop.

"What's your name?"

"Vito Corleone," Ray said.

"Come on. This is a friendly establishment. We like to know who we're dealing with."

"I'm not here to make friends," Ray said. "I'm here to pay a gambling debt."

"I'm Dom, you can give it to me. I'll make sure it gets to the right people."

Ray said, "Who're the right people?"

"Don't worry about that, my friend," Dom said.

Ray didn't know if they thought they were intimidating him, or they were just dumb.

The showroom walls were floor-to-ceiling glass, banners festooned across them with an advertising message that said: *The car of your dreams for a down-to-earth price.* Ray turned, heading for the door, but Anthony had moved quickly across the floor, cutting him off.

Anthony said, "We can't let you go till we figure this out."

Dom, the bigger of the two guys, was coming toward him. Had to be 250 pounds, but he had a gut and looked out of shape. Anthony was ten feet away, standing in front of the door that was all glass and said VENICE MOTORS in a typeface that looked Italian, featuring a stylized gondola and a gondolier holding an oar.

Ray stopped, watched Dom approach, Dom reaching out to

grab him. Ray took his hand and using the momentum of his body, threw him through the plate-glass window, the big guy landing on the concrete walkway outside the building.

Anthony charged him now. When he got close, Ray grabbed the front of his shirt, turned sideways and threw him over his hip. Anthony went airborne, landing hard on the tile floor. Ray walked out and got in his car. Saw Dom on a bed of glass, trying to get on his feet as he drove out of the lot.

He had Joey's address on Lake Shore Drive. He took Sixteen Mile Road/Metro Parkway to the east side and got on I94 for a mile and a half and got off at exit 273, North River Road, went left toward Harrison Township. He passed Selfridge Air Force Base on his left, a military installation. He could see runways and military buildings in the distance, set back a couple hundred yards behind a fence topped with razor wire. He'd read somewhere – in the event of war – Selfridge had missiles with long-range nuclear capabilities.

He could see the Clinton River on his right now, boats cruising along, houses close together, lining the water on both sides. It was a strange contrast of styles – old dilapidated single-story cottages next to huge new over-the-top, two-story brick colonials with three and four-car garages, rich and poor living side by side. He passed the Captain's Quarters Condos and a subdivision called Brigantine Estates and the Crews' Inn Restaurant, Marley Marine and Sundog's Marina: Bait, Gas and Cold Drinks. He turned on South River Road and took it to Lake Shore and caught glimpses of Lake St Clair between the houses that were big and new. Joey's was the last one on a dead-end street, bordering the lake on the north side and a Clinton River tributary to the east. His house was built in the middle of two lots, a five-thousand-square-foot colonial with a four-car garage.

Ray parked in the cul de sac just past the house. He watched a cigarette boat rumble past him on the river and then gun it as it hit the open water of Lake St Clair, two girls in jeans and sweatshirts standing on the rear seat with cans of beer in their hands. He sat there for twenty minutes, watching Joey's house, the front windows of his Jeep down, a breeze coming in off the lake. A dozen more boats came down the river heading for open water, a non-stop armada of partiers, drinking, listening to music, and having fun.

He could see the side of Joey's house, his backyard extending to the lake. He could see the dock and a boat on a hoist in a custom boathouse. He waited for an hour. He didn't see anyone come out of the house or go in. He got out of the car and walked to the front door and rang the bell. The garage was on the west side of the house, four varnished wood doors facing east. He rang the bell again and looked through a small round window into the foyer, didn't see anyone.

He went around to the back. Saw sailboats with trim white sails out on the lake and motorboats zigzagging, kicking up white spray. There was a patio made out of decorative pavers, a two-tone color scheme: rose and plum. There was a table with a closed umbrella through the center of it and four chairs. The back of the house had French doors that opened to the patio.

He picked the lock and went into a big room with a cathedral ceiling and big windows that looked out on the water. There was a furniture grouping, two couches and a coffee table and four leather armchairs in the middle of the room. There was a fieldstone fireplace against one wall, and in the corner, a sixty-inch Sony flatscreen on a custom stand. The room was spotless, everything neat and tidy. There were no newspapers or magazines, nothing out of place. It reminded him of a model home, furnished and decorated but nobody lived there.

He moved through the room down a hallway to the kitchen. There was a Krups coffee maker on the counter and a toaster, but nothing else. He opened the refrigerator. It was empty, cleaned out. He moved past the dining room to an office. He looked in. There was an antique desk. He went in and sat behind it and checked the drawers, opened each one. They were all empty. There was a glossy picture book on a table across the room that showed a little girl posing with her hand over her mouth and a title that said *A Day in the Life of Italy*.

He went upstairs and checked the bedrooms, four suites that had big attached bathrooms with Jacuzzi tubs. Two had spectacular views of the lake. Like the downstairs everything was perfect, beds made, carpet spotless. No clothes in the closets. No toothbrushes or combs or shaving cream or mouthwash in any of the bathrooms.

He went back downstairs through the kitchen into the four-car garage. The enormous space empty except for half a dozen moving boxes sealed with clear packaging tape. Whoever had cleaned the place out didn't have time to finish the job. He squatted and pulled tape off one of the boxes and opened it. There were framed photographs wrapped in newspaper. He unwrapped one. It was a shot of a dark-haired guy in a bathing suit, had to be Joey, posing on his boat. He unwrapped another one and saw the same guy in a golf outfit, grinning with three other guys, big white clubhouse in the background, looked like Oakland Hills. And in the third one, Joey wearing a softball uniform, same colors as the Oakland As, posing with the team.

He found Visa and American Express credit-card receipts in a manila envelope. He found the title to a 2009 Cadillac STS-V, a 2008 Corvette and a thirty-two-foot Century pleasure craft – everything in the name Joseph S. Palermo, Jr. on Lake Shore Drive.

He dug deeper and saw an Apple PowerBook. He brought it out and put it on top of a wardrobe box. He opened it and pushed the power button and waited till it booted up.

He checked the document file, mailbox and address book. Everything was empty, cleaned out like the refrigerator and the closets. He stared at the icons lined up on the bottom of the screen. He moved the cursor with his left index finger and clicked on Microsoft Entourage. It brought up Mail and he clicked on "Send & Receive." Nothing there. He checked Deleted Items. Nothing. Clicked on Sent Items. Everything was erased. He stared at the screen. Scanned the icons again. It didn't look like there was anything in the trash but he clicked on it and opened it, and under Name, he saw: Re-"I'm yours." He clicked on it and took it out of the trash and put it on the desktop and opened it. The message said, "I'll be a little late, but I can spend the night so we can take our time. Love, S." It was from Sharon34@hotmail.com, dated October 2nd 2008. Ray felt sick to his stomach.

He walked out to the boathouse. There were ropes and dock lines on the wood plank floor. He turned a lever on the hoist and lowered the boat into the water. He stepped down on the bow and walked back to the cabin and went below into the galley. He opened drawers and cabinets. Checked the refrigerator. Like the house, it was cleaned out, spotless.

He went forward, looked in the bathroom, tiny closet-size room with a shower and a toilet and sink. He moved into the bedroom or stateroom, whatever it was called. It was dark. He found the switch on the wall, flipped it and half a dozen recessed ceiling lights came on. There was a queen-size bed, comforter tucked neat and tight over it. He sat on the bed, glanced up at a Mitsubishi flatscreen on the wall, then looked through a porthole into the boathouse. He got up, looked at a framed painting of a sunset over the bed. He turned to go and the glint of something caught his eye. He got on his knees. It was stuck in the corner between the carpeting and baseboard. He picked it up and looked at it, a diamond earring. It looked like one he'd given to Sharon, remembered buying it at Astrein's in Birmingham for their tenth anniversary. Sharon couldn't believe he'd actually gone into a store and picked something out for her. He didn't tell her two attractive salesgirls helped and advised him. The earrings had even more significance because he'd missed their ninth anniversary, completely forgot it.

He was coming out of the boathouse when he saw the two meatheads from the used car lot on the dock, coming toward him. Dom's face, after taking a dive through the plate-glass window, was covered with band-aids. Anthony was a step ahead of him. He had a crowbar in his hand this time.

Ray reached back, felt the bulge of the Colt under his shirt in the small of his back, but he decided not to draw it. They were twenty feet away when Ray said, "What a surprise. You guys showing up at Joey's and you don't even know him."

"We know *you* though, don't we?" Anthony said.

He moved toward Ray now, raising the crowbar over his head. When he got close he swung big and wild and Ray stepped back and he missed him, swishing air, Anthony puffing, breathing hard.

Ray said, "Come on, you pussy, is that all you've got?"

Anthony came at him again, swinging and missing with his right hand, going all the way around with the crowbar and this time Ray stepped in, chopped him between his neck and shoulder, a karate shuto, and sent him in the lake.

Dom came at him, balancing prodigious weight on little feet. Threw a big angry, off-balance punch at Ray and Ray sidestepped it and hit him in the ribs with a body shot that drove him in the cold October water.

Ray moved down the dock, turned when he was halfway across the lawn and saw them drenched, coming out of the lake.

Seventeen

Angela put her purse on the kitchen counter and opened a bottle of Chianti Classico, her last '97 Antinori, and poured herself a glass. She was tense, nerves frazzled after a two-hour dinner with her father and his surprise guest, cousin Joey from America, visiting for a few months, staying at her father's villa outside Rome.

Joey had talked about himself through three courses: tagliatelle and fresh white truffles that the owner, Signor Moro, sliced on their pasta at the table. The *secondo piatto* was veal chops that were as thick as a Russian novel. That was followed by *insalata verde* and *formaggio*, tiramisu and espresso.

Joey had talked about his house on Lake St Clair in an area called Harrison Township. You should see the sunsets, Joey said. He talked about his boat and about his cars, talking with his mouth full. Her father did not seem to listen or pay attention. Sat hunched over his plate, shoveling food in his mouth, eyes moving around the room.

At one point, Joey said, "What's with him?" Pointing to Mauro, her father's bodyguard sitting at the bar. "What's the story, Unk, you don't eat with the hired help?"

He grinned and gulped more Amarone, drinking it too fast.

Her father said, "Do not ask about matters that are not your concern."

Angela liked that, her father telling him to mind his own

business. She could see that Joey annoyed him too.

Joey grinned, "Take it easy, Unk, I'm just having some fun with you, yanking your chain."

He rubbed his eyes and wiped his fingers on his pants.

Angela said, "What brings you to Rome?"

"You know, get away for a while," Joey said. "I been here four days, I've got to ask you where the hot spots are at? Deadest town I ever been to in my life. Lights out at like nine o'clock."

Angela said, "What are you looking for?"

"Action," Joey said. "What do you think?"

It had been a couple of years since she had seen him. He looked older, heavier, most of the weight around his middle like a tire that had been inflated, and his hair was thinning on top, but these imperfections did not seem to affect his confidence. He reminded her of an actor playing the role of a TV Mafia character.

When Joey got up to use the toilet, Angela said to her father, "What is the matter? You have not said a word."

"How can I?" her father said. "He never closes his mouth – even when he is eating."

He picked up his glass, sipped his wine. She could tell he liked it, his expression changing when he took a sip. His eyes looked across the room and then back to her.

He said, "Are you still seeing that street punk?"

"Are you going to bring that up again?" He did business with Roberto, but did not approve of him. She had been so careful, trying to keep it a secret, and he had somehow found out. She was going to say: I see who I want, but said, "Do we have to talk about this now, ruin the dinner, our evening?" Because of Roberto, he had stopped supporting her, so as far as Angela was concerned, she was on her own. She could see who she wanted.

Her father took another sip of wine and fixed his attention on her. "Are you doing okay? You have money to live?"

"I'm fine," Angela said. Which was not completely truthful. She was almost out of money, but with her share of the ransom she could keep going for a while. She just had to get it from Roberto.

"I want you to help me with Joey. You need money, I pay you to come over and take him out, get him away from me. He's driving me out of my mind."

"Why is he here?" Angela said.

"He is in trouble."

"What kind of trouble?" She looked up and saw Joey coming back to the table.

"I will tell you," her father said.

Angela said, "Why is he your problem?"

"What can I do? It's for my sister."

After dinner her father ordered a glass of grappa. Angela and Joey walked down the street to see the Trevi fountain. Angela took his arm and they moved through the crowd, around the side of the fountain to the front to get a better view.

Joey said, "What's this?"

"One of the hot spots, the big attractions of Rome," Angela said.

"All I see is a fountain. When I say action I'm talking about nightclubs."

Angela said, "No visitor can leave Rome without seeing the Trevi fountain. It's called Trevi because three streets meet here: *tre vie*. Do you understand?"

"I know," Joey said. "I seen it before." He was staring at the fountain. He pointed at a statue and said, "Who's that again?"

"Neptune," Angela said. "God of the sea."

"That's right," Joey said.

They walked up to the edge of the pool.

Joey said, "Look at all the coins in there."

"People throw in three thousand euros a day," Angela said. "For good luck."

He grinned. "Tell me you don't believe that bullshit."

A vendor, an aggressive little dark-skinned Asian, approached them with an armful of roses. "Want to buy?" he said to Joey, big smile.

"No want to buy," Joey said. "Get the fuck out of here."

The vendor kept smiling and said, "Want to buy?"

Joey said, "Say that one more time I'm going to pick you up and throw you in the fucking water."

"Take it easy," Angela said. "He doesn't understand you."

"Let's have some fun," Joey said. "Put Unk to bed, hit some clubs. What do you say?"

She told him she was too tired, but would pick him up the next morning, and show him the sights of Rome.

"Oh, boy," Joey said. "I can hardly wait."

~

Angela carried her wine into the bathroom, placed the stemmed glass on the sink and filled the tub with hot water. She was going to soak and relax, drink her wine. She could see the Colosseum lit up in the distance. This view was the reason she had fallen in love with the apartment. It was expensive, but her father was helping her in those days.

She took her clothes off and dropped them in a pile on the bathroom floor and stepped in the tub, taking her time, getting used to the hot water. When she was all the way under, water covering her shoulders, she heard a sound – like a door closing. She thought it was Roberto and was disappointed, she wanted to be alone tonight. More than that, she could see their relationship coming to an end. She had lost interest in him, but didn't have the energy to tell him tonight, so she would have to think of an excuse to get rid of him.

She said, "Roberto, is that you?" And then thought, who else would it be? "I'm in here." They were supposed to split up the money. With her share she was going to get away for a while – from her father who was trying to run her life, and from Roberto who needed someone to run his, but not her. She was thinking about Greece. Cruise the islands, lay in the sun for a week. Then she was thinking about going to Paris. Stay at a nice hotel, shop and eat and drink wine.

She finished her Chianti and reached her arm out of the tub and put the glass on the tile floor. Now she stood up and grabbed a folded white towel off a warming rack attached to the wall and wrapped it around her and stepped out of the tub onto the Persian rug, a gift from her father. She dried herself and slipped on a white terrycloth robe and went into the living room and put on a Magic Numbers CD, a British group she liked, and played *Love Is Just a Game*, singing along to it, thinking about Roberto again. As soon as she received her share of the money she would tell him the relationship was over.

Oh maybe I think, maybe I don't
Maybe I will, maybe I won't . . .

She danced into her bedroom and turned on the light. He was sitting on the bed, looking at her.

McCabe watched her park the Lancia on the street, and walk in the building, but it wasn't the one he thought, the entrance was on the next block on Via del Monte Oppio. Her apartment building was the last one, bordering two streets, with an unobstructed view of the Colosseum lit up right there less than a hundred yards away. He parked on Via della Polveriera and waited. He saw lights go on in an apartment and saw her in the window that was open. He got out of the car. There was a downspout that ran up the apartment wall a foot from her window. He climbed it with his backpack on. Reached out and touched the window, pushing one side all the way open. Now he reached over and grabbed the sill and jumped, arms through the window, body half inside the room, legs hanging over the edge, and shimmied his way in.

He got up and bumped the window and it closed with a *bang*. She must have heard it. He was in her bedroom. He crouched next to the bed, listening. Heard her call Roberto, but Roberto didn't answer. McCabe heard her turn the water on and off a couple times. Heard her walk into the other room and put music on. Heard her singing and was surprised how bad her voice was, worse than his and that was saying something.

She had a robe on and was drying her hair with a towel when she walked in the room, and turned on the light. She glanced at him sitting there and he sprang off the bed and tackled her, trying to pin her down, surprised how strong she was. She yelled and he put his hand over her mouth and she tried to bite him. He flipped her on her stomach, sat on her, pulling her arms back, and wrapped duct tape around her wrists. She yelled again and he put a piece over her mouth, and taped her feet together. He flipped her on her back. Her robe had come apart and he pulled it closed.

He could see her arms flexing, trying to rip the tape and pull her hands free.

McCabe said, "What's the matter? You're not glad to see me?"

She glared at him.

He said, "Where's the money?" He pulled the tape off her mouth.

"I don't know."

"Then you've got a problem."

He went in her closet and looked at her clothes and took out some things and threw them on the bed. He could see her eyes follow him. He went back in the closet, opened the top drawer of her dresser, looking at panties and thongs, and saw a small black pistol with a short barrel. He picked it up and went back in the room and said, "This what you're looking for?"

"You better go some place and hide," she said. "Hope they don't find you."

He put the tarp on the floor and unfolded it. He saw her watching him.

"You're making a big mistake," she said. "You have no idea."

He put the tape over her mouth again. "You're the one made the mistake."

Now he had to get her out of the apartment without anyone seeing them. He walked across the apartment and looked out an east-side window down at Via del Monte Oppio. It was 1:15 a.m. He looked in both directions. The street was deserted.

He found her keys and cell phone on a table near the front door. He put the phone in his shirt pocket and took the keys. There were two of them. He opened the door and tried the keys and found the one that worked. The second key had to open the door to the building.

The stairs were made of white marble and very narrow and there was a small elevator that ran through the center of the apartment building. He went down and got the car and parked in front with the hatchback open. Now he went back upstairs and wrapped her in the tarp, and carried her over his shoulder, down a flight of stairs to the car. She fought him the whole way, squirming, moving, trying to make noise. He opened the hatchback and slid her in and closed it. He hadn't seen anyone and hoped no one had seen him.

He went back to her apartment and got his backpack and her clothes. He filled two bags with food from her kitchen and took the stairs again, down to the car. He drove through the city and got on the autostrada, heading north to Viterbo, a fifty-minute drive at 1:30 in the morning with no traffic, following Pietro's directions to the house called Casale Vecchio, his summer home, McCabe replaying their conversation at the restaurant.

"I met a girl," he'd said.

Pietro had given him a sly grin. "A girl, eh? This is sounding good. An Italian girl?"

"A good-looking Italian girl."

"It is sounding better. And what, you want to bring her here for dinner?"

"You told me I should visit your house in Lazio. Now I have a reason."

He gave McCabe the keys and drew him a map.

It was originally a hunting lodge – the walls were made out of perperino, volcanic stones. It had a tile roof and was built in 1782 on a hill overlooking the lush green countryside of Lazio. He could see Viterbo to the north, the clock tower, Palazzo del Podesta sticking up over the rooftops of the city.

He pulled up the steep drive and parked and carried Angela inside and unwrapped the tarp on a rug in the main room. She was soaked with sweat and he could see fear or anger in her eyes, or both. He couldn't blame her, wrapped in a tarp for an hour. He felt bad about it. But he couldn't think of another way to get her out of the apartment without being seen.

He pulled the strip of tape from her mouth. She didn't say anything, just looked up at him. Her robe had come apart down the middle where the sash had loosened, exposing the soft curve of her breasts, her flat stomach and the thin dark strip of hair between her legs. He knelt next to her and pulled it closed.

"Don't touch me," she said.

McCabe was thinking, okay, you don't care if your robe's open, I don't either.

She said, "Where are we?"

"In the country," McCabe said.

"I have to use the toilet."

McCabe took the Swiss Army knife out of his pocket and pulled a blade open and cut the duct tape binding her hands and feet. Now he helped her up and gave her the paper bag with her clothes, and took her to the bathroom. It had a ten-by-ten-inch window that looked down a steep hill to a valley, and beyond it rolling hills extending to a dark ridge of mountains in the distance. The room had a toilet and a sink, a mirror and stone walls and no way out except the door. He closed it and waited.

Ten minutes later she came out wearing a pair of jeans and a white blouse, barefoot, red toenails on the gray tile floor. The clothes seemed to change her attitude.

She said, "Listen, take me back to the city. I will talk to them. I will see what I can do about getting your money."

"Is that right?"

"I will talk to Mazara," she said. "I will make sure you get some of it back."

Like that was it. It was over. She was ready to go home now. McCabe said, "I don't want some of it. I want it all." He'd put the bags of groceries on a coffee table in the center of a furniture grouping. He was hungry and reached in a bag, grabbed a loaf of ciabatta and a wedge of pecorino romano. He said, "You want something to eat?" Looked up, and she was gone. He moved toward the front of the house, down a hallway into the salon. Checked the front door. It was locked. Behind him stairs led to the second level. The stairs, like everything else, were made of stone. He ran up and stood at the top. There was a bathroom straight ahead and bedrooms on both sides, moonlight coming through the upstairs windows casting light across the floor.

He went right into a dark bedroom. The side window was open and he could see her on the roof, moving to the top of the pitch and then climbing over onto the other side, bare feet sliding on the curved tiles. He ran down the stairs into the main room, picked up the roll of duct tape, went into the kitchen and out the back door. A tile slid down the roof, hit gravel and broke in half.

He waited under the overhang. Heard the low hum of the wind and felt a cold breeze come up the hill past the house. Heard her on the flat roof above him. He stepped out in the yard now and said, "How're you going to get down?"

She had a roof tile in her hand and flung it at him. He stepped aside and it hit the ground. She said, "You're never going to get the money."

Now a bat flew over the roof and dove at her.

McCabe said, "Know what that is?"

She tried to swat it and missed.

"It's a bat," McCabe said. "Don't let it get tangled in your hair. It'll bite you and bats have rabies."

The bat came at her again and she screamed, and moved to the edge of the roof and got down on her hands and knees. She lowered her body over the edge and hung there still five feet from the ground. McCabe reached up, grabbed her and brought her down, and carried her inside. He took her to the bathroom and locked her in with a key that was sticking out of the lock. He went upstairs, got a blanket and pillow off one of the beds and brought them down and unlocked the bathroom door and threw them in.

"I won't sleep in here."

"You don't have a choice." He closed the door and locked it.

She pounded on it for a while, and yelled some things in Italian he'd never heard before. She wasn't making it easy, but why did that surprise him? He took the bags of groceries in the kitchen and opened a bottle of wine and poured some in a glass. He cut a couple slices of cheese and ripped off a chunk of bread and went outside. Light was breaking over the hills. He'd get some sleep and see what Mazara had to say. See if he wanted his girlfriend back.

Eighteen

McCabe opened his eyes, looking up at the beamed ceiling and stone walls of Casale Vecchia, and for a split second forgot where he was. He got up and went outside and took a leak in the bushes next to the house. It was a bright clear day, a cool breeze blowing up the hill. He looked out across the lush green countryside and saw the dark shapes and angles of Viterbo about five kilometers away.

He went back inside, splashed water on his face and brushed his teeth at the kitchen sink. He was tired, groggy. There was a clock on the wall. It was 9:30. He'd slept maybe three hours. He rubbed his eyes, yawned and stretched, trying to wake up.

He'd brought eggs, pancetta and bread from Angela's apartment. He found coffee in the freezer, and put it in the coffee maker on the counter and made a pot. He fried the pancetta in a skillet on the stovetop. Cracked six eggs in a bowl and found a whisk in a drawer and beat them. The ciabatta was hard so he put it in the oven to soften it. He scrambled the eggs and sprinkled in grated cheese. Drained the pancetta on a paper towel to get rid of the grease. Took the bread out of the oven and buttered it. He put the eggs, pancetta and bread on heavy white plates and poured coffee in two mugs, put everything on a tray and took it to the dining table in the main room.

He knocked on the bathroom door and said, "Want something to eat?"

She didn't answer. He put the key in the lock and opened the door. She was stretched out on the floor, blanket under her, looking up at him, yawning.

"Come out if you're hungry." He closed the door and went to the table and waited for a couple minutes, and when she still wasn't out he scooped up a forkful of eggs and put it in his mouth. He ate the scrambled eggs and pancetta, and when he was finished, wiped the plate clean with a piece of stale bread.

Ten minutes later, the door opened and she appeared, hair pulled back in a ponytail, crossed the room and sat at the table across from McCabe but didn't look at him. She stared at the plate of food, picked up her fork and took a bite of eggs and made a face.

"It's cold," she said.

"That's what happens when hot food sits too long," McCabe said. "You don't come right away."

She picked up the coffee mug and took a sip, eyes looking over the rim at him. She took a bite of her cold eggs and ate them and went back for more. She ate like she was hungry, and drank the coffee and ignored him. He watched her thinking how good she looked first thing in the morning. He said, "How do you like it?"

She didn't say anything, just kept eating.

He waited till she laid her fork on the empty plate and said, "How do I get in touch with Roberto Mazara?"

She glanced at him and said, "I don't know."

"You like it in there," he said indicating the bathroom.

"Because that's where you're going to be spending most of your time."

"Believe me," she said. "He's not going to give you the money."

McCabe said, "Want to bet? I got something of his and he's going to want it back."

"I don't belong to Roberto," she said, "If that's what you are saying."

"As long as he thinks you do," McCabe said.

"He is going to come after you," Angela said. "And he is not going to stop."

"That's okay," McCabe said. "But he better bring the money. All of it."

"I don't think he has all of it," she said. "I'm sure the money has been divided among his men."

McCabe said. "Where's your share? We can start there."

Angela said, "He has not given it to me."

"You're either lying or you're being scammed."

"Who are you, you think you can take on this armed gang?"

"I'm not Chip Tallenger from Greenwich, Connecticut. I'll tell you that. My dad's a retired ironworker living on a pension."

"The story in the newspaper said you were rich."

"I'm not," McCabe said.

"The amount of the ransom seemed insignificant," she said, "to someone so wealthy."

"Did you hear what I said?"

Angela said, "Why do you think I am going to help you?"

"You like sleeping next to the toilet?" McCabe said. He slid a pen and piece of paper across the table to her. "Write down his number."

She crumpled the paper in a ball, threw it at him and missed. He got up and went around the table at her, but she was already on her feet, holding the fork in her fist, arm raised, ready to fight him.

"Put it down." He moved toward her and she tried to stab him. He stepped back, and she came at him, swung again and he blocked her arm and took the fork out of her hand, and dropped it on the floor.

She made a run for the kitchen and he caught her before she got to the doorway, standing behind her, holding her arms. She tried to free herself, tried to kick him. He bent her back and dragged her to the bathroom, pushed her in, and locked the door. She was pounding on the hardwood, yelling in Italian.

There wasn't much he could do with her at the moment, and wasn't much he could do without her. He'd wait till she cooled down and try again.

McCabe went back to the table and picked up the fork. He took the dishes into the kitchen and washed them. He went back into the main room. The pounding had stopped. He stretched out on the couch and fell asleep.

Nineteen

Ten in the morning, Joey was standing outside the villa smoking a Montecristo No. 4, waiting for Angela. At eleven when she still wasn't there, he called her apartment and got her answering machine. "This is Angela," a breathy voice. "Leave a message. *Ciao*."

Joey said, "Yo Cuz, you're an hour late. Where the fuck're you at?"

At noon Joey went into his uncle's office. The old boy was sitting on a couch, watching some foreign movie, the mistress, Chiara, sitting next to him, looking bored. "Hey, Unk, something's wrong, Angela was supposed to be here two hours ago."

His uncle glanced at him and paused the movie. "You think something is wrong you don't know her. Angela is never on time in her life. I think she is still asleep." He said it with an edge to his voice.

Joey said, "I'll go surprise her."

His uncle seemed to like the idea. He perked up and yelled Mauro's name and a few seconds later the little guy ran in the room like he was sitting out there waiting to be called. In the faint light Mauro now reminded Joey of Sammy Davis Junior, his build and skin color. Joey grinned, almost laughed out loud, wondering if Mauro could sing and tap dance.

His Unk told Mauro to give Joey a ride into the city. Joey

left the old boy in his office with his mistress who looked like she needed attention, wondering now if he should pay her a visit, walk down the hall in the middle of the night, unsheathe the pork sword. Nothing against his Unk, but show her what a hard-on looked like.

In the car, a black Mercedes sedan, he looked across at Mauro behind the wheel. They were still on villa property, cruising on the pebble driveway that had to be a quarter-mile long. Joey said, "You take the oath?"

Mauro glanced over at him with a blank look on his face. This Sicilian hick had no idea what he was talking about. "Poke your finger, spill blood on a sacred image, picture of a saint?" Joey paused, thinking about his old man telling him it was one of the rituals of the Sicilian Cosa Nostra, how they did it in the old country. Then the picture was lit on fire, you had to hold it while you swore to obey the rules of the family.

His dad had said, "May your flesh burn if you fail to keep the oath."

Joey thought it sounded pretty goddamn stupid. He wasn't going to hold a burning piece of paper. His old man had wanted him to be "made," but after what had happened it would be a while, if ever. There was also the law of silence called *omerta*, his dad said meant don't talk to cops, tell them your business, like he'd tell the police anything about anything. Mauro, the little man, probably took it literally, thought *omerta* meant don't talk to anyone.

Driving through Rome Joey would point to some ruins and say, "Hey, Mauro, what's that?"

Little fucker'd go, "*Vecchia Roma*."

Give Joey a smartass two-word answer in Italian. Joey

wanted to give him a one-word answer: "*Vaffanculo.*" Fuck you. Or a three-word answer: "*Succhiami il cazzo.*" Suck my dick. That exhausted his knowledge of Italian but had come in handy in his old eastside Detroit neighborhood.

Joey liked looking at monuments and such, but it made him wonder what the Italians had been doing for the past two thousand years. They hadn't built anything close to the Colosseum or the Pantheon, or St Peter's. Most of the people, from what he could see, lived in second-rate apartment buildings outside the city the ancient Romans wouldn't have stepped foot in.

Mauro parked the Benz in front of a cool old building with arched windows and shutters. He could see the Colosseum right there. It looked a lot bigger up close, bigger than Comerica Park where the Tigers played. Bigger than Ford Field too. Jesus, six, seven storys high.

Mauro glanced at him and said, "The residence of the signorina."

That's the most he'd ever said at one time, got five words out of him – might be a Guinness Record. Joey also liked that he called Angela the signorina, like she was Italian royalty or something. But then again, as the daughter of Don Gennaro, maybe she was.

Twenty

McCabe went out and got in the Fiat and took the steep driveway down to a country road that wound around to the main road, Viale Fiume. The weather had changed, heavy dark clouds hung over the mountains as he drove through the hills, past sheep and horses grazing, passing through La Quercia, a village, arriving in Viterbo a few minutes later. He was surprised to see a modern mirrored-glass building on Via Cassia right outside the medieval city. He drove through Porta Romana, a giant archway built in the wall that surrounded the city, took a series of narrow one-way streets and parked on Via Roma in the center of the business district.

McCabe had seen photographs of Viterbo, but had never been there. He was surprised how big it was and how crowded. He walked downhill to Piazza del Plebiscito. Studied the two arcaded buildings that made up Palazzo dei Priori, built in the fifteenth and sixteenth centuries. Stopped in the tourist office and picked up a street map of the city. He sat outside at a café in the square, ordered espresso and sipped it, studying the map, looking for a place to meet Mazara and make the exchange, Angela for the money.

He walked to Piazza del Gesu and north to Piazza San Lorenzo, the religious center. He went south to Piazza della Morte, Death Square, which somehow seemed appropriate, but was too small, too remote. From there he took a series of winding streets to Piazza San Pellegrino in the medieval quarter, and back to Piazza del Plebiscito.

He stood staring at the buildings and got an idea, decided what he was going to do and how he was going to do it. He'd meet Mazara and ask for the money. Mazara would hand him the soccer bag, and he would tell them where to find Angela. But where could he keep her that was out of sight, but still close by? The car was probably the only option. But she wasn't going to lie there quietly in the back, so where else could he hide her? It was a little more complicated than he thought. He considered calling Chip, ask for his help, but he didn't want to involve anyone else. It was his problem and he'd handle it.

Now he had to buy some food. It would be a couple days before he got everything organized. He found a butcher shop, a macellria, and bought slices of Cacciatora and Felino, and a whole chicken with its head still attached. Bought a loaf of ciabatta at a panetteria. Bought fresh mozzarella at a formaggeria and tomatoes at a vegetable stand in the market. He forgot the wine and went to an *enoteca* and bought a bottle of Chianti, and a Tuscan Chardonnay. He carried his packages to the car, opened the hatchback and put them in.

Angela thought she heard a car and looked out the window. McCabe's Fiat was moving down the hill toward the road that went one way to Viterbo, and the other way to a village called Bagnaia. Beyond the road she could see the muted rectangle shapes of houses across the valley, a smoky haze hanging low over the hills, the vista reminding her of the Tuscan countryside.

It was 1:30, only thirteen hours since he had taken her from the apartment, but seemed much longer, like days had passed, trapped in the room, her prison cell, pacing back and forth, ten feet from wall to wall, anxious, frustrated, going crazy.

She pictured McCabe sitting on the bed, waiting for her as she walked in the bedroom, taking her down, and taping her hands and feet. She'd had a panic attack wrapped in the tarp. She could not move and had trouble trying to breathe, heart pounding, overcome by anxiety. Thinking of her mother helped calm her as it always did, helped her through tense situations. Feeling her mother's gentle touch, hearing her soothing voice, like she was a little girl again.

Angela had been asleep when he slid her out of the car and carried her in the house, waking when he unwrapped the tarp, drenched in sweat as if she had stepped out of her bath. He kidnapped her and then apologized, saying he had no choice, no other way to get her out of the apartment. Thinking back she liked that and was surprised when he brought her a pillow and blanket. And he had continued to surprise her, this student who was not afraid to challenge a Mafia gang. She admired his toughness and determination, but what chance did he have of succeeding? None. What he was doing seemed foolish and naïve. He had been lucky, but his luck was going to run out.

Her cousin Joey would be wondering what happened to her. He would say something to her father, and her father would say you can never count on Angela. She is always late. It was true. She had been late her whole life.

Mazara would have called looking for her by now, and had probably stopped by her apartment, and let himself in. She had given him a key, something she now regretted. He would make himself comfortable, drink beer and watch a football match on television. He would think she was in the city, shopping, or having lunch. It wouldn't be an issue until tonight or tomorrow when she still had not returned his calls or returned to the apartment.

Standing at the door, she moved the handle up and down. It was locked. Of course, it was locked, and the door was heavy and solid. She looked around the room for something to jam in the keyhole to try to unlock it. There was a brass doorstopper screwed into the baseboard molding. She unscrewed it and pulled the rubber cap off the end and tried to stick it in the keyhole, but it was too big.

Angela unfastened her belt, took it off and folded the buckle away from the clasp and stuck the clasp in the keyhole. She moved it around trying to find the pin. She tried for ten minutes and quit, frustrated, throwing her belt on the floor. She turned on the faucet and put her hand under it and scooped water up to her mouth, drank and turned off the water.

She looked out the window and saw a man walking along the road at least a hundred meters away. She opened the window as far as it would go and yelled, "Signore . . . can you hear me? Help!" She said it again, but he was too far. He continued on his way, never glancing in her direction.

She looked in the mirror, annoyed, irritated, angry at herself for letting this happen. She went over and picked up the belt, bent the buckle back and stuck the clasp in the keyhole again, moving it in a circular motion, doing this for almost fifteen more minutes, trying to find the pin until her hand ached, too tired to continue. She stretched her arms over her head and bent down and touched her toes.

Angela was thinking about her nanny, Carmella whose father was a locksmith from Siena. He had taught Angela how to set a pin, saying, you reach in the lock with something long and sharp, a piece of metal, and find the pin that's binding the most and push it up until you feel it set. That's how you pick a lock. She had tried it the one time and was able to do it, but that was long ago.

She stuck her belt clasp in the lock again, moving it to the right edge and then the left. She pushed as hard as she could and thought she felt something move.

Twenty-one

Sharon's boss called his cell phone. He didn't recognize the number and answered it. Her name was DeAnn Forbes. They'd met a couple times, but he didn't know her very well.

DeAnn said, "I'm worried about Sharon, we all are. Is she all right?"

"Stressed out. Just needs some time off." He had to be careful what he said.

"Imagine my surprise," DeAnn said, "when I got an email saying she was taking a leave of absence. I couldn't believe it. Sharon's our top rep and I had to try to explain to our clients what was going on and didn't have a clue. Ray, can you help me out, can you tell me what the hell's going on?"

What was he going to say? He'd been kicked out of the Secret Service, went home and Sharon wasn't there, and based on the mail and phone messages, she hadn't been around for days. He was thinking about the article in the *Free Press* about the guy who reported his wife missing. She worked in Puerto Rico during the week and came home on weekends to see her husband and two kids. The husband said they'd had an argument and his wife decided to go back to Puerto Rico a day early. The husband said she was picked up in a dark sedan. He didn't know anything more.

Two weeks later the Macomb County Sheriff's Department went to his house with a search warrant and found the wife's torso in a garbage can in the garage. The husband confessed he'd cut up her body in his dad's machine shop and strewn her body parts in a wooded area behind their house. A detective working the case said, when the wife's missing the husband is always the main suspect.

Ray said, "Sharon will call you, explain everything when she's ready."

DeAnn said, "Does she have cancer, can you tell me that?"

Ray said, "She's not dying." He hoped she wasn't.

DeAnn said, "Tell her we love her and she's welcome back whenever she wants."

Ray was suspicious, didn't believe it. Sharon would've called, not sent an email. That wasn't like her. She was conscientious and responsible, loved her job, and made a lot of money, more than he did and he was well paid for a federal agent. It didn't seem plausible that she'd just up and leave with someone like Joey Palermo, either. But she had to be lonely, starved for attention and affection. He certainly hadn't helped the situation. She was alone most of the time and when he came home he made her miserable. He couldn't see it before or maybe he didn't want to stop and consider her point of view. It was as if his life had been out of focus and now everything was in perfect register. He wanted her back and wondered if what he was feeling was possessiveness or love. Did he still love her? Did he ever?

But if she planned to go away with Joey she would've told someone, wouldn't she? Her sister? Her friends? The way she did it didn't make sense. That's why Ray had his doubts. Until he knew better he'd have to assume something was wrong, something had happened to Sharon.

He drove downtown to the McNamara Building, where

he'd worked for the first two years as an agent. Parked in an open lot across from the office, went in the building and asked for Jim Teegarden.

Teeg came down and got him, shook his hand and said, "Good to see you, Ray. This take you back?"

"Déjà vu all over again."

Teeg was compact and meticulous, dark hair going gray, wearing a blue Oxford-cloth shirt with heavy starch, gold cuff links, and a designer tie. They took an elevator up to the tenth floor, a bullpen of cubicles where Ray had worked. He said, "Looks exactly the same. Like I walked out yesterday."

"What'd you think, the Service was going to change?"

Teegarden had fifteen years in. He was a GS-15, same as Ray had been, and had his own office. Ray stood at the window, glancing at the GM Building a few blocks away, and beyond it the Detroit River and the shoreline of Canada. With the casinos and new construction Detroit looked better than ever. But Ray didn't care, he liked it the way it was. Liked its rustbelt, blue-collar charm.

Teeg said, "Here's Joey, take a look."

He had a stack of photographs in his hands, sliding three off the deck like he was dealing cards, and arranged them on his desk that didn't have anything on it except a phone. Ray stood there looking down at a black-and-white shots, a close-up of Joey's face. Nice-looking guy, heavy beard, dark hair slicked back, Joey grinning, Joey smoking a cigar in the second one, getting in his car in front of the Messina Spaghetti Company, his office, a two-story cinderblock building on Grosbeck.

The next series showed Joey in his boat on Lake St Clair; Joey outside the Roostertail, the riverside, partying with his buddies, and Joey on a street in downtown Detroit, making his daily collections.

Teegarden put three more shots on top of those, showing Joey with a baseball bat. He was in a batter's stance, and it looked like the inside of a restaurant. There were tables in the background but nobody sitting at them. Another shot showed Joey swinging for the fence. And in the third one, Joey was outside the restaurant, big smile, bat resting on his shoulder.

Teegarden said, "Surveillance photos, courtesy of the Federal Bureau of Investigation."

Ray said, "He ever play ball?"

Teegarden said, "He only swings at things that don't move – inanimate objects, and people."

He slid three more photos off the deck: busted-up cases in a jewelry store, smashed car windows on a dealership lot and the shattered storefront window of a fur shop. He could read the name on the door in the left side of the frame: Dietrich Furs.

Ray said, "He likes to break things, I see."

Teegarden said, "You don't pay for protection, this is what happens."

"They've got pictures of what he did and people he threatened, right? What's the problem?" Ray said.

"Call the police," Teegarden said, "and you might end up like this."

Teegarden showed him a guy on the floor of a party store, head resting in a pool of blood.

"I see your point." Ray didn't understand how Sharon could fall for someone like Joey Palermo. She was too smart, too aware.

Next, he put down pictures of two fat, balding old men wearing black horn-rim glasses.

"This is Vincenzo 'Vito Uno' Corrado," he said, pointing to the photo on the left. "The boss of all bosses. And this is Joey's father, Joseph 'Joe P.' Palermo, the under-boss."

Ray said, "They all have cute nicknames, huh?"

"They'd have a field day with you," Teegarden said. "I could see Ray 'His Eminence' Pope in a second."

Ray said, "That's not bad. I'd have to be the top wop with that name."

"Vito's got stage two prostate cancer," Teegarden said. "And Joe P.'s got a heart condition, takes Coumadin."

"What's Coumadin?"

"Blood-thinner medicine."

"Doesn't say much for the vitality of the Detroit Mafia," Ray said, "does it? What's Joey's title, where's he fit in?"

"Runs a street crew, he's a lieutenant. They go into a store, tell the proprietor he needs protection. The guy objects, tells them they're crazy, you saw what they do."

Ray said, "Interesting business model."

"Is he still bothering Sharon?"

"He calls the house," Ray said. "Leaves messages."

"He obviously doesn't know what you do, or did."

"I'm not sure," Ray said.

"What's Sharon say?"

"She doesn't."

Teeg stared at him probably wondering what the hell was going on, but didn't say anything.

Ray said, "Where's old man Palermo live?"

"Bloomfield Village," Teegarden said.

"You have an address?"

"What're you going to do?"

"I don't know." And he didn't, but if anyone knew where Joey was, his dad did.

Ray cruised by the house, a 4,500-square-foot red-brick colonial with a circular drive on a street called Glengarry in the heart of the Village, one of the wealthiest areas of suburban Detroit.

"What a country," Teeg had said. "The mob under-boss living among affluent professionals: doctors, lawyers and auto executives."

He drove one block over and looked between two houses and saw the back of Joe P.'s place. Ray drove home and had an early dinner. He cooked a strip steak on the grill and had a baked potato and a bottle of Sam Adams. He got in bed at seven and set his alarm for 2:00 a.m. He woke up before it went off, 1:57, got up and put on black Levis and a black turtleneck. He unlocked the gun box in his closet and chose the Walther PPK over the Colt because it was small and light, easier to carry.

Ray went back to Bloomfield Village and parked on Williamsbury. It was very dark, the moon a sliver. He felt odd, out of his element. He opened the car door – he'd disconnected the interior lights – and got out and pressed the door closed. He walked between two houses that were big and spaced apart, looked like there was an extra lot between them. Both had swimming pools that were covered for the season. It was so quiet the only thing he heard was the sound of his footsteps on the hard grass. It was cold and clear and smelled like fall and when he let out a breath he could see it.

The back of Joe P.'s place was straight ahead. Ray hopped a white picket fence and crossed the yard to the back of the house. There was a brick patio with nothing on it. He noticed a small sticker on one of the windows that said: Protected by Alert Security Services. Ray didn't believe it. Why would the under-boss of the Detroit Mafia need a security system?

There were French doors that opened onto the patio. He tried the handles, no give at all. The doors were locked top and bottom with deadbolts. He moved along the back of the house to the garage, three-car attached, single door and a double. Next to the garage doors was a glass-paneled entry door.

Ray looked in but couldn't see much. He turned and stood facing the backyard and threw an elbow and broke the bottom left pane. He watched and listened, didn't see or hear anything. He reached through the broken pane and unlocked the door and went in. There was a dark-colored Lincoln Town Car and a silver Ford Edge. There were trashcans, and patio furniture taking up most of the third space.

He tried the door to the house. It was locked but it moved, gave half an inch or so. He flipped a switch on the wall and six recessed ceiling lights came on. He studied a pegboard attached to the wall that had rakes and shovels and brooms and saw a crowbar. He went over and picked it up off the hook and went back to the door and jammed the tapered end of it into the seam between the edge of the door and the jamb, and bent the crowbar back, heard the wood groan, and the door came open.

Ray went through the kitchen and dining room and living room into the foyer. It had a marble floor and a grand sweeping staircase that rose up to the second floor. He started to go up the stairs and stopped, glanced left into a room with paneled walls and a fireplace.

He went back down, crossed the foyer and went in the wood-paneled room. He sat behind the desk, and turned on a small lamp that was on the desktop. It had to be Joe P.'s office, the room fifteen by fifteen, two chairs and a table against the far wall in front of a window that looked out on the front yard. He checked the drawers looking for something from Joey, a letter, a postcard, but didn't find anything.

It was 4:05 when he took out his cell and dialed the number on the desk phone, Ray reasonably sure it was Joe P.'s private business line that only rang here, the number different from the one Teegarden had given him. The only unknown: who else was in the house? Joe P. and his wife for sure, but what about his bodyguard, a big dude named Angelo who had played defensive end for another Joe P., Joe Paterno at Penn State.

The phone on the desk rang, and even though he was expecting it, the sound startled him. God it was loud. It rang ten times before he heard voices at the top of the stairs.

"I know it's the middle of the night. Don't worry about it, go back to bed."

Ray heard someone come down the stairs, and come across the foyer, and come in the room, a silver-haired guy about five seven, wearing a bathrobe and black glasses with big frames that reminded him of Aristotle Onassis. Joe P. reached over the desk for the phone and brought it up to his face and said, "This better be fucking important."

Ray said, "It is."

Joe P. turned and said, "You have any idea who I am?"

He put the phone back in the cradle.

Ray drew the Walther PPK and said, "Who else's in the house?"

"My wife."

Ray said "What about Angelo?"

"He don't stay with us."

A voice from upstairs said, "Joe, who you talking to?"

"I'm on the fucking phone, will you go back to bed."

Ray said, "That's no way to talk to the little lady."

Joe P. said, "What do you want, the silverware, a TV? Help yourself and get the fuck out of here."

He talked tough for an old man in a bathrobe. Ray said, "Where's Joey?"

"I don't know. Why don't you call him. I'll give you his number."

Ray pulled the hammer back on the PPK. "Let's start over, okay? Pretend I just walked in, haven't said a word. Where's Joey?"

Joe P said, "You think you can come in here, intimidate me in my own house? I got twenty clowns like you work for me."

Ray crossed the room and placed the barrel of the Walther against Joe P.'s cheek, felt teeth under wrinkled skin and said, "Then you know I'll shoot you dead, eh goomba? Pull the trigger, blow your fucking head off. Then go upstairs, find out what Mrs P. knows. See if she wants to talk, be a little more co-operative. I started with you because I figured you'd understand the gravity, the serious nature of the situation," he said, giving it a little bureaucratic embellishment.

"Who you with?"

"Want me to say it again?"

"What do you want him for?"

"I want to talk to him."

Joe P. didn't say anything. He probably thought he was still thirty and in shape. That's the way it worked. In his head, Ray still thought he was twenty-one. "All right, you don't want to talk, let's go upstairs."

Joe P. leaned back against the desk. Could barely hold himself up. He coughed and grabbed his chest, struggling, trying to stay on his feet but couldn't, and went down on the floor, legs kicking for a few seconds, then he stopped moving, eyes bulging out of their sockets, staring up at Ray. The clock next to the phone said 4:23 a.m.

Twenty-two

McCabe drove up the hill and pulled in and parked next to the house. He carried the groceries into the kitchen and put them away. He went through the main room to the bathroom and knocked on the door. She didn't say anything. He put the key in the lock and turned it and pushed the handle down and opened the door a crack and swung it all the way open. She was standing at the window looking at him.

"You want to get out of here? Give me the number," McCabe said.

She looked angry, didn't say anything. He'd be angry too, cooped up in this little room, like he was in Rebibbia. That was the idea, wasn't it? "You like it in there, enjoying yourself?" He reached for the handle, started to close the door.

She said, "Okay."

"You can come out," McCabe said, "but try anything like you did before, that's it. You're going to grow old in there."

She did and he led her to the dining table in the main room and sat next her. Gave her a piece of paper and a pen. She wrote down a number and handed it to him. He took her cell phone out of his pocket, turned it on and it started *beeping*. She had gotten at least a dozen calls. Angela stared at it but didn't say anything. He dialed the number. Heard it ring a couple times. Heard Mazara say, "*Pronto*."

McCabe said, "Looking for Angela?" He glanced at her. "Say something."

"Roberto . . ."

She said it just the way he wanted her to – helpless, afraid.

"Where are you?"

McCabe said. "You want her back, it's going to cost you five hundred thousand euros."

Mazara said, "What is this?"

"What do you think it is?" McCabe said.

"I talk to Angela."

"You can talk," McCabe said, "when you bring the money."

"I don't have it," Mazara said.

"Kidnap someone, rob a bank, you'll figure something out," McCabe said. "You've got forty-eight hours." Give him enough time but not too much.

Mazara said, "You do anything to her . . ."

McCabe closed the phone, cut him off. He didn't want to hear Mazara's hard-guy threats. Just wanted to hook him and let him hang for a while.

Angela said, "What did he say?"

"He's going to think about it," McCabe said.

"He said that?" She shook her head. "I don't believe you."

"No, he didn't say that. He didn't say anything."

"What about you, McCabe?"

She gave him a sultry look, kept it on him and said, "Would you pay to have me back?"

"Why? You don't mean anything to me."

She was pouting now, looking offended, and McCabe reminded himself she was playing him like she did the first time, and he was falling for it again. He wasn't that dumb, was he?

They went in the kitchen and had lunch at 3:00 in the afternoon, bread, salami, Caprese salad and warm Chardonnay that wasn't bad, McCabe sitting across the table from her, occasionally glancing at her but not talking. There wasn't much to say. She ate everything, drank two glasses of wine and finished the meal with a piece of bread.

When he was finished, she picked up the dishes and took them to the sink and washed them. He stood next to her and dried them like they were a married couple in their country home. But he was alert, on guard, didn't trust this sudden change in attitude, watching her, making sure she didn't reach for a knife.

McCabe said, "I'm going into Bagnaia." He wanted to check it out, see if there was a better place to meet Mazara and make the exchange.

She didn't say anything, but turned her head and looked at him with big sad eyes and pouty lips.

"You can take me with you," she said.

He considered it for a few seconds and realized he was slipping into the stupid zone again. He said, "No way."

"Then leave me here. Don't lock me in that room. Where do you think I will go?"

Anywhere. To the neighbor's to make a phone call. To La Quercia. To Viterbo. Back to Rome. He held her in his gaze. "You know what's going on here, what's happening?" If she did, she didn't acknowledge it, one way or the other. "You're my bargaining chip. With you I've got a chance of getting the money back. Without you I've got no chance at all."

He took her back to the bathroom. She went in, but didn't say anything, wouldn't look at him. He closed the door and locked it.

~

McCabe was gone longer than he planned. He'd driven through Bagnaia, checked it out and stopped at the gardens at Villa Lante, but didn't find a location that would work. He'd stick with his Viterbo plan.

He drove back to Pietro's place, parked the car and went inside. He unlocked the bathroom door and swung it open. Expected her to be standing there, but she wasn't. Did he forget to lock the door? No, he rewound and saw himself doing it. Locked it and checked the handle to make sure.

He crossed the room and opened the gun case, three shotguns in their custom slots, one missing. He gripped the barrel of a twelve-gauge, lifting it out.

"Put it down," she said somewhere behind him.

He glanced over his shoulder and saw her holding the shotgun across her waist, barrel leveled at him, flat and horizontal like she knew what she was doing.

McCabe's dad had been a duck hunter, he knew shotguns, knew the stance. He put the gun back in the case and turned toward her. "You had your chance. Why didn't you go? Or are you waiting for them to pick you up?"

He moved toward her and she raised the shotgun, stock against her shoulder, twin blue steel barrels pointed at his chest.

She said, "I think you should stay right there, do not move."

She was on the other side of the room about fifteen feet away.

"You going to shoot me?" He took another step toward her, nervous, not sure what she was going to do, staring down the end of the barrels. Saw her cock the twin hammers back with her thumb.

McCabe said, "Think you've got the nerve?" Challenging her, daring her to do it.

"Take another step," she said, "you'll find out."

He did. Moved toward her, saw her fingers twitching on the triggers. He reached out, grabbed the shotgun, taking it out of her hands. He closed the hammers and put it on the rug.

She came at him now wild and out of control and he wrapped his arms around her and took her down on the antique rug, his body on hers, holding her arms at her sides against the floor, looking at her, faces a few inches apart. He kissed her. That's what he'd wanted to do since he'd brought her here, since the first time he saw her.

She kissed him back, and they were making out, McCabe into it, lost in the moment, and she was too, eyes closed, holding him tight. Now she opened her eyes and they were looking at each other, both a little embarrassed. What the hell had just happened? McCabe slid off her and she sat next to him, legs bent under her. "Were you going to shoot me?"

"It isn't loaded," she said, reaching for the shotgun, breaking it open, showing him the empty chambers.

"You looked serious," McCabe said, "like you were going to blow me away."

"That was the idea." She paused, her brown eyes locked on him. "Admit it, now you're wondering if I called Roberto, aren't you?"

"If you did, he'd be here by now," McCabe said.

"I didn't."

"Tell me what's going on, will you? I don't get it."

"I made a mistake," Angela said. "I caused you a lot of trouble, a lot of problems and I feel bad about it."

It sounded sincere, but he wasn't convinced, expected Mazara to come through the door any second. He said, "How'd you get out?"

She smiled. "I am not going to tell you. I might have to do it again."

"I guess there's no point locking you up," McCabe said. "I'm not sure what to do with you. I can't lock you up and I can't trust you."

"Why don't you pour me a glass of wine while you're thinking about it."

Later, in the kitchen, she said, "I was attracted to you the first time I saw you that day at Rosati."

"If you were, I didn't see it."

Angela smiled. "Under the circumstances, I didn't see much future. What you did, getting my bag back, was very heroic. I was wondering what it would be like to go out with you, get to know you."

"Come on," McCabe said, doubting her, although he'd felt the same way.

"It's true," Angela said. "There was something about you."

"Well I couldn't take my eyes off you," McCabe said. "Coming toward me in Piazza del Popolo."

She started to smile and stopped herself. "You said I reminded you of Manuela Arcuri. I don't look anything like her."

"That day you did. Like Manuela in *Hearts Lost*. Ever see it?"

"I don't think so."

"You should." He turned his attention to the bottle of Chianti, cut the foil off the top with a paring knife, and screwed a corkscrew through the center of the cork and pulled. It came out with a *pop*. He put the bottle on the tile countertop and looked at her. "How'd you know where I was going to get off the bus?"

"Sisto, with the red hair, waited outside the entrance to the school and followed you," Angela said.

"How'd you know I'd go after the two guys on the motorcycle?"

She smiled. "That was completely unexpected. But it worked to my advantage. I didn't have to try to meet you. You did everything, you made it easy."

"What if I didn't go with you?"

"But you did," she said and smiled again.

"I couldn't resist you, huh?"

"You did seem interested."

He flashed back to that day at the *enoteca*, McCabe taken by her. He would have walked her to Florence if she'd asked, walked her to Venice.

She glanced at the Chianti. "Are you going to pour the wine some time today?"

"Oh, you want some wine?"

He filled two stemmed glasses about a third of the way and handed one to Angela. She took a big gulp. "Take your time," McCabe said. "Don't drink so fast. Sip it, and taste all the things that are going on." She'd said something like that to him at the *enoteca* and now he was giving it back to her.

She smiled. "Now you are a connoisseur, uh?" She sipped

the Chianti and swished it around in her mouth. "How was that?" Angela said. "Did I do it correctly?"

"I think you've got the hang of it," McCabe said.

"I have to tell you. After we collected the money . . ." She paused. "Sisto said you saw our faces, you would go to the police and identify us. They were talking about killing you."

McCabe said, "And let me guess, you talked them out of it?" Was she telling the truth?

"They were serious," Angela said.

Her face was, too.

"I told Mazara, if they harmed you," Angela said, "I would go to the police myself and turn them in."

"So you saved my life and I should be grateful, is that what you're telling me?"

"Now that you mention it."

"I'll see what I can do." He sipped his wine.

"I like you, McCabe." She came up next to him and held his hands. "I don't want anything to happen to you. But if you continue with this you are going to be hurt or worse." She let go of his hands, stepped back and picked up her wine glass.

"I'll take my chances," McCabe said.

"That's what I expected you to say."

"Why'd you bring it up?"

"I was hoping you would change your mind," Angela said.

"You think I'm going to give up, you don't know me."

Twenty-three

Joey went up to the door and scanned the names in the directory and saw A. Gennaro, apartment 2B. He pressed the button, but nothing happened. He pressed it again. Still nothing. He tried another apartment, waited and heard the door buzz open. He walked up a narrow staircase that wound around the elevator shaft to the second floor, and knocked on Angela's door, waited and knocked again. He stood there looking at the door painted green with a high-gloss finish. He turned and looked behind him at another apartment across the hall. Just two on the whole floor.

Downstairs, he heard the door to the building open and close, heavy and solid. Heard someone coming up the stairs. Joey walked halfway up to the third floor and waited, listening. He could see the shape of a man through the steel mesh of the elevator shaft, standing in front of Angela's door. Joey started down, and saw him open the door and go in the apartment.

Joey walked down and knocked on Angela's door, waited a couple seconds and it opened. The guy saw him and tried to close it, but he was ready, put his weight into it, pushing his way into the room. It was the douche bag owed his uncle money. He couldn't believe it, Joey trying to remember his name. "The fuck're you doing here? Where's Angela at?"

Guy didn't say anything, stared at him like he was deaf.

Was this clown Angela's boyfriend? Must be if he had his own key.

"Where's my Unk's money?"

"I do not have," he said.

"You do not have?" Joey said. "You better fucking have."

Joey wished he had his baseball bat, show this dick with ears who he was dealing with here. Joey moved toward him, hit him in the face and knocked him on his ass. He could feel the adrenalin surge, squatted, put a knee on his chest and pinned him against the carpet. "Where's she at?" Joey said, the guy's name coming to him now. Mazara, that was it.

"The American took her," Joey thought he said, easing up a little so he could breathe.

"What American?"

He told Joey about the student they'd kidnapped. Thought he was the son of a wealthy American senator, Charles Tallenger, but instead they had picked up the wrong one, and he had taken Angela.

This was getting good. Joey'd been down since he left Detroit and this charged him up. He felt like his old self again. He'd find this amateur fucking yahoo student, bring Angela back and, who knew, maybe take over his uncle's business while the old boy sat on his ass. Joey was thinking – hold on a second – maybe this was fate. Maybe this was destined to happen. He'd looked up his horoscope online that morning. It said making your mark on the world isn't for the faint of heart. Plans always change. Be open to new voices directing you. It was as if it was talking directly at him, telling him he was on track, showing him the way.

Joey let him up now and his phone rang. Mazara flipped it open and brought it to his ear.

Joey said, "That him?"

Mazara nodded.

"Gimme the fucking phone," Joey said.

Mazara handed it to him.

Joey put it up to his ear. "You have any idea, my friend, who you've got there?"

The voice on the other end said, "Who're you?"

"Guy who's going to cut your nuts off," Joey said, "you don't let Angela go right fucking now."

"You want her back," he said, "get five hundred thousand euros, put the money in a white Adidas soccer bag. Think you can remember that?"

Joey said, "I wish you luck 'cause you're going to need it." The phone went dead, asshole hung up on him. He glanced at Mazara. "Where's the money at?"

"It was cut up like a pizza. Everyone they take a piece and now it is gone."

"That's what I'm going to do – cut you up, you don't get the money back, including what you owe my uncle, and bring it to me. I don't want to hear any fucking excuses."

Joey was thinking, with these modern-day dumbass Italians, he'd get a piece of the action, maybe even get it all. He had Mauro drive him to the Excelsior on Via Veneto, this famous hotel on this famous street. He went to the reception desk and got a room with the passport that said he was Salvatore Bitonte, a hairdresser from Detroit, but not a fag.

He had to get out of the villa for a while, be on his own. He looked at his watch, a gold Rolex President. It was 1:55. No wonder he was starving. He went to the restaurant next door, place called Doney, had bombolitti with artichokes, bread and two glasses of Batar, a nice Tuscan white, and for dessert, coffee and strawberries with limoncello mousse, kept Mauro waiting in the car, Joey didn't care. He paid cash for the meal, put the receipt in his shirt pocket and went outside.

When Joey got back to the villa his uncle was acting strange – like what else was new? He wasn't listening to opera or studying one of his paintings. He was sitting behind his big wooden desk he said once belonged to Mussolini, his hands folded like he was praying.

Joey said, "Yo, Unk, what's up?"

His uncle got up and came across the room, taking tiny steps, an odd look on his face. "I do not know how to tell you this . . ."

Joey was thinking the old boy was upset 'cause he blew his woofers listening to *Rigoletto*.

"Your father is gone," his uncle said in a soft voice.

"What?" Joey didn't understand him.

"Giuseppe is dead."

It was strange. His father had died and he didn't feel anything at all. "What happened?"

"Was his heart," Unk said, still holding his hands together.

No surprise there. His old man had had angioplasty twice and was taking a blood thinner. Unk put his arms around Joey, hugging him. Joey didn't like this old guy, who smelled like mothballs and BO, touching him. That was another thing about the modern Italians, they could shower a little more often, Jesus Christ. He looked down at the top of his Unk's balding silver hair, the skin on his head tan like his arms and face.

Joey's first impulse was to go home. Sneak back in the country the way he'd snuck out – go to the funeral, see his mother. It was risky, but he had to do it. The family would respect him for coming out of hiding to honor his father, wouldn't they? Respect him, or think he was an idiot for coming back?

Then he thought, maybe his old man got what he deserved. Instead of helping Joey, he'd sent him away, banished him to cover his own ass. Now with Joe P. out of the picture, Joey was on his own. No one would help him. No one would go near him.

His uncle finally let go of him and called Mauro. The little guy came in the room, and his uncle said something to him in Italian. Mauro hurried out and came back a few minutes later with a small-stemmed glass that had clear liquid in it.

"Drink this."

Joey took the glass and sipped it – sambuca. The warm licorice liquid going down slowly like motor oil, taking his breath away, his uncle staring at him, and Mauro standing there like a statue. Joey said, "I'm going to Rome, spend a few days in a hotel. I need to think."

"This is no time to be foolish."

He wanted to say, Oh, okay, Unk, thanks for the great fucking advice. Joey went upstairs, changed his clothes, hung his shirt and pants in the closet, packed a suitcase, a small bag with enough stuff for a few days. Joey poked his head back in his Unk's room and said, "Yo, Unk, backo shortolo."

Joey was happy to get out of the villa. He felt free for the first time in weeks. Mauro drove him back to Rome and dropped him off at the Excelsior. He felt good walking in the lobby, checking out the thirty-foot ceiling with giant chandeliers and expensive-looking furniture. The room was big and expensive-looking too. It ought to be for $750 a night, the euro still kicking the dollar's ass.

He went to his room, laid on the bed, relaxed and looked at the *Herald Tribune*, checked the NFL scores, the Lions had lost another one, now 0 and 7, Jesus. Worst team in football. He turned on CNN and watched for a few minutes, wondering what the hell was going on in the world. He felt out of touch, hadn't seen a newspaper or TV for six days.

There was a knock on the door. He opened it and saw a good-looking blonde reminded him of Sharon, standing there, same hairstyle, same height and build. He smelled perfume. Jesus, like she took a bath in it.

She said, "Signor Bitonte?"

"Call me Sal," Joey said.

She came in and moved past him and sat on the queen-size bed and he closed the door and said, "What's your name?"

"Lia."

"Lia, huh? Okay, Lia, let's see what you got." Joey's rule: when he was alone with a babe, she had to be naked. He liked to look at her body. At first girls would resist and pretend to be shy, but the truth was they couldn't wait to show him the goods. He dated one chick with huge bozos liked to stand in front of the window and shock people driving by. At first she was like – no way. You think I'm going to prance around in my birthday suit?

Another one liked to walk out to the end of the driveway and get the newspaper in a robe with nothing under it. When the wind blew it open she'd pretend to be embarrassed. Oh, don't look. I'm naked under here.

It was Joey's belief that all women were whores. Some like Lia were up front, straightforward about it. They came to your room and you paid for their services. Girlfriends got paid in other ways: gifts and dinners and trips. But they all took your money, one way or the other.

Lia got up and took her clothes off and Joey looked at her and grinned and said, "*Succhiami il cazzo*."

She got on her knees, knelt before him. See, his command of Italian was coming in handy again. As it turned out, Lia was nothing special, going through the motions, giving him a C- blowjob and a C+ fuck. When they were finished he paid her €250 and booted her out. He needed to be alone for a while. He went to the mini bar and took out a bottle of Grey Goose and made himself a Martini.

He sat on the bed, leaned back against the headboard, more relaxed now, the edge taken off, and thought about Sharon, Sharona his nickname for her. She'd been the exception to the all-women-are-whores rule. She refused to parade around in the nude, and when he gave her a present, she told him it wasn't necessary and meant it. She was a keeper. That's why he asked her to marry him. He'd dated dozens of girls and realized that meeting the *one* was like luck roulette.

He pictured Sharon with the blonde hair and the black beaver that was like a mohair sweater he couldn't keep his hands off of. She wasn't the best-looking girl he'd ever dated, but she was the sexiest. She was also girlish and feminine and funny. Only one he'd ever gone out with made him laugh. He saw himself showing her the sights of Rome, and then taking her to Positano on the Amalfi Coast, this beautiful picturesque town, and he got horny again just thinking about it.

It was his father who'd arranged for his passport that was the real thing, and snuck him into Canada – through the Detroit–Windsor Tunnel in the back of a panel truck so there'd be no record with Canadian customs. He was driven to Toronto where he got on a plane with his new identity, headed for Frankfurt, Germany, biggest goddamn airport he'd ever seen in his life. From there he flew to Milan and was picked up by Mauro who tóok the Autostrada del Sole 350 kilometers to Rome in a little less than four hours.

He'd been in Italy now for six days and he had a craving for Coney dogs and thick rare cheeseburgers. He missed Edy's mint- chocolate-chip ice cream too and the idea of staying with his uncle, hearing opera every day had him on edge. But the situation with Angela presented an interesting opportunity. Joey had a vision. Saw Mazara and his crew working for him, Joey sitting back, relaxing, getting rich. Yeah, he'd take some of that.

Twenty-four

It was just before 9:00 p.m. when he opened the refrigerator and took the chicken out and put it on the counter, its long neck and head still attached. "You want to make something – a side dish to go with this?"

Angela said, "I don't know how to cook." She came toward him and clinked his glass with hers. 'But I know how to do this," and took a sip.

"An Italian girl who doesn't cook . . ." McCabe said. "That's got to be a first. In ancient Rome learning to cook was a girl's duty."

"Does this look like ancient Rome?"

"What was your mother thinking?"

"She died when I was young." She put her glass down and pulled her hair back behind her ears. "We lived in a small house, one floor, on the outskirts of Palermo."

McCabe said, "You don't look Sicilian."

"My mother was from Cinque Terra. She had blonde hair. It was just before seven in the morning." Angela paused, took a breath. "I heard a knock on the door and wondered who would be coming to our house so early. I was getting ready for school. We didn't have to wear our uniform that day. I had a new pair of jeans and a blouse, but my mother said I could not wear jeans to the Ave Maria School – even on special days. I heard the door open and then voices, men arguing with my father. My mother told me to stay in my room and went out to see what was happening. I wanted to see, too, so I crept down the hall and peeked into the salon. There were two men aiming guns at my father. One was stocky and losing his hair, almost bald. The other man had a big mustache. That's all I remember, a face with a mustache. They tied up my father and then my older brother, Massimo, who was fourteen, and then my mother. The men made them sit on the floor. I could tell by the way they spoke, their accent, they were not Sicilian."

McCabe said, "Who were they?"

"Calabrians. The bald one kept saying, '*Dove il denaro? Dove il denaro.*'"

McCabe said, "Where's the money?"

"My father said, 'What money?' He didn't know what they were talking about. Mustache walked over and put a knife to my brother's throat. I remember my father saying, 'I don't know.' I was more afraid than I had ever been in my life. I could hear my heart thumping in my chest. I thought the men could hear it too. I thought it might explode." She paused and sipped her wine. "The bald man asked my father again for the money. My father said, 'Don't you think I would tell you if I knew.' This time Mustache did not hesitate, put the knife under my brother's chin and cut his throat. My mother screamed and now Mustache moved to her with the knife." Angela's eyes were wet. "My father begged them but it did no good and the man cut her throat. I was shaking. I went back to my room and got under the bed and closed my eyes as tight as I could, and put my hands over my ears." Angela took a breath. "I remember the sounds my father made when they stabbed him –" She paused again. "They thought he was dead."

McCabe said, "They didn't hurt you?"

"They didn't find me. One of the men, I don't know which one, came in my room. I could hear his feet on the wood floor, coming toward me. I put my hand over my mouth. I could see his shoes, ordinary black shoes that were scuffed and needed polish, and the bottom of his dark trousers. That was the scariest time of all, thinking they were going to kill me. I closed my eyes and pretended I was invisible, and a few minutes later I heard the front door close."

"But your father was alive?"

"The men walked out and I could hear him moaning, in agony, shirt covered with blood. I ran to our neighbor's house. An ambulance came and took him to the hospital. He had been stabbed four times and should have died."

"He must be tough," McCabe said. "That's where you get it, huh?"

"A few months later we moved to Rome. Carmella, my nanny, raised me." She picked up her glass, sipped some wine. "You would think an experience like this would have brought me and my father closer together, but just the opposite. I think he has always resented me because my brother was killed and I wasn't. Massimo was his favorite."

McCabe said, "Did he talk to you about what happened?"

"I asked him who the men were and why they came to our house," Angela said. "He wouldn't tell me anything. He's never said a word about it."

"I saw you with him coming out of Al Moro and I could tell by watching you something was wrong."

"You could see that? Every time I talk to him we argue," Angela said.

"Who were the men with you," McCabe said, "walking behind you?"

Angela said, "The little one is Mauro, my father's bodyguard. He, too, is Sicilian, from my father's village."

"He doesn't look like a bodyguard."

"That's what happens – you underestimate him – and then it's too late. The other man is my cousin from Detroit. Maybe you know him."

"What's his name?"

"Joey Palermo."

"Are you a Palermo too?"

"No, Gennaro."

McCabe was thinking – wait a minute. He remembered the Rome cop, Captain Ferrara, telling him about Carlo Gennaro, the boss of all bosses in Rome. It couldn't be the same family. He said, "Your dad's name isn't Carlo, is it?"

Angela said, "How did you know?"

Twenty-five

They were sitting on the portico, looking across the valley at the Cimini Mountains, blue sky, high clouds, Viterbo in the distance. The half wall next to them had vines crisscrossing it like green veins. She glanced at McCabe and said, "Do you know what Viterbo is famous for?"

McCabe said, "Of course, do you?"

He made it sound like a challenge.

"It is the city of popes," Angela said. "*La Città dei Papi*. More popes are from Viterbo than anywhere."

"Anagni is the real city of popes," McCabe said. "I can think of four who were born there: Innocent III, Gregory IX, Alexander IV and Boniface VIII– all between 1198 and 1303."

Angela said, "You know your popes." She sipped her wine. "Then what is Viterbo?"

"The residence of popes," McCabe said. "They lived there because it was safer than living in Rome. The emperor wanted to kill them. That's why the walls were built around the city."

She saw a truck driving by in the distance.

McCabe sipped his wine and said, "You know about the papal election of 1268?"

"Let me think," she said, putting him on. "No, I don't remember."

"Eighteen cardinals went to the bishop's palace to elect the new pope," McCabe said. "A year and a half went by and they still hadn't picked someone, so the people of Viterbo, the Viterbesi, locked them in their conclave and fed them bread and water till a new pope was chosen."

She was leaning back in her chair, legs bent, feet on the stone wall for balance.

"Are you falling asleep yet?" McCabe said.

"I was starting to doze off now that you say it."

His glass was empty and she poured him more Chianti and held his gaze. She said, "You going to tell me your plan to get the money, or talk about the history of Viterbo?"

"I'm going to do as the Romans do."

"Who said that, Caesar?"

"St Ambrose."

"Who is St Ambrose?"

"The Bishop of Milan."

Angela studied his face. "Is this for real?"

"You want to hear it?" He paused. "St Augustine went to Milan and learned that the Church didn't fast on Saturday as they did in Rome."

"When was this?" Angela lit a cigarette and blew smoke toward the mountains.

"AD 387." McCabe sipped his wine. "So St Ambrose said, 'When I am at Rome, I fast on Saturday. When I am at Milan, I do not. Follow the custom of the Church where you are.' And over time it became 'When in Rome, do as the Romans do.'"

"So you are going to do it their way, uh?" She flicked her cigarette ash on the patio stones. "What does that mean?"

"I'm going to meet Joey in front of Palazzo dei Priori," McCabe said, "if you know where that is."

"In the square," Angela said, "Plebiscito. There are usually a lot of people there."

"That's why I chose it," McCabe said.

"Okay, you meet him in the middle of town," Angela said. "Then what happens?"

"I invite him in the Palazzo, the council chamber, show him the ceiling. It's covered in frescos painted by Baldassare Croce in 1592, depicting the mythological origins of Viterbo and other historical events."

She smiled, not expecting that. "What are you really going to do?"

McCabe said, "Ask him for the money. He isn't carrying a white Adidas soccer bag, it's over. We try again another time."

"If he has the money," Angela said, "and I believe he will, he is going to want to see me. You must know that, right?"

He looked at her but didn't say anything.

"How many people have you kidnapped?" She could see him start to smile. "It doesn't seem like you know what you are doing." Angela paused. 'You have to make them think you have a partner – you are not alone."

"I've got another idea," McCabe said.

"I hope so."

"You'll be in a hotel room in Piazza San Pellegrino. I tell Joey to meet me in the square, he looks up, sees you in the window."

"You know what happens then? He sends Mazara in the hotel and up to the room to get me."

"He's supposed to come alone," McCabe said.

Angela said, "You think he's going to play by the rules?"

Her expression serious now. "If you really want this money I suggest you think about it a little more."

McCabe said, "You kidnap someone, you don't expect them to give you advice on how to collect the ransom."

Angela said, "You sound like you need some help."

"Whose idea was it to take me?" McCabe sipped his wine, eyes on her.

"Mazara was telling me about this rich American he met in Rebibbia and read about in the newspaper. He was thinking of kidnapping him, making some easy money. He told me what he was going to do. I listened, and said, 'That is never going to work.' He said, 'You have a better idea?'"

"Sounds familiar," McCabe said.

"I planned everything. I arranged to rent the farmhouse and volunteered to try to meet you, hoping you would notice me and you would be interested."

"How'd I do?" McCabe said.

"I also chose the transportation and the route the senator would take, sending him to three churches. The last one was Santi Giovanni e Paolo because it was built over a house of worship, and there are tunnels and underground passageways that would give us a perfect way to escape with the money.

"I knew the carabinieri would be involved, brought in for counsel, and they would use a tracking device or a transponder to follow the money and they did. We agreed to split the ransom five ways. Mazara told his crew I deserved a full share. 'For what?' Sisto said. 'Shaking her ass. That's what she does, what she is good at.'"

"Sounds right to me," McCabe said.

"Be careful, you want my help or not?" The wind blew her

hair and she straightened it and tucked it behind her ears. "Mazara didn't tell his crew that I was the one who had planned and organized everything, so, of course, they thought he did it. I was thinking, based on all I had done, I deserved at least half of the money, let them divide the rest."

McCabe said, "Why'd you do it?"

"I have bills to pay like everyone." She could see he didn't believe her.

"Your father is head of the Roman Mafia and you need money?"

"He found out I was seeing Mazara and cut me off."

"They give you your share? You can hand it over, save a step," McCabe said.

"I told you. I have received nothing," Angela said. "Not a single euro." She picked up her glass and drank some wine. "Did you talk to Joey, tell him the details? What you want him to do?"

"Not yet," McCabe said.

Angela said, "When do you think the exchange is going to take place?"

"Tomorrow," McCabe said.

"And you have not talked to him?"

"No."

"How do you know he will be ready?"

"He better be."

"McCabe, do you think this is just going to happen? They are just going to arrive in Viterbo and hand you the money? Say, here you are. Good luck."

McCabe grinned now and said, "What're you getting so excited about? It's all going to work out."

"You know your first idea might be okay," Angela said.

"You mean taking Joey into the council chamber?"

Angela said, "Palazzo dei Priori."

"It's a municipal building," McCabe said.

"Exactly."

"How're you going to get in?"

"I know a way," Angela said. "You want me to tell you?"

Twenty-six

Ray trained the binoculars on a girl in a peasant dress, getting out of a VW microbus in a 7-Eleven parking lot. Her brown hair parted down the middle and held in place by a headband, barefoot, the tops of her milky white breasts visible as she leaned forward, stepping out of the front passenger seat, closing the door and going in the store. It was like being in a time warp. Seeing her reminded him of the time he was on a detail to protect Tipper Gore at a Grateful Dead concert. Al was a US senator at the time, Bill Clinton's vice-presidential candidate on the Democratic ticket. The girl looked like the Deadheads he'd seen that afternoon and night in their pastel tie-dyes, braids, beads and flowers, hippies throwing Frisbees and playing hacky-sack in the RFK Stadium parking lot.

Ray had just completed his first year as an agent. He was on temporary assignment in the Washington office. Protective Services was short-handed, so that's how he happened to be sitting on a riser, stage left next to Tipper Gore on June 14th' 1991.

He remembered the caravan of spotless black Chevy Suburbans following two Virginia State Troopers, driving into the parking lot past the VW bugs and microbuses, Deadheads looking like some bizarre tribe, staring at Ray and his fellow agents like they were aliens.

He'd called Sharon after the concert and told her about it.

"There were guys wearing these weird headdresses just standing in front of the stage, smiling, and guys dressed as skeletons and some as Uncle Sam."

"They were high," Sharon said.

Ray said, "They were more than that. I saw a guy drink water out of a bong."

"God's herb," Sharon said.

"God's herb, huh?"

Sharon said, "You and Tipper expand your consciousness? Drop any blue Osley?"

Ray said, "What's that?"

"Acid."

"Sure," Ray said, "we do it all the time in the Service."

"Did you feel a connection with the band?"

Ray said, "I wouldn't go that far."

"Did you feel like part of the family?" Sharon said.

"No, I felt like I was protecting the wife of a vice-presidential candidate."

"Why'd Tipper want to see the Dead?"

"She said she likes their music."

Sharon said, "How'd she like it after a twenty-minute Jerry solo?"

"Not too much I guess," Ray said. "We didn't stay very long."

"They do 'Big River'?"

"I don't know," Ray said.

Sharon said, "How about 'Dark Star'?"

"You're enjoying this," Ray said, "aren't you?"

They'd gotten along in those days, liked each other and had a good time. Sharon sold space in *Rolling Stone* and got a big kick out of Ray, the straightest guy she knew, going to a

Grateful Dead concert with Tipper Gore.

He saw Teegarden glance over at him.

"What're you looking at?"

"Nothing," Ray said. He lowered the binoculars and glanced at Teeg. They were in his Jeep parked behind Desmond Funeral Home on Crooks Road in Troy. The 7-Eleven was next door. They were watching people leave after Joe P.'s visitation.

"Think it's a coincidence?" Teegarden said. "I give you the man's address, the next day he's dead."

"Yeah," Ray said, "I can see why you might be a little suspicious, but the *Free Press* said he died of natural causes."

"Massive heart attack," Teeg said.

"I'd say it was a stroke of luck," Ray said.

"Is that supposed to be funny?"

Ray grinned. "You think I'd be that callous and insensitive?"

Teegarden shook his head.

"I'm looking for Joey," Ray said. "This seems like the perfect opportunity to find him."

Teegarden aimed his binoculars at the rear entrance of the funeral home. "You see them? They're all here," he said. "There's Vito Uno himself."

"Guy in the black suit, I'll bet," Ray said deadpan, looking at a dozen guys in black suits.

Teegarden looked over at him. "You're in a good mood, I see."

Ray flashed a grin.

"Vito's the tall silver-haired guy. Walking with his brother Santo 'Big Sam' Corrado, his consigliere."

"Who's that in the tan outfit?" Ray said, pointing to Anthony from the used car lot.

"Antonio 'Tony the Barber' Barbara."

Ray said, "He cut hair?"

Teegarden looked at him with a hint of a smile. "He's an enforcer works for Joey, or did. His weapon of choice is a straight razor."

"That's Mrs P., I'll bet." Ray trained his binoculars on a silver-haired woman with a black scarf over her head. He remembered her from a framed photo on the desk in Joe P.'s office.

"Angela Palermo," Teeg said. "How'd you know it was her?"

"She looks like a grieving widow."

"What are you, an expert on grieving widows?" Teegarden lowered his binoculars. "I see the whole Detroit Mafia but I don't see Joey. Which is odd. His dad passes, he should be here don't you think?"

Ray said, "Where's Joe P. from?"

"Sicily. Town called Ribera."

"Maybe that's where Joey is," Ray said. "You see *The Godfather*? Michael Corleone shoots the New York cop, hides out in the village where his father was born."

"Seems kind of obvious, don't you think?"

"Yeah, probably." But Ray was thinking you never knew. "Maybe he's somewhere they can't get in touch with him."

"Where's that? I could call you from the summit of Mount Everest."

Ray agreed, expected Joey to be there. He didn't show up at the funeral either, a high mass at St Hugo's Church celebrated by Monsignor Tocco, the good monsignor praising Joseph Palermo for his strong Catholic faith and his many contributions to the parish and the community.

Ray stood in back, every seat taken, and watched Mrs P. and

the other family members in the first pew, but no sign of Joey. He wasn't at the gravesite, Holy Sepulchre on Ten Mile in Southfield, black Caddy limos lined up on the road near the grave. Again, well attended by the top brass of the Detroit Mafia.

"Who's the old guy in the gray suit next to Mrs P.? Right there. He's got his arm around her." Whoever he was, he obviously knew her well to be holding her like that.

"I don't know," Teegarden said. "Never seen him before but I'll find out." He picked up his camera with the long lens, like the kind sports photographers used, and aimed it at the guy and Ray heard the speed-winder clicking.

"He's probably a visiting dignitary. Could be from a Chicago or New York family, paying homage to Vito Uno or Joe P. himself."

"How about the skinny dark-skinned guy?" Ray said.

"No idea," Teeg said. "Not a clue."

"Get him, too, will you?"

Teegarden aimed the big camera again and clicked a couple of shots, and looked over. "Seen enough?"

Ray nodded. He started the Jeep and made a U-turn and drove through the cemetery. On the way downtown he told Teeg Sharon had disappeared.

"I knew something was up," Teegarden said. "Your sudden interest in the Palermo family. You obviously haven't gone to the police, have you?"

Ray said, "Would you?"

"Probably not." Teeg paused. "They'll think you had something to do with it."

"I came to the same conclusion," Ray said.

"Let me see what I can find out," Teeg said.

Ray pulled up in front of the McNamara Building and Teegarden got out and stood in the open door. "I'll call you."

And he did about an hour later, Teeg saying he'd scanned the shot of Mrs P. and the mysterious stranger.

"Know who he is? Joey's uncle, his mom's brother from Italy. But wait, it gets better. He's Carlo Gennaro. That name mean anything to you?"

"No," Ray said.

"He's Don Gennaro, head of the Roman Mafia."

Maybe that's where Joey was, staying with his uncle the don. Sharon too. The more he thought about it the more plausible it seemed. Ray glanced at Teegarden. "You don't happen to have his address, do you?"

"What're you going to do? Every time I give you an address somebody dies."

~

Ray got online and booked a Northwest flight, Detroit to Rome. He booked a room at the Hotel del Senato on Piazza della Rotondo near the Pantheon. He'd stayed at the Grand Hotel on Via Del Corso one time, protective detail for the vice president. The Grand was big and opulent and expensive and had excellent accommodations for an advance detail, and twelve agents on three shifts, but he didn't need that on this trip. The del Senato was described as having small clean rooms with great views of the Pantheon, and they served breakfast. It sounded perfect.

He drove to Borders and bought a Berlitz Italian phrasebook and dictionary, and a Michelin map that detailed Rome and its outskirts. Joey's uncle lived near Mentana. Ray Googled it and found out Mentana was a small town northeast of Rome about twelve kilometers. Had a population of 16,288, and the mayor's name was Guido Tabanella.

He stared at a framed photograph of Sharon on the desk next to the computer, Sharon with dark hair, smiling at the camera. The picture really capturing her: sexy and good-looking. He thought about their wedding at St Regis Church and the reception at Pine Lake Country Club, Sharon's parents showing him off as their celebrity son-in-law, caught up in the Secret Service mystique.

Ray and Sharon didn't want a big wedding but her parents insisted on it – 350 people, half of whom Ray had never met, mostly Sharon's dad's Chrysler buddies and the entire Vanelli family, which had the population of a Sicilian village. Sharon had picked a band, the Howling Diablos, she knew, and after all the formality: speeches, dinner, cutting the cake and throwing the bouquet, they drank and danced, first Ray taking off his rented tux jacket, and then his cummerbund, then his ten-pleat, wing-collared Egyptian cotton tuxedo shirt, swinging Sharon around in his sweat-soaked undershirt to the raised eyebrows of her dad's friends and fellow club members. Ray and Sharon didn't care, it was their wedding.

They honeymooned in Hawaii, the first stop, followed by a week in New Zealand, cruising the South Island, stopping in pubs and meeting the locals who seemed to genuinely like Americans. Someone would buy them each a pint and they'd buy one back, and two hours later they would stagger out and go to their hotel and make love.

When they got back from the trip Sharon's parents gave them enough for a down payment on the house in Beverly Hills. The future looked bright. They were in love and it looked like only good things were ahead for them.

He thought back, trying to pinpoint when things started to go wrong, when they'd started drifting apart. Clearly, his being away from home for extended periods of time put a strain on their relationship. Even so, they'd been able to keep it together for ten years, at least. Over the past twelve months he'd been drinking more and paying less attention to her. He could see she didn't know what to do, either, baffled by his surly belligerence. They couldn't have a conversation without getting into an argument. The job had stressed him out of his mind and he didn't realize it at the time. He'd felt that way for so long it was just normal. Looking back, now he understood, he got it, and wanted to tell Sharon he was messed up, and wanted to apologize.

Ray left the next evening at 7:05, flew coach, a seat on the aisle. He drank Cabernet, watched part of *Slumdog Millionaire*, fell asleep and woke up when the plane landed in Amsterdam. He had an hour-and-forty-five-minute layover and then a two-hour flight to Rome, arriving at Leonardo da Vinci airport at 1:05 pm. The last time he'd flown to Rome was on Air Force One, and he hadn't had two Dewar's on the rocks and three mini bottles of red wine. He was hung over and jet-lagged.

Ray took a taxi to the del Senato, a good-looking, six-story pink building with white accents on the southwest side of the Pantheon. It had a small elegant lobby with a chandelier, and a smaller bar that didn't appear to be open. It was a lot nicer than the write-up in the guidebook. He checked in, went to his room and dropped his bag on the floor and went to the window. He could see the east side of the Pantheon, and the muted white building on the opposite side of Piazza della Rotonda, and the obelisk in the center of the square.

He went to the bed and pulled down the gold-striped spread and stretched out on the mattress, his body heavy and tired, and looked at the clock on the bedside table. It was 3:30 in the afternoon.

When he woke up four hours later it was dark. He looked out the window, saw the Pantheon in the piazza below, the square crowded with cars and street vendors and tourists, the sounds coming through the open window. He showered and dressed and took the elevator down to the lobby and handed his key to a dapper old guy in a blue suit behind the desk, and went outside.

He stood in front of the Pantheon studying its pillared facade built in AD 125, looking as sturdy as a New York sky-scraper. He studied the columns, wondering if they were Doric or Corinthian. Thinking about the last time he'd been here. He was on detail with the vice president and his wife, the two of them, and a priest from Rome, a papal attaché named Father Grimaldi, their guide, plus three other members of the detail. They'd gotten a private tour of the Pantheon, and what had really impressed him was the opening in the ceiling, a circle called the Oculus, the Great Eye; it was the only source of light in the whole place.

It had rained earlier the day they were there and the marble floor was wet, the area roped off. Father Grimaldi told them the Pantheon had been designed with a drainage system below the floor, diverting the water that came in through the opening. Amazing.

Ray walked toward Piazza Navona, saw a taxi and got in and

took it over the Tiber River to Trastevere and wound through the narrow streets to Piazza Sant'Egidio. He told the driver he was going to Museo di Roma. The man looked at him like he was crazy and said, *museo non aperto*, telling Ray what he already knew. It wasn't open. He paid the driver ten euros for the eight-euro fare, got out of the taxi and walked down a narrow cobblestone street that had huge stone urns sprouting green plants. He could see laundry hanging on a rope strung between the buildings that were a shade of magenta.

He approached the café, Ombre Rosse, and stood across the street, scanning the people sitting outside under canvas umbrellas, under tall leafy trees that seemed to grow out of the cobblestones. Ray didn't know who was meeting him. He went inside and moved past the small wood-topped bar where customers stood drinking espresso out of little white cups, and beer out of stemmed glasses. He walked into the main room that was small and crowded and loud. There was an open table in the corner. He sat and ordered a glass of red wine. He looked around but no one seemed to notice him. Looked at a framed sepia-tone photograph on the wall next to his table. Six men from another time, sitting in chairs, four of them looking at the camera and two more grinning and glancing to the their right.

The waiter brought his wine in a short-stemmed glass. He watched the door, studying everyone who came in. He sipped the wine that tasted bitter, watching a dark-haired girl, mid-twenties, get up from the bar and come into the room. She was petite, five two, shoulder-length dark hair, attractive, bag on a strap over her shoulder. She didn't look at him but walked to his table.

She said, "Signor Pope, my name is Paola. May I join you?"

Ray got up and pulled the chair next to him out and she sat down. She was better-looking up close, dark eyes and high cheekbones and flawless skin.

"Would you like a drink," Ray said, "glass of wine?"

"*No, grazie*," she said. "I have this for you."

She had a heavy accent. She slipped the bag off her shoulder and rested it in her lap. She unzipped it and took out a manila-colored package and handed it to him. It was padded, a few inches thick and must've weighed four pounds.

"What you order. *Buona notte*, Signor Pope."

She got up and moved to the door. Ray looked around to see if anyone was watching him. No one seemed to be. He signaled his waiter, asked for the check and paid for the wine. Now he tucked the manila envelope under his arm and walked out of the café and went around the corner down Via della Paglia to Santa Maria in Trastevere, the square quiet and deserted at 10:30 at night.

He took a cab back to his hotel and went up to his room. There was a lamp on the bedside table. He turned it on and sat on the side of the bed and pulled the tape off the envelope, opened it and slid a shrink-wrapped SIG Sauer SP 2022 on the bedspread, along with three twelve-shot magazines. Thirty-six rounds.

Ray unwrapped the SIG. It was 7.4 inches long and weighed 30.2 ounces fully loaded. He picked up a magazine and slid it in the grip. In his opinion it was the best handgun you could buy, balanced, accurate and dependable. He cradled the weapon with two hands and aimed across the room at a bust, the likeness of Julius Caesar.

His BlackBerry started buzzing in his pocket. He took it out and looked. It was a text message from Teegarden confirming that Sharon had arrived in Italy on October 12th. She had flown New York–Rome on KLM. Now finally, he had a line on her. He couldn't believe it. There were a lot of times in the past week he doubted he'd ever see her again, doubted she was alive, but had held out hope. A friend of Teeg's at the FBI had done him a favor, contacted Italian immigration. Nothing about Joey yet. He'd stay on it and follow up when he had something concrete.

Twenty-seven

They went inside and she stood next to him and watched him cut slices of bread and cheese on the tile countertop in the kitchen. "McCabe, you don't say much about yourself. Are you really from Detroit?"

"Nobody says they're from Detroit unless they are."

"After visiting, I can understand. You have brothers or sisters?"

"A sister," McCabe said. "Two years older. Married, two daughters, works for an ad agency."

Angela said, "What is her name?"

"Jane," McCabe said.

"What about your parents?"

"My mother died when I was a freshman in high school, lymphoma, cancer of the lymph nodes."

"So you know what it feels like," Angela said.

"I thought it was unfair, but I didn't feel sorry for myself. I didn't think poor me. What can you do? You force yourself to stop thinking about it, move on."

"What about your father?"

"He's a retired ironworker. A few years ago he was on a job, trying to maneuver a thirty-foot I-beam into position. It had been drizzling that day and the steel was wet and he fell forty feet and landed on top of a plywood pedestrian walkway. Broke his hip and shoulder on the left side and his pelvis. He was supposed to be wearing a safety harness, but wasn't. He was in critical condition for a week and eventually got better and came home but he couldn't go back up on the high steel, and retired at forty-five on a modest pension."

She touched his hand that was flat on the countertop, sliding her fingers over his. He lifted his hand and turned it around and lightly gripped her palm, gliding his fingers over hers now.

She said, "What is it about holding hands."

"I know what you mean," he said.

She put her wine glass down on the counter and put her arms around his neck and kissed him. He brought his hands up under her tee-shirt, and reached behind and unfastened her bra. She raised her arms and he pulled the tee-shirt up over her head. He glided his fingers over her breasts, bent down and kissed her nipples, hand sliding down her flat tan stomach, reaching into her capris, fingers probing and sliding into her.

Then they were pulling at each other's clothes, trying to take them off, like they couldn't do it fast enough, and went down on the rug on the kitchen floor, Angela on top now, breasts pressing against his chest, feeling the heat from his body. Angela kissed him and reached between his legs, holding him and guiding him inside her.

She traced the scar over his left eye. They were upstairs in bed, McCabe on his back, sheet angled across his chest, Angela next to him on her stomach. He could feel her body against his, and the light touch of her fingertip on his face.

Angela said, "How did this happen?"

"I got hit with a puck," McCabe said.

She made a face, looked concerned like it had just happened

and he was in pain. "How many stitches do you have?"

"Fifteen."

"Fifteen? That is a lot."

She kissed the scar. He had another one on his right cheekbone, a white ridge of tissue that snaked down under his jaw. She touched it, moved the tip of her index finger over it. "What about this one?"

"High sticking," McCabe said. "I played for the Muskegon Fury in the United Hockey League. Also called the U-Haul League because we were hauled around in a bus. It's a couple steps below the NHL. We played the Rockford Ice Hogs and the Fort Wayne Komets and the Bloomington Prairie Thunder." He could see she had no clue what he was talking about. "Instead of hockey, it should've been called boxing on ice."

"Is this where you learned to fight?" Angela said.

"No," McCabe said, "but I got a lot of practice. There were four or five fights every game. Ever thrown a punch on skates?"

"Let me think," Angela said, rubbing her jaw for effect. "No, I don't think so."

He liked her smartass attitude, and the way she looked at him. "We beat Fort Wayne in the finals, won the Colonial Cup my first year. That's like the Stanley Cup of the UHL, if that makes any sense."

"I'm impressed," Angela said.

"You should be. I was making four hundred dollars a week as a rookie, living the good life." He grinned to show her he was kidding. "We had a salary cap, a limit of $250,000 for the whole team. That's all the league allows. To put it in perspective, the lowest paid player on the Detroit Red Wings makes $475,000."

"If you didn't play for the money," Angela said, "why did you?"

"I loved the game, and it's a pretty good life for six months a year. I lived in Muskegon, the beer tent capital of the world, a rundown blue-collar town on Lake Michigan. We traveled by bus and stayed in cheap motels – what a surprise, huh? We played at Walker Arena in front of five thousand fans. There isn't a lot to do in Muskegon in the winter, so people came to see us."

"The United Hockey League does not sound so good."

"It was a blast and it was a legitimate way into the NHL." He paused. "My goal since I was a little kid was to play for the Red Wings."

Angela said, "How old were you?"

"Nineteen, one of the youngest guys on the team. I played defense."

"Were you good?" She rubbed her hand through the hair on his chest.

"I was rookie of the year," McCabe said. "But the beginning of my second year I got checked on the boards and tore my AC joint." He pointed to his shoulder. There was a long rope-like scar that started at his collarbone and angled over his left shoulder where he'd had the operation – ligaments and tendons damaged. "That was it, the end of my hockey career."

She touched his shoulder gently with her fingertips. "I'll try not to hurt you."

He couldn't lock her in the bathroom and he couldn't trust her, so sleeping with her seemed like a good compromise. They made love again, slower this time. There was no hurry. McCabe liked her dark eyes and hair and olive skin that looked like she had a natural suntan. He liked the way she smelled, and liked her body, the way they fit together, like they were made for each other.

McCabe opened his eyes and saw the sheet folded back He got up and put on his jeans and went downstairs, walked barefoot through the main room into the kitchen. She wasn't there, either. He went outside, stood on the pebble drive. The car was gone, and now he felt like a fool.

He went in the kitchen and opened the refrigerator, picked up a bottle of Pellegrino water and took a swig. She could've been back in Rome. He could hear her saying, "I turned on the charm and he fell for it." Without her the show was over. What had happened between them seemed real. If she was acting, she was a pro. He thought back about what he did and what he might've done differently, and decided there was no reason to second-guess himself now.

Viterbo was four or five kilometers away, La Quercia maybe half that distance. He could walk and catch a bus back to Rome, and figure out what to do from there. He was upstairs getting his things when he heard the car, looked out the bedroom window and saw his rented Fiat coming up the driveway, pulling in next to the house. He walked in the kitchen as Angela entered with a basket of groceries, singing a song he'd never heard, or maybe it was because her voice was so bad.

"It's market day," she said, studying him. "What's the matter?"

McCabe just stared at her, trying not to give anything away, but she saw something, sensed his concern.

"You looked so peaceful I did not want to wake you," Angela said. "You thought I went away?" She studied his face.

"You did. I can see it in your eyes. If I was going to do that I would have done it before."

He went over and took the basket from her. It was heavy. He looked inside and counted four bottles of wine, cheese, fruit, meat and bread. "How long you think we're going to be here?"

"You never know," she said.

"I called Joey after you fell asleep, told him we'd be ready tomorrow. I said you have the money? He said, 'Wait and see.'"

Angela said, "What did you say?"

She took the wine bottles out of the basket and lined them up on the counter, two reds and two whites.

"I said, you want Angela back? He said, '*Succhiami il cazzo.*'"

Angela said, "You know what that means?"

McCabe said, "Uh-huh. I didn't think he spoke Italian."

"He doesn't."

She took the cheese and meat out of the basket and put the packages in the refrigerator, closed it and looked at him.

"How well do you know him?" McCabe said.

"He's my cousin. I met him when I was thirteen. My father sent me to visit my aunt Angela, Joey's mother. I flew to Detroit with Carmella, my nanny. Uncle Joe and Aunt Angela picked us up at the Metro Airport and drove us to their home in Bloomfield Hills. Joey came over the first night and had dinner with us. I could see he was interested in Carmella, but that was all. Nothing happened.

"The next day we visited the famous places of Detroit: Greenfield Village and Motown, where the music was recorded. We saw the factory where the Model T was built and the General Motors Building. There is not so much to see. We went to a baseball game. I had my first hotdog."

"What did you think?"

"I loved it."

McCabe said, "How do you think Detroit compares with Rome? I mean architecturally, culturally."

"You are funny," Angela said. "We drove with my aunt and uncle to Harbor Springs on Lake Michigan."

McCabe said, "Where the rich people go."

"They have a big house on the water with a sand beach and a motor boat. Joey came to see us and was there for a couple of days, staying because of Carmella. Thinking back, he was insecure, you know, because she was so beautiful. He reminded me of a schoolboy. He liked her but didn't know what to say to her or how to act. He would make fun of the way she spoke English, and the way she dressed. Joey is not a good person."

"That's the impression I get," McCabe said. "How old was Carmella?"

"Twenty-two. And Joey, at the time, was twenty-five. The last night we were there he went to her room in the middle of the night and he forced himself on her."

McCabe said, "Why didn't you go to your uncle?"

"You would have to understand how they thought of him. Joey was their little prince."

"What did Carmella do?"

"What could she do? She was embarrassed. She was ashamed. Who was she going to talk to? What was she going to say?'

McCabe said, "Tell them what happened."

"Do you think my aunt and uncle would have believed her? Would have taken her word over Joey?" She paused. "I tell you this because Joey is not going to make it easy. I hope you know that."

"Don't worry," McCabe said. "I'll be ready."

Twenty-eight

Mazara said he'd go to the hotels in Viterbo, show the photograph of Angela, ask if anyone had seen her. Joey said, you kidnap someone you don't take them to a hotel. Was this guy playing with a full deck? McCabe had her someplace outside the city. Someplace quiet and secluded – a house in the country. That was the only thing that made sense, the only way he could've pulled it off.

Joey was sure McCabe had someone helping him too, another student maybe. How could he have done it by himself? How could he have gotten her out of the apartment without anyone seeing them? Joey and Mazara had knocked on every door in her building, and asked if anyone had seen Angela leave the night before, Mazara doing the talking, telling the neighbors Joey was her cousin from America, and he had come a long way to see her. One guy said he saw her walking down the stairs about 8:40 p.m., but didn't see her again. Nobody else could remember seeing her at all.

Joey had told Mazara if he did exactly what Joey said he'd help square things with the don. What could he say? Joey liked being in Italy now, liked the action, catching a buzz on what was happening.

Mazara had picked him up at the Excelsior, and now they were on the autostrada heading for Viterbo, Mazara driving, Joey relaxing in the front passenger seat, checking out the countryside, feeling good about himself.

He said, "Got my Unk's money?"

"There," Mazara said, pointing his thumb over his shoulder at the bag on the back seat. It was a white soccer bag that said *Adidas* on the side. Joey turned, got on his knees, reached over the seat, picked up the bag and put it in his lap. He unzipped it and saw banded packs of bright-colored bills that looked like play money.

"How much?" Joey said.

"Four hundred and thirty-seven thousand euro," Mazara said.

That's all that was left after paying the don €60,000, and he still owed him €90,000 more, thirty per cent. His crew had already spent three thousand from their shares, and Roberto said they were angry and didn't want to give any of it back. Joey wanted to count it, see if he was telling it straight, but it was too difficult to do in the car.

Mazara had gotten him a Beretta Nine and a fancy five-shot twelve-gauge with a walnut stock you'd shoot skeet with. He wanted something simple and sawed off, a sixteen-inch barrel he could carry under a coat.

The Beretta was in his belt under the Tommy Bahama, the gay shotgun was in the trunk. They were cruising past fields of crops on both sides of the highway that reminded Joey of the farms he'd see driving to northern Michigan. He saw stone farmhouses, and occasionally a little walled village in the distance. They were listening to Italian rock music that sounded like shit. "You call this music, what the hell is it?"

"Negramaro," Mazara said, "they are very popular in Italy. The singer, he was a plumber before he start the group."

"With a voice like that he should go back to unplugging drains. What else you got?"

Mazara handed him a CD, and flashed a smile. He said, "Eminem from Detroit."

Joey said, "I know where he's from. It doesn't make him sound any better. I can't listen to rap." He hated it. Joey imagined hell as a never-ending hip-hop concert. "You got anything good? Frank Sinatra, maybe." In his head he could hear Frank singing:

> I get no kick from champagne
> Mere alcohol doesn't thrill me at all . . .

"Or how 'bout Tony Bennett?"

Mazara looked confused. "No."

"Why am I not surprised?" Joey looked out the window and saw a farmer on an old-fashioned tractor, dust trailing in his wake, looked over at Mazara and said, "How long you been seeing Angela?"

He ignored the question, kept his eyes straight ahead, two hands on the steering wheel, holding the Fiat steady. He zoomed in close to a semi, put his signal on and sped around the truck that was carrying pigs, a foul smell coming through the interior of the car. "Jesus," Joey said.

"*Miale*," Mazara said. "*Porco*," and pinched his nose with thumb and index finger.

"No shit," Joey said. The inside of the car smelled like a sewer.

Mazara looked over at him and cracked a smile.

Joey said, "You're banging Angela, aren't you, Bob? *Scopatta.*"

Mazara's grin faded fast. He looked away from Joey, turned

his head, staring straight at the highway again, the muscles in his face tightening.

"I don't blame you, she's a nice piece of ass even if she is my cousin." Joey saw an aqueduct in the distance. "You have any idea what the don would do, he found out you were knifing his little girl?"

Mazara kept his head straight, but Joey saw his eyes dart over at him. He looked nervous now.

"Listen, partner, I'm not going to say anything, okay? That's between you and Angela. But if the don finds out . . ." He didn't finish. It was more fun this way, let him imagine what would happen.

Mazara could not believe this situation he was in, the strange sequence of events that had him driving Joey, the loudmouth American, to Viterbo. First it was the don challenging him about the money. He remembered the man's harsh words and his angry expression, remembered being nervous, sweat rolling down his face.

Then Angela was kidnapped, taken from her apartment by the American student, McCabe. What kind of student was he? What kind of student did that? Mazara was concerned about him taking advantage of her. And although they were not married he wore the *corno*, the horn on a chain around his neck to prevent her from being unfaithful. He also gestured, making the horn sign, the *mano cornuta*, extending his index and little finger while holding down his two middle fingers and his thumb to repel adversity.

And then Joey coming to Angela's apartment while he was there. It was too strange. Getting the money back was another problem, telling his crew the don wanted a larger percentage of the ransom.

Sisto had said, "This is your problem. We did not negotiate with the man. You make the mistake, the money should be taken out of your share."

"I will go to the don's villa," Noto had said, "and cut his throat like a pig."

Mazara had considered the same course of action, but the don was the most powerful man in Rome, and if they did not succeed, and even if they did, they would be hunted and killed. He was thinking about this as he drove to Viterbo, listening to Joey taunt him, trying not to lose his temper, but it was very difficult. He grabbed his *cazzo* for good luck.

They drove into Viterbo through the opening in the wall that Mazara said was the Porta Romano, the door to Rome. Huh? The building above it looked like a castle, and reminded Joey of Epcot Center at Disney World, but it was real, built in the Middle Ages. When was that?

Mazara wound through narrow empty streets, the walls of buildings made of gray stone, rising up on both sides, making the streets seem even narrower. The town looked deserted. Then they turned a corner and wow, this street was wider and there was traffic, a lot of it, and people everywhere, like they'd just driven into a different town.

He could see distant parts of the city as the elevation changed, domes and towers, far and near, giving him a better sense of how big Viterbo actually was. Now in the hectic business center the buildings were fancier, painted yellow with green trim.

Joey said, "Know where you're going?"

"I think this is Piazza San Lorenzo," Mazara said.

He pulled over in a space on the street and parked. Joey got out and walked to this big open area surrounded by buildings, a church and bell tower on one side. This is where McCabe had told him to go, but why here? Not many people around, a few tourists taking pictures.

Mazara's phone rang. Joey opened it, brought it to his ear and said, "You better have Angela."

"You better have the money," McCabe said.

Joey said, "You really think you can pull this off?"

McCabe said. "I see anyone who looks familiar it's over, say goodbye to your cousin."

"Let's see how good you are," Joey said. So McCabe was somewhere close by, watching him. The phone went dead. He turned in a complete circle, looking for an American student. It was hotter than hell, Joey squinting, glancing around, the sun beating down on him. He'd already pitted out his shirt.

A fat blonde tourist eating an ice-cream cone walked right into him and got chocolate ice cream on the front of his teal Tommy Bahama Easy Breezer. "Why don't you open your fucking eyes," he said, trying to wipe the ice cream off with his hand.

The fat lady said, "Rude."

He said, "What's a big load like you doing eating ice cream, anyway? Seen a mirror lately?" Joey knocked the cone out of her hand and kept moving. The phone rang again. He took it out and brought it to his ear.

"We're going to take a walk," McCabe said.

"You want the money?" Joey said. "You better quit fucking around."

"I haven't even started," McCabe said.

Joey could feel the adrenalin pumping now, thinking what he was going to do to this guy when he caught him.

"Walk out of the piazza and head right down Via San Lorenzo," McCabe said. "I'm going to stay on the phone, keep you company till you get to where you're going. How's that sound?"

"You're pressing your luck," Joey said.

"You better get moving. You've got five minutes," McCabe said. "And you don't look like you're in very good shape."

"You'll see what kind of shape I'm in."

McCabe was going to run Joey around Viterbo, try to separate him from Mazara and his crew, knowing they were around somewhere. He watched Joey walk along Via San Lorenzo, the soccer bag angled across his right shoulder, cars cruising by, phone pressed against his ear.

Occasionally McCabe would say, "Joey, how you doing? You okay?" Or, "How about this weather? You believe it's late October? Or, how about those Lions? I hear they're 0 and 7, think they'll win a game this year?"

McCabe told him to go through Piazza della Morte, Death Square, with its spindle-shaped fountain, and take a left on Via Macel Maggiore and a right on Via San Pellegrino. He could hear him breathing hard, and could hear the anger in his voice when he spoke. He was in front of Joey, watching him come down the street, checking to see if anyone was following him. He appeared to be alone, but he knew Mazara and his gang were somewhere close by, he could feel them.

McCabe walked Joey all the way to Piazza San Pellegrino. Let him rest for a few minutes, McCabe standing out of sight on the side of the church. Joey shifted his weight and moved the soccer bag to the opposite shoulder again. It must've been heavy. He turned in a complete circle a couple of times, glancing around the medieval square. There were a dozen or so people scattered across the piazza, looking at places of interest and taking pictures. No sign of Mazara and his boys. McCabe said, "Joey, hey, you ready? Let's go."

McCabe guided him to Piazza del Plebiscito, a couple hundred yards back to the center of town, and watched him in the crowded square, drenched with sweat, Joey turning his head side to side, looking around like a penguin in an island shirt.

"Where're you at?" Joey said. "Where's Angela? Let's do it."

McCabe decided to make his move now and came out of the courtyard and headed into the square toward Joey, Joey with his back to him. As McCabe got close Joey must've heard him or sensed him and turned around. "You better have money in that bag." He looked exhausted, sweat streaming down his face, legs apart, hands on his thighs, breathing hard. "Where's Angela at."

McCabe said. "First let me see what you've got. You put phone books or newspapers in there, thinking you're clever, I want to know now before we waste any more time."

"First, I want to see my cousin and if she's got so much as a scratch –"

"Listen," McCabe said. "Nothing's going to happen till you open the bag."

Joey unzipped it and showed him a pile of banded, bright-colored euro notes.

"That's all you get, just a peek till Angela's standing here, I can see she's okay."

McCabe felt relieved now, thinking it was going to work out. He pointed to a second-story window in Palazzo dei Priori, the Renaissance building in front of them. "There she is. You see her?"

Joey was squinting, looking up, the morning sun hot and bright overhead.

"I don't see nobody."

"Right there in the window," McCabe said, pointing, assuming she was there because that was the plan, that's where she was supposed to be.

Joey said. "Is that her? Okay, yeah."

"Give me the money," McCabe said. "I'll bring her down."

Angela walked along the hall, looking in offices. She was on the second floor of Palazzo dei Priori, and she'd been right, all the municipal employees had gone for lunch and siesta. She had entered the building and walked up the stairs. No one had said a word or had given her a second glance.

She went into an office with a view of Piazza del Plebiscito. There was a cluttered desk with two chairs in front of it, and one behind it, the desktop covered with stacks of papers. There was a computer, an IBM, and a printer, an HP, on a credenza behind the desk. She looked out the window at the congested square. She saw a policeman at the far corner of the building, posing with two female tourists.

There were so many people it took time to locate Joey, but there he was with the soccer bag, standing in front of the building, talking to McCabe like old friends. Then she saw Mazara approaching, and Noto pushing his way through the crowd. She saw Sisto directly below her, moving along the front of the building. From this overhead angle she could see it all happening, three of them going toward McCabe, closing in on him, surrounding him, and she knew they had no intention of giving him the money.

Twenty-nine

Out of the corner of his eye McCabe saw someone come up behind him. He tried to move but he wasn't fast enough and now Noto's arms were wrapped around his, locking him in place like a human vice.

Joey looked at him and said, "You're in the wrong business. You really think I was going to give you the money?"

"No, I thought you might do something stupid like this, and you did."

Joey looked at Mazara, and pointed to the second-story window. "She's up there, go get her."

It was quiet in the Palazzo, the only sounds coming from Piazza del Plebiscito. Mazara gripped the Tanfoglio in his left hand as he moved up the stairway to the second floor. Checked four offices. No one in any of them. Looked in the fifth and saw Angela standing at the window. He watched her for a few seconds, wondering what she was doing. She turned and saw him, put her finger in front of her mouth, telling him not to say anything.

He went in, aiming the gun, checking the room. She seemed calm and relaxed, not what he was expecting of a hostage kidnapped for days. What was she doing in this office in a municipal building by herself? It was strange. Something was not right. He approached her and whispered, "Where are they?"

She looked at him and shook her head.

"Don't move," Mazara said in a quiet voice. "You are safe now." He walked out of the room, thinking Angela did not look as if anything was wrong, nor did she seem happy to see him. He moved along the hall checking the remaining offices on the floor. He saw no one. What kidnapper leaves their hostage before the ransom is collected?

When he went back to the room she was gone.

McCabe saw Mazara appear, coming out of Palazzo dei Priori, moving toward them. Joey turned and saw him and said, "Where the hell's she at?"

"She was in an office, right there," Mazara said. "And then she was gone."

Joey said, "What're you talking about?"

"Angela, she vanish like a ghost," Mazara said.

"A ghost, huh?" Joey grinned and glanced at McCabe. "Where is she, Slick? Still in the building?"

"Now you're starting to get it," McCabe said. "You want Angela, you've got to give me the money."

Joey handed the soccer bag to Mazara. "Hang on to this and keep an eye on him. I'm going in to have a look," he said, walking toward Palazzo dei Priori.

McCabe's mistake, he figured they'd do something, but didn't think they'd jump him in a public place, local police thirty yards away. But it wasn't over. The bag of money was right there and he was going to get it. Now a tour group, about thirty people, walked by them and stopped, crowding together in front of the arch that led to the courtyard behind Palazzo dei Priori, the mass of people separating them from Joey. McCabe lifted his heel and brought it down in the center of Noto's left foot. The big man grunted and let go of him, hobbling, trying to stay on his feet.

Sisto rushed him, and McCabe hit him with a straight right and he went down. Mazara came from behind, surprising him, almost knocking him off his feet. McCabe swung an elbow into his face and Mazara went to his knees. The strap slipped off his shoulder and the bag fell on the ground. McCabe went for it, picked it up, and took off running across the square, dodging people, trying to get through the crowd. He banged into a guy taking a photo and sent him flying.

He ran out of the piazza and down Via San Lorenzo to his car parked on the street, opened the door, threw the bag on the passenger seat and got in. He started the Fiat, put it in gear and saw Sisto and Mazara, coming toward him. He waited for an opening in traffic, pulled out and there was the little guy they called Psuz standing in front of the car, aiming a shotgun.

McCabe gunned it, engine winding, driving right at him. Psuz stepped out of the way, disappeared, and McCabe saw him in the rearview mirror. Saw him level the shotgun: firing and blowing out the rear window, firing and blowing off the passenger side mirror, firing and blowing out the passenger side windows, glass flying, glass all over him, all over the dash and front seats.

McCabe jerked the steering wheel left, then right, and floored it, speeding on a narrow one-way street toward Porta San Pietro, a straight shot out of the city. He drove through the arched exit, went left on Via Cassia, passed Porta Romana, cars lined up, bumper to bumper, waiting to enter Viterbo, the once holy residence of popes.

Joey was about to go in the building, looked back and saw McCabe take off with the soccer bag. He was gone five seconds and they'd lost the money. Now he was about thirty yards behind Mazara and Sisto, running, sucking air, trying to catch them. He heard a shotgun blast and then two more. Saw Mazara get in the front passenger seat of the Opel, and got there as they were pulling out. Joey was on the driver's side, aiming the Beretta at Sisto behind the wheel. Sisto stopped and Joey opened the rear door, jumped in and slid across the seat behind Mazara, pressing the barrel of the Beretta against the back of his head. "The fuck you think you're going?"

"He take the money," Mazara said.

"I know he take the money you fucking bozo." Joey hit him on top of the head with the barrel.

"He was lucky," Mazara said, turning in the seat, putting his hands up to protect himself.

"He was lucky? There were three of you, you can't handle a college kid. Jesus." Joey drove his fist into the seatback. In Joey's mind it was a no-brainer, a slam-dunk. What were they doing? Standing there holding their dicks while McCabe got away with €437,000.

Sisto stopped and picked Psuz up down the street that was as wide as an alley, Psuz getting in next to him saying, "He go this way, we catch him."

"You better catch him," Joey said.

Sisto gunned it, speeding along the narrow street, going through Porta San Pietro, stopping at the main road. Joey looked to the right and saw a gas station and beyond it a mirrored-glass building that looked out of place next to the old city.

"There," Mazara said, pointing left.

Joey saw the blue Fiat in heavy traffic up ahead. "What do you think Don Gennaro's going to say when I tell him what happened?" That got their attention. Mazara, still rubbing his head, glanced back at Joey.

"Why do you tell him?"

"Why do I tell him?" Joey shook his head. "Dude, his little girl, my cousin's been kidnapped in case you forgot, and she could be in serious fucking trouble. Oh, and you lost his share of the money. That's why I tell him." He leaned back in the seat, trying to get comfortable. There wasn't much legroom.

Psuz was next to him with the shotgun, barrel pointed at the floor, the stench of gunpowder filling the car. Psuz had bleached blond hair, a dark beard and dark eyebrows, and gave Joey the creeps. He grinned at him and Joey said, "What's your problem?"

Mazara looked back and pointed straight through the windshield. "You see? There, the blue Fiat?"

Joey saw it turn right up ahead, and they did too on Viale Fiume, a two-lane country road. They passed irrigation canals and flat dirt fields that had been harvested. They passed farmhouses in the distance and sheep grazing.

Mazara said something to Sisto in Italian and Sisto grinned, and looked at Joey in the rearview mirror.

"What'd you say?" Joey said.

"No more telling us what to do," Mazara said it like he was trying out the line, waiting for a reaction.

"Is that right?" Joey said. "Let me remind you, if it wasn't for you clowns we wouldn't be in this situation. We'd be on our way back to Rome with Angela and the money." Joey decided to keep the Beretta handy, even the odds if they were thinking about a mutiny.

Psuz was grinning at him again. Joey brought the Beretta up and aimed it at him. "You don't quit looking at me like that I'm going to put this in your mouth, let you suck on it like a big dick. You'll probably like it."

Mazara looked over his shoulder and said, "Be careful what you say. Psuz was in the Bersaglieri, a sniper in Italian army, can kill you from three hundred meters."

"Yeah, right." He didn't look like a sniper. He looked like a rump ranger.

"No, is the truth."

They passed through a little village, La Quercia, and saw a sign that said Bagnaia 6 kilometers. Joey lowered the pistol and rested it on the seat next to him. Glanced at Psuz. A sniper, huh? Maybe he'd come in handy. They passed a truck and a couple of cars, and came up behind a dark-blue Fiat. The rear window was blown out and the sheet metal was puckered with buckshot.

Sisto pulled out in the oncoming lane, trying to drive next to the Fiat, but the Fiat sped up and they couldn't quite catch it, didn't have the power to pass it, and swung back and got on McCabe's tail again and rammed him. The impact jarred them, Joey jerking forward, the shoulder belt straining, but holding him. Sisto accelerated and rammed McCabe's car again, and then pulled out, gaining on the Fiat this time, almost next to it.

~

McCabe saw Joey leaning out the rear window of the Opel with a gun in his hand. He heard the blast and felt the left rear tire blow, and felt the back end slide out. He hit the brake, trying to slow down, get the Fiat under control but couldn't, and then lost it, the back end going all the way around, and he was spinning, doing a 360. He turned the wheel, trying to correct his course, trying to straighten out the car, and he went off the road and over the embankment, rolling now, hands squeezing the steering wheel, conscious of his body going head-over-heels twice as the car rolled, blowing out all the glass.

The Fiat landed right side up, but was still moving, slamming head-on into a tree with impact. McCabe was conscious of the airbag blowing in a split second, hitting him in the face, knocking him back against the headrest, nose and forehead stinging. Conscious, too, of the dull pain in his arms and shoulders from holding the steering wheel so tight.

McCabe was dazed from the collision. The windshield was gone, roof caved in, hood buckled, and he could hear a hissing sound from the radiator that must have been punctured, steam escaping under pressure. He looked out the driver's side window and saw the Opel on top of the embankment, backing up fast. He was woozy but knew he had to move. It was difficult with the airbag pressing against him. He pushed the seat back as far as it would go, unhooked his belt, brushed glass off the soccer bag, and pushed it out the passenger side window. He glanced back toward the road and saw the Opel in profile on top of the embankment, skidding to a stop in reverse seventy yards away.

He pulled the handle up but the door wouldn't open,

wouldn't budge. He used his arms to pull himself up and slid over on the passenger seat. He went head first through the open window, holding on to the doorsill, flipping his body around, going down on his knees, looking through the empty window frames. They were out of the car, four abreast, starting down the embankment.

Cars were slowing down, people trying to see what was happening. Behind him was the tree line, a narrow wooded area he'd seen from the road that went uphill a hundred yards to a stone house and outbuildings on the other side of the trees.

He picked up the bag, put the strap over his shoulder and went into the woods about fifty feet, stopped and saw them standing around the Fiat, and McCabe started to run.

Joey said, "Jesus Christ, you believe this fucking guy?" The Romans were looking in the car windows. "You going to stand there, pull pud, or go find him?"

These guys were so fucking lame it hurt.

Mazara said something in Italian and the three of them moved into the trees, Joey behind them, holding the Beretta down his leg. He didn't think these bozos would try to take him out but you never knew. He could hear the hum of traffic behind them as he followed the Romans into the woods.

They'd sure as hell better find him and do it fast. There was considerable personal gain at stake here too, beyond just the money. Joey saw himself giving McCabe to his uncle, saying, you want the guy kidnapped Angela? Here he is. My pleasure. You don't have to thank me. Just give me my own territory, I'll show you how it's done.

Joey saw himself making the rounds, persuading the Roman

shopkeepers they needed protection. It wasn't hard. They didn't want to pay him he'd pull out the Closer, a twenty-nine-ounce white ash Louisville Slugger. His advice to young racketeers: choose a bat you could control, never pick up more wood than you could swing. Joey with his height and weight could handle a thirty-ouncer without any problem, but he liked the twenty-nine better. He knew it didn't make any sense, but one ounce made a difference.

The other piece of advice he'd give about hitting: loosen up a little before you swing for the fence. Stretch your muscles. Joey preferred a Louisville Slugger model C271 pro stock, but on occasion used his Pete Rose autograph with the man's signature on the barrel of the bat, and the words *Hit King* under it, and 4,256, his record number of major-league hits. It was a little corny but he liked it 'cause he liked Pete Rose, admired him, and having the man's autograph on the bat gave him confidence. He was thinking about the bat, watching Mazara and the other two clowns walk through the woods when he heard a siren in the distance, the sound like a siren in a Second World War movie. The three Romans stopped, turned and looked at him, and they all started moving back to the car, Joey thinking, Jesus, that's all he needed – get arrested in fucking Italy.

When Mazara walked out of the office looking for the kidnappers, Angela had run down the hall and down the stairs. Instead of going into Piazza del Plebiscito she entered the courtyard between Palazzo dei Priori and Palazzo del Podestà. She had joined a tour group of Dutch students that had stopped to study the Etruscan sarcophagus lids on display.

The tour guide explained the historical significance of the ancient coffin lids, but Angela wasn't listening. She was glancing behind her through the students, looking for Roberto.

She stayed hidden in the group until they moved into Piazza del Plebiscito. She didn't see McCabe or Joey or any of them and started across the square. She heard the distant discharges of a shotgun, and then panic, people running toward her. Angela was concerned about McCabe, hoping Joey and Mazara didn't do something crazy. Two Polizia sedans sped past her down Via San Lorenzo, lights flashing, sirens yelping. She had seen a taxi queue on Via Roma, and ran there and got in the rear seat of a yellow Fiat sedan and told the driver she was in a hurry. Drive toward Bagnaia, I will direct you. She could see his face in the rearview mirror, dark eyes studying her. He looked Tunisian or Moroccan. She took a fifty-euro note out of her purse, leaned forward and handed it to him. He nodded and started the car.

"*Subito, signorina.*"

They drove out of Viterbo and through La Quercia, zipping along, Angela thinking about McCabe again and realizing she had not stopped thinking about him. McCabe was tough, but there were five armed men after him. There was nothing she could do. No way to contact Joey or Mazara. And even if she could, what would she say to them? She was staring out at the countryside and felt the taxi slow down, and looked through the windshield and saw brake lights ahead. Cars traveling in both directions were stopping now.

The driver glanced at her, his solemn eyes in the rearview, and said, "I don't know."

It could have been anything, a collision, sheep crossing the road, a farmer driving a tractor slowing traffic. After a few minutes they started moving slowly, creeping along, Angela nervous, worried, looking out the window. She hit the button and the window went down and she lit a cigarette. She saw the driver's eyes looking at her in the mirror again but not saying anything to his fifty-euro customer. She blew smoke out the window and watched it disappear.

She could see flashing lights up ahead, two police cars parked on the side of the road. As they approached Angela looked down the embankment and saw four Polizia de Stato standing next to a dark-blue Fiat. It was McCabe's car, there was no doubt in her mind. The top was crushed, sides dented. Was he in the car? Was he hurt? If he was hurt they would have called an ambulance. So where was he? And where were Joey and Mazara?

Thirty

McCabe walked upslope through the trees, the strap over his left shoulder, bag resting on his right hip. When he reached the top of the rise, level now with the farmhouse, he could hear sirens in the distance, getting closer. He looked down the hill at the highway and saw Joey, Mazara and Sisto get in the car, and take off just before two police cars arrived, lights flashing.

He walked out of the trees and saw laundry on a clothesline next to the house. He looked down the hill and saw four uniformed police getting out of the two cars, walking down the embankment to the rented Fiat, what was left of it, traffic heavy, congested, barely moving.

McCabe moved up to the top of a steep rock-strewn hill fifty yards to the right of the farmhouse, picking his way through brush and Mediterranean scrub. He stood on an outcropping of rock, breathing a little from the climb, and lifted the strap over his head, put the soccer bag on the ground and stretched. The view was something, green rolling hills extending to a dark ridge of mountains that rose in the distance.

Angela had obviously seen what was happening from the window of Palazzo dei Priori, and had taken off. If something went wrong, they had agreed to meet back at the villa. He turned and looked off across the hills, saw Lago di Vico to the south and the Marta and Leia, tributaries of the Tiber, winding through the landscape east of the lake. La Quercia was due west, and beyond it, Viterbo. He knew where he was, and where he had to go. He scanned the terrain and thought he saw Pietro's villa on a hilltop to the east.

Psuz moved through the trees: cork wood, white oak, sycamore and holly oak. He had grown up in Lazio, the village of Gallese on the other side of the Cimini Mountains. His father had taught him how to hunt, and how to track game. He knew the trees and the vegetation and the rocky terrain. He had moved up the hill at least one hundred meters when he heard the sirens. He glanced back through the trees and saw Joey, Mazara and Sisto running to the car, getting in and driving away, leaving him. But now the American would also see them and not be expecting him.

Psuz saw McCabe come out of the trees and walk to the top of the hill and stand there looking down at the police, wondering what he would do, and then he disappeared, went over the hill and was gone. Psuz ran up and looked and saw the American moving down the slope and went after him, thinking if he could move fast enough he could circle around and get ahead of him, be waiting for McCabe at the bottom. Surprise.

Pietro's villa didn't look far, a few miles, but it took McCabe over an hour to get there, late October sun beating down on him. He hiked through the hills and crossed the main road, Viale Fiume, and walked through the trees along Strada Pian di Nero. When he got to the base of the hill, looking up at the villa, he decided to circle around and come up behind it.

There was a stone outbuilding that was built about fifty

yards from the main house. It was the size of a three-car garage and had a couple bedrooms, a bathroom and kitchen for Pietro's cook and housekeeper. The villa was on the other side of the gravel apron where Pietro parked his cars, but there were no cars there now. McCabe scanned the windows across the backside of the villa, didn't see anything suspicious, didn't see anything at all. He moved to the door, opened it and went in the kitchen. Stood and listened but didn't hear anything. He put the soccer bag on the table. Went in the main room, opened the gun case and grabbed the barrel of a Perazzi twelve-gauge. He loaded it and took it into the kitchen and laid it on the table next to the bag.

He opened the refrigerator, took out a cold bottle of Pellegrino water and poured a glass. Drank it leaning against the counter, thinking about Angela again, wondering what happened to her. Picturing her face the last time they were together, seductive brown eyes looking up at him.

"I saw your car."

It was her voice. At first he thought he'd imagined it, but there she was, standing in the doorway that led to the main room.

She came toward him, tears in her eyes. "I thought you were dead."

McCabe said. "It takes more than getting shot at and rolled in a car to stop me."

"Always the tough guy, uh?"

"I'm kidding."

She gave him a dirty look and opened a drawer and took out a towel and went to the sink and wet it and dabbed his face and it stung. "Easy," McCabe said, pulling away from her.

"Oh, you do feel pain, uh?" She showed him the towel that was stained with blood.

"I'm okay," McCabe said.

She touched his cheek again with the cool cloth. "I was worried about you. Do you understand?"

He gave her a slight nod.

"That's the best you can do?"

He brought her to him and put his arms around her and held her close.

"That's better," she said. "I knew Joey was not going to give you the money."

"You called it," McCabe said.

"No, I saw it all happening from the window of the Palazzo, four of them surrounding you." She looked up at him. "But you still have me. I'm your bargaining chip. You remember saying that?" She paused. "Listen, we can try again."

"We don't have to," McCabe said. He glanced at the soccer bag on the table. She went over and unzipped it, looked inside, turned to him and smiled.

"Were you going to tell me?"

Thirty-one

Ray got up and took a shower and went down and had cappuccino and biscotti, sitting outside at the hotel café, the Pantheon looking somehow different in the morning light, tourists already gathering in front of it, taking pictures at 8:30 in the morning.

He sipped the coffee and studied a map of Rome and Lazio. He found Mentana and circled it with a yellow marker. When he was finished with breakfast he asked for the check and left a five-euro note on the table. He walked into the square and took the first right, a narrow street that wound around to Via del Corso. He was carrying a black computer bag with a strap over his shoulder. It held binoculars, a flashlight, the SIG Sauer and the two twelve-shot magazines.

He stopped at a *tavola calda* and bought two ham sandwiches, a liter bottle of carbonated Panna water and a Coke, and put all that in the bag too.

He took a cab to Auto Europa at 38 Via Sardegna. He had reserved a Fiat Croma, a four-door sedan with a stick shift and air-conditioning. The rental agent, a short, balding man about Ray's age, gave him a city map and highlighted the route to Mentana. It was twelve kilometers, about seven and a half miles. It looked easy, just take the GRA that looped around the city, and look for exit A12.

But it wasn't easy. He got lost three times and finally pulled into a BP gas station. An attendant came out of the booth, walked up to the Fiat. Ray said, "*Dove e Mentana*?" Giving it his best pronunciation.

The attendant pointed to the highway and said, "*Dritto, a destra, dritto*."

Ray took out his dictionary and looked up the words. *Dritto* meant straight and *a destra* meant to the right. So to get to Mentana he had to go straight, take a right and continue straight.

It was a scenic drive into the green rolling hills, vineyards on both sides of the highway, stretching to the dark heights of the Apennine Mountains, clouds hanging on their peaks. Fifteen minutes later he was driving up a steep hill into the walled village of Mentana. He parked in a municipal lot next to the castle and walked into town up Via Monte San Salvatore. There was no one on the street. It was deserted except for a couple of cats that disappeared down a dark alley. He saw laundry hanging from rope strung between buildings. He wondered where all the people were, and then realized it was siesta; they were having their main meal of the day and then taking a nap. No worries. No stress. This was how the Italians had been doing it for thousands of years.

He passed a bakery and a meat market and a cheese shop and three *enotecas* – all closed – and the Hotel Belvedere that was open. He walked uphill to the end of the street, looked at the Garibaldi Monument commemorating the Battle of Mentana in 1867, a piece of Italian history Ray was not familiar with. He walked around the monument and sat on a brick wall, looking down at the valley that extended below him east and west. To the north he could see the peak of Mount San Lorenzo. He slipped off the backpack and took out the binoculars and scanned the countryside. Don Gennaro's villa was in the hills south of the mountain. Ray didn't have an address but he had directions Teegarden had gotten from his contact at carabinieri headquarters.

Head north out of Mentana. When the road forks follow it left toward Monterotondo, another town a few kilometers away. The don's villa is about 500 meters northwest of the fork on the right side of the road. Look for a driveway flanked by stone pillars and a steel gate. There was a map that showed Mentana and the main highway that went north. He saw the fork in the road, and an arrow indicating the location of the don's villa.

"His estate's on 250 hectares," Teegarden said.

"What's a hectare?" Ray said.

"I knew you were going to ask me that," Teegarden said. "Two and a half acres."

"That's a big piece of property," Ray said, "You've got photos of the place, don't you?"

"How do you know that?"

Ray said, "You don't do things halfway."

"Just do me a favor, don't tell me what you're going to do," Teegarden said. "I don't want to know, okay?"

He handed Ray eight-by-ten prints, aerial photographs of the estate: the villa, vineyards, olive grove, outbuildings, and private road that led to the highway. There were also surveillance photographs of the villa, different angles, all shot with a long lens and printed in black and white.

"There's the man himself," Teeg said. "Carlo Gennaro."

"I remember him from the funeral."

He handed Ray another shot that showed the don in a bathing suit, sitting on the patio behind the villa next to a good-looking girl in a bikini, drinking a glass of wine. She looked about thirty.

Teegarden said, "Doesn't look like much, but he's got style, the hair and sunglasses."

He reminded Ray of an Italian actor, an older version of Marcello Mastroianni or someone from that era. "I can see how you might tend to underestimate him," Ray said. "Although I like his taste in women. Who is she?"

"Chiara Voleno, a model."

"Not bad," Ray said. "What do you know about Carlo Gennaro?"

"He's Sicilian," Teegarden said. "His wife and son were killed twelve years ago by a rival gang. Stabbed Carlo four times and assumed he was dead."

"That's usually enough to get the job done."

"The men who did it were found decapitated in an apartment, the don sending a message."

Teegarden handed him a photograph of the crime scene, two bodies without heads and blood everywhere. "The newspapers called it the Ribera Massacre."

Ray said, "Why did he come to Rome?"

"He has a daughter who hid the morning the mom and son were killed. I guess he decided to distance himself from his enemies, go where it was safer. Twenty per cent of the shops in Rome now pay him. *Pizzo*, it's called, protection money. He makes fifty thousand dollars a week."

"That's two and a half million a year," Ray said.

"And it's only a small part of his business. He's invested in real estate, clinics, retirement homes, supermarkets, funeral parlors, bakeries." Teegarden paused. "He's also a cultured Mafioso. Loves opera, has an extensive art collection. Makes his own wine and olive oil."

"A real Renaissance man, huh?" Ray said.

"Which is more impressive when you find out he quit school after fifth grade."

Teegarden handed him another print.

"The villa's half a kilometer from the road. He has his own private drive that's guarded twenty-four hours a day. The only other way in is a two-track path that cuts through the vineyard. The don has two barns where he keeps his equipment, and a stone building where he makes and stores his wine. He hires locals to come and pick the olives and grapes during harvest. Grape season's over but olives are harvested in November. You could hang around and taste the new crop."

"The daughter live with him?"

"She isn't in any of the photos so I'd say, no."

Ray had been driving along a wall of oak trees, and saw something on the right. He looked back at the entrance to the don's estate, saw the ancient stone pillars flanking the driveway, iron gate closed, car blocking the driveway on the other side of it. He drove three hundred meters past the estate, and now there were vineyards on his right, the branches thin and bare after the harvest. Ray looked for a place to pull over and saw a dirt path that led into the field. He hit the brakes and took a right and drove in far enough so the car couldn't be seen from the road. He walked out and checked.

He hiked back to the don's property through a forest of oak trees, leaves turning yellow at the edges, marking the distance off with three-foot strides, counting three hundred and knew he was close. He went twenty yards further and heard voices. Still inside the tree line he saw two guys standing at the pillared entrance to the estate, a dark sedan, some kind of Fiat parked, blocking the driveway.

They reminded Ray of two Italian guys from high school, Giancotti and Veraldi. Ray watched them for a couple minutes. Giancotti was on his cell phone, pacing, having an animated conversation. Veraldi was smoking a cigarette. He took a final drag, dropped the butt on the gravel drive and stepped on it. They were both right-handed and had guts and thinning hair. They weren't muscular or even especially big. Giancotti had a Beretta in a holster on his belt. He was wearing sunglasses and a long-sleeved white dress shirt tucked into jeans.

Veraldi, with an HK MP5 sub-machine gun on a strap over his shoulder, concerned him more. Ray didn't worry about them hearing him; they were making too much noise. He started moving again, due north this time, toward the villa, heading through the trees. He paced off four hundred yards and came to an olive grove that extended into the hills for as far as he could see.

To his right was Don Gennaro's sprawling villa that made Joe P.'s suburban colonial look like a shack. It had stone walls and a tile roof and had to be seven thousand square feet. Behind the villa was an enormous stone veranda that wrapped around the back of it, and had two levels. He took out the binoculars and focused on a dark-haired girl, had to be the model, stretched out on a lounge chair, sunbathing next to the pool. She was either wearing a flesh-colored bathing suit or she was naked.

He scanned the edge of the grove and saw two guys wearing berets, white shirts and black vests, peasants with shotguns slung on straps over their shoulders. They were talking and grinning, watching the girl. While they were distracted Ray decided to make his move. He came out of the woods and went left into the grove, circling around behind the guards for a better view of the villa.

The sun was almost straight up and it was hot. No wonder the girl wasn't wearing a bathing suit, she was trying to stay cool. He moved through the grove, smelling olives, the trees heavy with them. When he was directly behind the villa he slipped his bag off and took a few gulps of the Panna water and put the bottle on the ground. He was about fifty yards from the veranda. He couldn't see the guards but assumed they were still watching the girl. He was too, studying her with the binoculars. She got up and moved to the pool and stuck her toe in the water and stood there posing. Knew she had an audience. She stretched and touched her breasts that were big and perfect, and had brown nipples the circumference of silver dollars.

He walked up the hill behind him, higher ground for a better angle. He scanned the vertical second-floor windows that opened like French doors and had balconies. He could see beds and furniture in the first room, a maid cleaning in the next one, and a skinny guy built like a teenager on the third balcony, hands on the railing, staring at the grove as if he knew someone was out there. Ray recognized him from Joe P.'s funeral.

He panned right across three more windows, looking for Sharon and Joey, but didn't see anyone, just rooms of furniture.

When he panned back the other way the skinny Sicilian was gone. Ray looked down and saw the guards on the edge of the veranda. They were probably trying to get a better view of the girl who was getting out of the pool, skin glistening, hips swaying, teasing the men as she went back to her lounge chair.

Ray saw the Sicilian come out of the villa now and move down to the lower level of the veranda where the guards were standing, said something to them and pointed in Ray's direction. He could see them coming toward him through the trees. He moved down the hill, picked up the backpack, gripped the SIG and started to run.

Mauro stood against the railing, windows open behind him, feeling the warmth of the sun. He had just returned from America, the funeral for Joey's papa in Detroit, Michigan. The don was asleep, tired from the journey and he was too. It was a long way to go in a short time, two days, but if the don asked that of him he did it. He was looking down at Tulio and Franco. Like Mauro they were Sicilians from Ribera. They were told to watch the villa, but instead were watching Chiara climb out of the pool, their eyes never leaving her. This had been going on since the hot days of summer. She would come out to the veranda late in the morning when she awoke. Always wearing the robe. Always untying the sash, and looking surprised when the sides of the robe opened, knowing Tulio and Franco were nearby, usually in the grove but always watching. She would take her time, playing to them before removing it, posing without clothes.

Mauro enjoyed looking at this woman as much as anyone, but she was a distraction for the men. How could they do their job with a naked woman standing in plain sight? He was going to say something to the don, but the don would say, if she is a distraction, why are you looking at her?

He saw the sun reflecting off something in the olive grove. At first he thought one of the workers had left a tool out there on the ground, but there had been no workers in the grove for quite some time, months. Workers had come to pick the grapes, but the olive harvest was not for another week. The reflection disappeared. There was a simple explanation. Probably nothing. He turned to go in the room, looked back and saw it again.

Mauro went down to the main floor through the villa, and outside, moving across the veranda to the lower level. Tulio and Franco glanced at him as he approached, turned and moved to the edge of the grove, trying to appear alert, doing their job. Mauro whispered to them, "Listen, I think there is someone out there, an intruder, you stand here looking at her, what are you doing?"

They were embarrassed, eyes staring at the ground.

The three of them spread out and walked into the grove, Tulio on one side of him, Franco on the other. Mauro saw a Panna bottle on the ground. He picked it up and unscrewed the top and heard the *psssss* sound of gas escaping. He looked at the men. "Did one of you leave this?"

They shook their heads.

Mauro took out his cell phone and dialed Pascal and Fausto at the villa's entrance and told them to be looking out for a possible intruder moving in their direction. Mauro had no idea if there was an intruder or what direction he was going, but he was taking no chances.

*

Ray was trying to figure out how they'd gotten on to him so fast. Did they have motion sensors? Video surveillance cameras? He was running through the olive grove, thinking about the water bottle he'd left, angry at himself for not paying attention.

He made it to the forest, ran sixty, seventy yards, stopped and listened, could hear them coming behind him. He used an oak tree for cover, looking back, seeing them appear one at a time, spread out, spaced twenty yards apart, moving toward him, two holding shotguns. He looked at the compass and saw he was heading south toward the entrance to the villa.

He changed direction, moving again, this time heading east. He went fifteen yards, stopped and looked back. One of the guards was getting close. Ray wasn't sure if the man had seen him or not. He turned and saw Giancotti and Veraldi, closing in on him from the opposite direction, Ray now caught in the middle. He went down on his knees and then his stomach, hiding in a patch of leafy foliage, gripping the SIG Sauer. He lay there holding his breath as Veraldi approached, carrying the machine gun. Veraldi stopped, looking around, his leg a foot away. Ray waited till he moved past him, till he was out of sight, got up and ran.

Thirty-two

"You done good," Joey said.

Psuz looked at him and grinned.

"I've got to tell you I had my doubts. I thought no fucking way Jose, but you did it."

"In the *casa*," Psuz said, pointing to a tan-colored stone house on the hill behind them.

Joey was still in the back seat, door open, catching a breeze that swept across the valley. He was staring out at the countryside, seeing little houses in the distance, tiny shapes, squares and rectangles with orange roofs. It was 2:00, sun dipping toward the mountains.

Joey lighted his last Montecristo No. 4 with the gold Alfred Dunhill lighter, puffed and got it going, and got out of the car. He clamped the cigar between his teeth, inhaled a little and blew out smoke the wind took as soon as it came out of his mouth. Psuz had called Mazara and told him he followed the American and knew where he was. Joey didn't believe it till he got there. Blondie had surprised him. Now Sis, Mazara and Psuz, his three Italian buddies, were looking at him, waiting for Joey to tell them what to do.

"He was going to capture the American, give him to you," Mazara said to Joey. "But he want you to have the honor."

Joey nodded. Okay, that was more like it. The Romans finally showing him some fucking respect. It was about time.

He glanced at Psuz. "You're positive he's up there?"

"I see him," Psuz said, pointing at the villa.

"Just making sure," Joey said. He sucked on the cigar, tasted tobacco juice, swallowed it, inhaled and blew out the smoke.

"We can go now?" Mazara said.

"Bob, that's what we're going to do, okay? Take a chill pill." Joey knew the smart thing to do was wait till dark, but he wanted to get it over with, get the money, give McCabe to his Unk, and go back to Rome have a nice dinner, a Florentine steak maybe, or a big bowl of spaghetti Alfredo. Drink some wine. Celebrate. The only question: how was he going to get up the hill? Taking the car would be like calling McCabe and telling him he was on his way. He could walk, but said to himself, who're you kidding? It had to be a hundred yards to the top. He'd never make it. "You three sneak up. I'll watch. When I see you at the top I'll drive up. We'll surround the place, bring him out and that'll be that."

They just stood there staring at him with these goofy looks on their faces.

"There a problem? Something you don't understand?" Joey said. He pointed at the villa. "What're you waiting for? Go get him. *Andi-fucking-amo*."

Now they seemed to get it. Sis and Mazara took off zigzagging up the scrub-covered slope in front. Psuz grabbed his shotgun and went around the hill to the opposite side of the villa, surprise McCabe if he tried to sneak out that way. Joey liked giving an order and seeing the Romans hop to it. Maybe there was hope for them after all.

Ten minutes later Sisto signaled him from the top. Joey got

in the Opel, sped up the driveway, parked on the flat gravel area next to the house, and got out with the gay shotgun Mazara had given him. Psuz was standing at the edge of the parking area, staring up at the roofline as if he were expecting McCabe to jump out a window or slide down the tiles.

Mazara was moving through the kitchen, two hands on the Tanfoglio. He entered a big room with walls of stone and beams in the ceiling. The floor was made of wood planks covered by a rug. He saw Sisto coming in the front of the house, coming through the salon, Sisto pointing to the ceiling, the gesture, saying McCabe could be up there. But only a fool would do that and this McCabe was not a fool. Mazara followed Sisto up the stairs. There were two bedrooms. He looked out the window to the west and saw Viterbo a few kilometers away.

He crossed the room and looked out toward Bagnaia, a village to the east. He went back downstairs and saw the telescope on a tripod in the main room in front of a window. He didn't notice it before. He went over and looked through the lens, turned it to the left and saw them, two figures he recognized as McCabe and Angela, a couple hundred meters away, at least, running along the road. Mazara didn't see anyone pointing a gun at her, or forcing her to run. It looked like she wanted to go with McCabe. Seeing this confused him. He grabbed his crotch for good luck, told himself she was just doing what she was told, a prisoner, waiting for an opportunity to escape.

McCabe went upstairs to get his backpack, looked out the bedroom window and saw them starting up the hill in front of the villa. Further to the right he could see the rear fender of the Opel parked on the side of the road. How'd they find him? He ran downstairs. Angela was in the kitchen, pouring a cup of coffee. "They're here," McCabe said.

"What?"

"Coming up the hill."

They went out the front door and over the wall and down the eastern slope toward the road, stopped a couple of times and took cover behind stands of oak and sycamore trees. Sisto and Mazara were coming up the hill toward the villa as they were going down. At one point they were only about twenty yards away. McCabe also saw Joey drive up in the Opel, but by that time they were walking along the road. Angela had her thumb out and a car was stopping.

Angela got in front and McCabe in the rear seat behind her. The driver was a thin middle-aged guy, hair going gray, looked like an accountant, white shirt and tie. He smiled at Angela and said something in Italian.

Angela glanced at him, her expression seductive and innocent. It was the same look she'd given McCabe at the wine bar the afternoon they met, and now the man was hooked just as McCabe had been. He said something to Angela in Italian. She turned her head and looked back at McCabe.

"He wants to know where we are going. What should I tell him?"

"Soriano nel Cimino."

Angela told the driver and he glanced at her and said something in Italian. She looked back at McCabe and said, "He's going to Montecampano. Soriano is out of his way, but he said he would take us."

"I think he likes you," McCabe said. And on cue the accountant looked at Angela again, and smiled. She was good-looking, but there was something down-to-earth and approachable about her that gave even a middle-aged accountant the confidence to hit on her.

Angela said, "He wants to know if you play football."

"Tell him no, I kidnapped you and the bag is filled with ransom money."

She did, and he laughed.

They went through Bagnaia and passed the sculpted Renaissance gardens of Villa Lante. After that, the driving became more difficult and the views more spectacular as they climbed the steep grade into the mountains. The driver kept glancing at Angela, grinning and talking. His name was Dante Lanzetta and he worked in the Palazzo del Plebiscito. How was that for coincidence? Dante told them they had to see the Sasso del Predicatore. McCabe remembered reading about it, a huge stone monument called the Preacher's Rock. He'd like to see it but didn't think they'd have a chance to do any sightseeing on this particular trip.

Thirty minutes later they drove into Soriano nel Cimino, a hill town with a population of about eight thousand. It was 3:30, sun hanging on top of the mountains. He could see the narrow shape of the clock tower and the walls and battlements of Orsini Castle. They were on Via Santa Maria, approaching the town center. McCabe told Dante he could let them out anywhere along there, and he pulled over.

"Where they at?" Joey said to the three Italians. They gave him blank looks. What else was new? "I don't believe it. We don't find them, I've got to tell the don his little girl's been kidnapped and you bozos let it happen." He grinned, couldn't hold it back. They were in the villa kitchen.

Mazara said he'd seen Angela and McCabe get in a tan Fiat and drive off in the direction of Bagnaia. Sisto went out to the car and came back with a map. He unfolded it and spread it out on the table. Roberto pointed to where they were. He traced a line with his index finger.

Joey said, "Okay, genius, so where they going?"

"I think to the autostrada and back to Roma."

Joey couldn't disagree with him. Jesus Christ, there was nothing around them except for small towns scattered through the hills. Would McCabe risk checking into a hotel? Joey doubted it. The carabinieri would be looking for him too. "Let's go. You can drop me off in Mentana, talk to the don yourself, tell him what happened to Angela, and where his money's at. I'm sure he'll be anxious to see you."

Then Mazara surprised him, looked up from the map and said, "You want McCabe? I have a way."

"Is that right?" Joey said. "What do you got? Let's hear it."

Mazara told him, laid out his plan and it sounded good, sounded realistic and doable.

Joey said, "Now you're talking." He agreed not to say anything to his Unk, let it play out a little longer. What difference would another day make?

Thirty-three

"Do you know where McCabe is?" Arturo looked at his eyes, believing after twenty-eight years with the carabinieri he could see dishonesty in a man's eyes.

"No," Chip Tallenger said. "I have not seen or talked to him since Thursday evening."

If he was lying, Arturo could see no evidence of it. He did not look down or look away or even blink, his eyes calm and steady. "What time did McCabe come to the room?"

"Nine, nine-fifteen. Picked up a couple things and left," Chip said.

"I must've seen him a few minutes later," Signor Rady said.

"*Per favore*," Arturo said to him. "If you please. I want to find out what happened."

"McCabe's no longer a student at this university," Signor Rady said. "I'm telling you this because he's no longer our responsibility or concern."

"Yes, but Signor McCabe is still my concern, so if you will indulge me."

"Okay," Signor Rady said, "but I don't see –"

Arturo had contacted Signor Rady about meeting with Chip Tallenger, a confidential discussion, but Rady insisted on being there, imposing his authority. This was university property and Signor Tallenger was a student, registered and enrolled, so Rady had to be present. They were in his office, once again, at the small table.

"I can't help you," Chip Tallenger said, although his eyes seemed to be saying he wanted to.

"You see the automobile, the Fiat rented by Signor McCabe?"

"Not till it was on TV."

"If you know something," Signor Rady said, flashing an angry look at Chip, "you better tell him. By protecting McCabe you're only going to make it worse."

Chip looked at Arturo. "Who's after him?"

"Signor Rady, give us a moment," Arturo said.

"I can't do that, Captain. If this matter involves one of my students, it involves me."

Now he was concerned. Arturo could feel the blood pressure rising. "Why was McCabe in Lazio?"

"No idea," Chip said.

"Why was McCabe at Signor Carsella's villa?"

"Who's Signor Carsella?"

"The man who owns Cucina da Pietro, the restaurant you walk out the gate is one hundred meters down Via Trionfale."

"I didn't know his last name," Chip Tallenger said.

"You know his villa?"

"That he has one in the country somewhere in Lazio, that's all. McCabe mentioned it. Pietro said he could use it. I've never been there. Never seen it. Why don't you ask the man who owns it?"

As it happened, Signor Carsella had contacted the carabinieri after seeing a live broadcast from the crime scene. Police were looking for an American student named William McCabe. Two days before McCabe had asked if he could use Signor Carsella's villa, saying he was with a woman, making the situation all the more intriguing. Arturo had asked Chip Tallenger who this mysterious woman might be. Chip had no idea. She was not a girl from the school or they would know. Now McCabe was in trouble or worse and Arturo had no motive, and no evidence beyond the rental vehicle. It was a coincidence Arturo was involved at all. He had gone to his office that morning to finish filing a report. He was planning to take the day off, his first in some time, months.

Luciano had seen him and said, "Captain, you remember the American student who was kidnapped?"

Of course he remembered. His name was McCabe.

"Someone tried to kill him."

And just like that Arturo was phoning his wife to cancel plans to spend the afternoon and evening, first shopping with her, which he did not care about missing, and then dinner at Colline Emiliane, which he did.

Luciano drove and they arrived at the scene on Viale Fiume, two kilometers east of Viterbo, at 3:15. There were four state police, and a television news crew from Rome already there, a reporter broadcasting live. How did they hear about it so quickly? Arturo was surprised the local police had been so careless. It was a crime scene after all.

Luciano told everyone to move back away from the vehicle until they had time to complete their investigation. Arturo studied the damaged Fiat resting at the edge of the woods. There was blood on the airbag that had deployed, and blood on the gray-and-blue cloth front seats, and bloody fingerprints on the passenger side door.

"Captain, you believe someone could walk away from this?"

"I don't know that someone did." He glanced up the hill past the tree line and saw a house. "Stay here, I'm going to check something."

He walked through the woods, looking for McCabe on the way, breathing hard, feeling the climb in his fifty-year-old legs. A man came out of the house as Arturo appeared coming out of the woods, crossing the yard, Arturo in jeans and a black tee-shirt under a sport jacket, his carabinieri badge on a lanyard around his neck.

The man's face was brown and wrinkled from the sun, and he wore a dark-blue beret. Arturo asked if he had seen what happened earlier and the man said no, but his wife had. The man called her name and she emerged from the house, a plump round woman wearing dark stockings and a black dress with an apron over it.

She told Arturo she was outside hanging laundry, right there, she said, pointing to a rope strung between two trees. There was a noise like an engine backfiring, and she looked down at the road, telling him about the car spinning out of control. Telling him about the men with guns getting out of another car, and about the man coming up the hill through the woods.

Arturo showed her the photograph of McCabe taken the night he was arrested.

The wife nodded. "It is him."

"Was there a woman with him?"

She shook her head. "No, but there was a man with a shotgun following him."

~

Later they had gone to investigate Signor Carsella's villa a few kilometers from the crime scene. On the way Arturo said, "So how is everything with Carmen?"

"Don't ask, Captain," Luciano said.

"Another argument?"

"This might be the end. We have not spoken for two days."

"If you were married you would have to work things out," Arturo said. "This is what I have been trying to tell you."

They drove up the steep hill toward the villa.

"I don't want to work things out."

Arturo said, "What do you want?"

"If I knew that," Luciano said, "it would be a lot easier."

Luciano parked next to the main house. "Have a look," Arturo said, pointing at the outbuildings.

Arturo got out of the car and entered the villa, walking into the kitchen. Yes, clearly someone had been here. There were wine glasses on the counter with wine still in them, and food in the refrigerator. There was a bloodstained towel in the sink, evidence of a possible crime, but not much to go on.

He checked the cellar, well stocked with wine but nothing else. He checked the main room and the salon and the toilet room. Went outside, stood on the portico, gazing at the lush countryside.

He went back inside and up the stairs. In one room a bed was unmade, sheet and blanket folded back. There was a backpack on the floor. Arturo opened the compartments and found clothes and a pocketknife. In the bathroom there was a shaving kit and a toothbrush next to the sink, signs McCabe had been there, but no sign of McCabe. He heard Luciano come up the stairs and said, "Did you find something?"

"Nothing. Now what, Captain?"

Arturo was wondering the same thing.

Thirty-four

"It's over," Angela said, relief in her voice. She was stretched out on one side of the queen-size bed. "I can't believe it."

They were in a small hotel on the outskirts of Soriano. It had been two hours since they had escaped from Pietro's villa. McCabe felt relieved too until he dumped the money out next to her, and counted it twice, getting €437,000 both times. "Sixty-three thousand's missing."

"You really thought you were going to get it all back?" Angela said. "I'm surprised they didn't spend more. Only three thousand."

"What're you talking about?"

"Mazara gave sixty thousand to my father. He was supposed to give him thirty per cent, 150,000, and thought he could get away with it. So my father will be looking for him if he isn't already."

She explained how it worked, how Don Gennaro received a share of everything, all of the criminal activity in Rome. McCabe had busted his ass to get the money and now this. "Where's he live?"

"What are you going to do?"

"I don't know," McCabe said.

"You think my father is going to give you the money? Are you crazy?"

McCabe said, "I tell him I've got you. He wants you back,

he gives me the sixty thousand euros."

"I think he would prefer the money," Angela said. "You know I want you to have it, but listen to me, this is not going to work. I am trying to help you, give you some advice. Don't go anywhere near my father. Listen, I don't want anything to happen to you."

That's how they left it. He put the money back in the bag, and ordered room service, appetizers and a couple bottles of Peroni. They'd spend the night in Soriano, and try to get a ride in the morning. He took out Angela's cell phone and dialed Chip's number, heard it ring and heard Chip say hello.

"I need you to do me a favor," McCabe said.

"I don't believe it," Chip said. "Spartacus, you're a popular guy. I saw you on TV, your yearbook picture, and the car you rented that looked like somebody had taken a sledgehammer to it. Captain Ferrara stopped by school a little while ago and asked me what I knew."

It was good to hear his voice. McCabe said, "What'd you tell him?"

"My roommate's lost his mind and disappeared."

"That's probably not too far from the truth." McCabe told him what happened, what he'd done.

Chip said, "You didn't really kidnap the Mafia don's daughter? Tell me you're making this up."

"It does sound strange," McCabe said, "doesn't it?" He looked out the window, saw a half moon lighting up the sky over Orsini Castle.

"That's an understatement," Chip said. "I don't want to rain on your parade, but maybe she's playing along, that ever occur to you?"

"No, Dr Phil," McCabe said.

"That's your ego talking," Chip said.

"What do you know about it?"

"I've watched a lot of TV, seen a lot of movies. Girls like that are used to getting what they want. They're used to the good life. What do you have to offer?"

"I'll ask her."

"But I think you've got a bigger problem," Chip said. "These guys you've gone up against are bad. You read about them in the paper, remember? They're not just going to give up. They're not going to go away. I hope you know that."

Yeah, he knew it.

"Can the Mafia princess talk to her father on your behalf, put in a good word for you?"

McCabe said, "From what she tells me they don't get along too well."

"I'd give it a try," Chip said. "That, or call Captain Ferrara. The way I see it those are your options."

"Or I could take the money and leave the country," McCabe said.

"How're you going to get it through customs and airport security?"

He had a good point.

Chip said, "Or I guess you can always shoot your way out."

"That's a possibility," McCabe said. "We'll talk about it when you get here."

Chip said he'd pick them up at ten the next morning.

Thirty-five

Ray had driven back to Mentana, and rented a room in a small hotel with a view of the countryside and Mount San Lorenzo. He needed a place to hang out and wait. He sat on the bed, thinking about Sharon, going over what he knew. According to Teegarden, the FBI had tracked her to Rome, arriving October 12th.

He also knew that if you were a foreigner staying at an Italian hotel your passport had to be recorded with the police, and there was no record of a Sharon Pope checking in any hotel in Rome. And there was nothing at all about Joey. His name had not appeared on any airline or cruise ship manifest, arriving in Italy or any European country in the past ten days. But he could've come here another way: by chartered yacht or jet. Or maybe he was traveling under an alias.

Ray's gut told him Joey was in Italy and he was staying at his uncle's estate. No proof, not much to go on, but he was going to exhaust that possibility before he did anything else.

At seven he went to a small café with white tablecloths, and had grilled coniglio that tasted like chicken, roast potatoes, green salad, bread and a glass of house red. He was the only customer at that early hour and finished his meal, had his coffee and paid the bill before anyone else came in. It was 8:15 and dark when he went outside. He walked back to the hotel to lie down for a couple hours.

He yawned and closed his eyes, but couldn't sleep and laid there in the dark, mind racing, thinking about Sharon. At midnight he got up, went in the bathroom and splashed cold water on his face, and brushed his teeth. He put on a black sweater and black jeans and a dark-blue jacket. He put the two extra magazines in his jacket pockets and slid the SIG Sauer in his jeans behind his back.

He walked down two flights of stairs, went through the lobby, and handed his key to the night clerk. He went outside and got in his car and drove back toward Don Gennaro's villa, 3.7 kilometers from Mentana. He'd clocked it coming and going the first time. When he'd gone 3.5 kilometers he slowed down and looked for a place to pull in the woods and did, backing in so he had a clear view of the road, and a fast way out. He heard a car approaching, and saw the flash of headlights as it zoomed past him.

He looked at the clock on the dash. It was 12:27 a.m. He took off the jacket, folded it on the passenger seat. Gripped the SIG Sauer, got out of the car and waited for his eyes to adjust. It was difficult to see in dense woods under an overcast sky, strangely quiet too, not a sound. He used a compass to guide him through the woods and got to the villa fifteen minutes later, hanging back in the tree line, watching the front of the place that was dark, all the lights off. He was about to come out of the woods and cross the twenty-yard expanse of grass to the villa, but saw something move, a shadow near the entrance, and a man appeared, coming out of the darkness with a dog, looked like a German shepherd, on a leash, lit a cigarette and blew smoke in his direction. He didn't like the idea of a dog.

That changed everything. They'd obviously screwed things down. Security was a lot tighter after his visit that afternoon.

Ray went around the side of the villa where woods met olive grove and moved through the trees close to the veranda. Two more men with shotguns were standing on the upper level, smoking. One was holding a dog on a leash. Ray moved back through the grove to the far side of the villa and noticed two first-floor windows open a couple inches. The bottom of the window was five feet off the ground. He reached up, opened both sides and slipped the gun in his waist behind his back and hoisted himself up and in. He stepped down onto the kitchen floor next to an industrial stove, stood and listened, heard a clock ticking. He pulled the windows closed, moved into the dining room with its tile floor and long wooden table, moved through an archway into a room the size of a hotel lobby, with a fireplace you could walk into and furniture groupings, with framed paintings on the walls, with statuary and antiquity around the perimeter, moved through an archway into an elegant smaller room with a grand piano, and moved through a final archway into the foyer. There was a spiral staircase with an ornate railing that curved up to the second level.

Ray climbed the stairs and walked down a long hallway with bedrooms on both sides. He went all the way to the end and opened the door. There was a four-post antique bed with a canopy over it, and Don Gennaro in the middle of it, snoring away.

The model was in the next room on the right. He could see her left shoulder and part of her back, sleeping naked in a bed similar to the don's. There was no one in the next three rooms.

The beds were made and the closets were empty. There was no one in the sixth bedroom, either, but there was a framed photograph of Joey on the desk, Joey in a tux, grinning, a champagne glass in his hand.

There were clothes hanging in the closet, shirts, pants and a couple sport coats. He found receipts in two of the shirt pockets, and slipped them in his jeans. He didn't see any women's clothes, nothing of Sharon's, no sign of her. Maybe they were traveling. He looked out the window, the clouds had scattered and he could see a half moon now, illuminating the veranda, the guards still standing there with the dog. He wasn't sure what to do. He walked out of the room, looked down the hall and saw someone at the top of the stairs, coming toward him.

Mauro had not slept for twenty hours, and yet he was not tired. He had walked around the villa every hour, checking with the guards. They had not seen or heard anything suspicious, although one of the dogs was barking at a deer that wandered out of the woods, but deer were common enough. He thought about what happened earlier and admitted to himself that it was possible no one had been in the grove.

There was also the business with Roberto Mazara. That too was on his mind. Mazara had stood in front of Don Gennaro and said he would bring him the money he owed within forty-eight hours, and then had disappeared. Only that morning Mauro had visited the man's apartment in Trastevere. He was not there and no one in the other apartments knew anything about him.

He had walked from the don's office into the foyer, listening to the silence and thought he heard something upstairs – a door closing? He was not sure and went up to check.

There were sconces on the walls on both sides of the hallway, lights set to dim, but giving illumination. He saw the dark shape of a man come out of Joey's room and reached for the knife.

Ray saw him take something out of his pocket and heard the metallic snap, and saw the flash of the blade. Even in the subdued light Ray recognized him as the skinny Sicilian that had chased him earlier that afternoon, and recognized the knife as a stiletto. Ray could draw the SIG Sauer and blow him away, but that would attract attention and things would get crazy. He wanted to get in, find Sharon and get out without any trouble. That wasn't going to be possible now.

The Sicilian came at him, circling to the right, right arm extended, fist gripping the handle, blade angled forward, pointing at him. Ray raised his arms in a karate stance as the Sicilian moved toward him, faking right, going left, slashing air.

Ray stepped back, watching his feet. He was quick, moving like a boxer. Punched with the blade, like he was throwing a jab, connected and Ray felt the sting as it went through his forearm, and knew he was in trouble. The Sicilian stepped right, jabbed and missed, but kept coming. Jabbed again, and this time Ray timed it, grabbed the wrist of his knife hand and threw him over his hip into the wall. He bounced off and Ray chopped him on the back of the neck and he went down and didn't move.

Ray ran for the stairs and retraced his steps back to the kitchen. His arm was throbbing, sleeve soaked with blood. He pulled it up and looked. Enough light from the moon now to see a deep puncture wound that looked like it went through his left forearm, blood streaming out, rolling down his arm. He scanned the kitchen and saw an apron and ripped off a strip of fabric, and wrapped it tight around the wound, tied it and pulled the bloodstained sleeve down over it.

Ray pushed the window open and went through it, and dropped to the ground. He crouched next to the wall of the villa, listening, but didn't hear anything and took off, running through the grove to the woods. He'd gone a couple hundred yards when he heard the dogs. The pain in his arm was getting sharper, more severe. He switched the SIG Sauer from his left hand to his right. Figured he was halfway to the car, and took off again. There was enough moonlight to see where he was going, running, slipping between trees and moving around them.

He saw light ahead where the forest ended. Heard the dogs, saw the Fiat, dogs closing in, got to it and opened the door, got in and closed it as they hit, two German shepherds banging into the side of the car, jumping at the window, jaws snapping, trying to get him through the glass.

He started the Fiat and floored it out of the woods, dogs chasing him down the road for thirty, forty yards then giving up. He drove back to Mentana. Found a first-aid kit in the armrest between the rear seats and took it with him in the hotel, bloody arm covered by the jacket, stopping at the front desk to get his key, and taking the elevator to his room.

He went in the bathroom, turned on the light and took off his jacket and sweater. He cut off the blood-soaked cloth with a scissors in the first-aid kit, and examined the wound. He was cut deep and needed stitches. But where was he going to get stitches in the middle of the night in Mentana, Italy? He squeezed disinfectant into the cut and wrapped his arm with gauze and surgical tape from the first-aid kit, and took four Motrin for the pain.

Ray heard his BlackBerry beeping in the bedroom. It was a text message from Teegarden saying Sharon had checked into the Hotel d'Inghilterra on Via Bocca di Leone 14, two days ago. That might explain why she wasn't at Carlo Gennaro's villa and why Joey wasn't there either. He was probably with her.

Ray looked at his watch. It was 2:40 a.m. His arm throbbed. He could see a spot of blood blotting the bandage, getting bigger. He was tired but the news about Sharon energized him. He'd drive back to Rome, get some sleep and surprise her in the morning.

Thirty-six

9:00 a.m., Ray got out of bed, showered, dressed and rebandaged his arm. It looked bad, swollen and still oozing blood. He would have to go to a doctor, have it looked at. He'd only slept a couple hours, if at all, his mind racing, thinking about what he was going to say to Sharon. It had been almost two months since he had seen her. He could understand why she had left him, but after thirteen years of marriage, why didn't she call, tell him her plan, leave a note? It was way out of character. That's why he'd come to Rome. That's why he was standing in front of the Hotel d'Inghilterra forty-five minutes later, stomach queasy, hands sweating, wiping his palms on his pants. He wanted to get it over with, hear what she had to say, and get on with his life.

He walked in the tiny lobby with its black-and-white tile floor. There was a trim middle-aged guy with salt-and-pepper hair behind the dark wood reception counter. Ray told him who he was and showed the man his passport. He had just arrived in Rome and wanted to surprise his wife. What room was she in?

The clerk said 410, but he was too late. Signora Pope had checked out last night. Ray asked if he could see the room. Maybe he would find something, a clue about where she had been or where she was going. The clerk handed him the key, said it was okay but the room was scheduled for cleaning, and the maid might be there already.

He took the small elevator up to the fourth floor and found room 410. The door was open. The maid's cart was in the hall as predicted. He entered and looked around. The maid was in the bathroom. She saw Ray, excused herself and walked out. There was a queen-size bed with end tables and lamps. There was a desk and chair against one wall, and two chairs and a table in front of the window that looked out on Via Bocca de Leone.

He sat at the desk, glancing down at a brochure listing the hotel services. Next to it was an empty Eclipse gum sleeve, a flavor called Polar Ice, and an empty Marlboro Lights pack. Sharon didn't smoke, or maybe she did and he didn't know it. He looked down and saw an empty shopping bag on the floor, heavy high-gloss silver paper and the name DOMUS in black type, big on the front, and an address: Via Belsiana 52.

Next to the bag was a waste basket. He reached in and took out a folded piece of paper. It was a boarding pass, KLM Flight 8934, New York–Rome, Sharon Pope, seat 14E. Okay, so she really was here. He'd still had his doubts. He got up and checked the closet. Nothing but empty hangers.

There were a couple of wet towels on the floor in the bathroom, and cotton balls black with mascara in the waste basket. He pictured Sharon standing in front of the mirror before she went to bed, wiping off eyeliner while he brushed his teeth.

He went back to his hotel, wondering what to do, and remembered the receipts he had found in Joey's shirts at the villa. He dug them out of the jeans he'd worn, and studied them. One was from a *tavola calda*, €1.50 for a cappuccino. The second one was a restaurant tab from Doney, Via Veneto 125, dated October 13th. Doney, he noticed, was at the Westin Excelsior Hotel.

*

11:10 a.m., McCabe was looking out the window, watching the street below for Chip's black BMW, wondering where he was. If you were coming from Rome this was the road you'd take into Soriano. He tried calling him and got his voicemail.

Just after noon he felt Angela's phone vibrate in his shirt pocket. He took it out, saw Chip's number on the screen, flipped it open and said, "Where the hell are you?"

"Right here," Joey said. "I'll put him on but first I want to ask how you're doing? Relaxing up there, enjoying the clean mountain air? I guess we just missed you at the villa. Don't worry, we're not coming after you. This time you're coming to us."

"McCabe," Chip said, "they broke my fucking hand –" panic in his voice.

"That's not all we're going to break," Joey said back on now. "Chipper's a little upset right now, and I won't lie to you, he's in a lot of pain, but he's learned a valuable lesson and I hope you have too. We're not fucking around."

"I'm not either," McCabe said. "Tell me where and when."

"We'll let you know," Joey said. "Listen, what happens to Chipper is up to you. Do something like you did before, it's over."

The phone went dead. McCabe could feel a surge of adrenalin like he was back on the ice, nothing quite like it, ready to take somebody's head off.

Joey was standing in a basement room under a vacant restaurant in Trastevere, Chipper tied to a chair, hands behind his back, head slumped forward looked like he was sleeping. They were near the river and the air was wet, musty. There were marks on the walls showing where the Tiber had flooded the room on a number of occasions, oily lines where the paint had broken down and separated from the pigment. Naked bulbs hung from the ceiling. Empty wine racks lined one wall, and furniture was piled up in the corner, tables stacked on tables, chairs on chairs. The floor was brick, broken in places, exposing the damp earth below.

Mazara was sitting on one of the old restaurant chairs, smoking a cigarette. Grabbing Chipper had been his idea, and Joey had to admit it wasn't bad. He remembered Mazara saying, you want McCabe? I tell you how to get him.

Joey had said, "Don't tell me, do it."

They'd driven back to Rome, dropped Joey off at the Excelsior, and gone to Chip's school, Loyola University, ended up sleeping in the car, waiting till they saw a black BMW pull out, 9:07 a.m., Chip behind the wheel, and followed him. When Chip stopped at a traffic light, Mazara and Psuz walked up to his car, broad daylight, bandanas over their faces, opened the door, yanked him out and threw him in the trunk of the Opel. Joey had finally found something these clowns were good at. Mazara had called to tell him and Joey had gotten in a cab and come right over.

The odd thing, at first, Chipper didn't seem concerned or afraid, had sat in the chair mouthing off.

"Listen," Chipper said. "You know who I am?"

"No, who are you?" Joey said.

"Charles Tallenger III."

He said it cocky like the rich Grosse Pointe assholes he knew. "No shit," Joey said. "Charles Tallenger III. Wow. I'm impressed."

"My father is United States Senator Charles Tallenger."

Joey'd heard of him. Sure. Remembered seeing him on TV one time, running for something, got beat by the good-looking babe with the glasses from Alaska.

"Let me go and all is forgiven," Chipper said.

"All's forgiven. You believe this guy?" Joey said to his Roman buddies. "See, we don't give a fuck who your dad is or who you are. We just want to know where McCabe's at."

"I don't know," Chipper said, losing the attitude. "Honestly."

"Well since you're being honest I believe you. But these guys still think you're bullshitting us," he said, indicating Mazara, Sisto and Noto.

"I don't know where he is," Chipper said, cocky attitude creeping back in his voice. "What don't you understand?"

"Okay," Joey said to Mazara. "He's yours."

The Romans picked him up and carried him to one of the round restaurant tables, stretched him out and held his right arm down, hand flat against the wood, fear in his eyes.

"Hey, what're you doing?" Chip said. Voice cracking, a couple octaves higher than normal.

"What's it look like?" Joey said. "You had your chance."

Sisto walked over and picked up a crude-looking hammer out of a toolbox and came back to the table, Chipper's eyes following him the whole way. He was afraid now, squirming and trying to free himself as Sisto raised the hammer.

"McCabe's in Soriano, in the mountains. I'm supposed to pick him up."

"How 'bout that," Joey said. "Forgot where his buddy was at, regained his memory just in the nick of time."

Sisto brought the hammer down and busted his hand.

Chipper yelled and they let him go and Joey watched him roll around on the table in pain, holding his broken knuckles. Jesus that must've hurt.

12:45 p.m., Ray was at the reception desk in the Excelsior Hotel, asking what room his dear friend Joseph Palermo was in. The clerk checked the computer in front of him and said there was no guest by that name in the hotel. He had the guy try Sharon Pope too and got the same response. Ray unfolded a Xerox photo of Joey and showed it to him. The clerk's eyes lit up. He smiled and said, "Signor Bitonte." He had seen Joey leave the hotel but he had not returned.

Ray left Joey a note, then sat in the lobby for a while, reading the *Herald Tribune*, an article about Somali pirates seizing a luxury yacht in the Gulf of Aden off the north-eastern coast of Africa, and were holding the crew for ransom. It seemed hard to believe these ragtag pirates getting away with it.

He checked the football scores. Michigan State beat Wisconsin and were 6 and 1. He finished the paper and watched a good-looking woman walk past him in tight jeans, moving toward the front desk. He sat there for a few more minutes, stood up, went outside and got in his car that was parked on the street in front of the hotel.

1:48 p.m., Joey walked up the steps and went through the revolving door into the Excelsior, moving across the lobby to the front desk, his Bruno Maglis clicking on the tile floor. He stopped and got his key and the hotel guy handed him an envelope. It was cream-colored Excelsior stationery.

"For you, Signor Bitonte."

Joey thought it was from his Unk, probably asking when he was coming back to the villa. Joey put it in his pocket, got on the elevator and pressed the button for the seventh floor. He took the envelope out and ripped it open. There was a folded piece of paper. He pulled it out and looked at it. Two words in capital letters: WHERE'S SHARON?

Joey freaked. Jesus! Had to be the husband, the Secret Service agent. But how the hell'd he find him? Joey felt the elevator slowing down, heard the bell ring, and the doors open. Expected to see a guy aiming a gun at him. It was the wrong floor, the fifth. Nobody there. He got off and ran to the stairs. The agent could've been waiting for all he knew, watched him get in the elevator. Maybe even knew what room he was in.

Joey took the stairs, went down to the basement and ran along a hallway, passing workers in their hotel uniforms. He slowed down and walked through a stock room, past banks of shelves to a loading dock with stairs that took him down to street level. He was on the east side of the hotel. Raised his arm, signaled a taxi that was heading toward him. It stopped and he got in.

Thirty-seven

McCabe checked the time on Angela's cell phone. It was 3:28 p.m. He moved along Via Sistina, up the hill past the Hassler Hotel where Senator Tallenger had stayed, Rome's best, past the taxi queue, half a dozen Fiats parked, the drivers standing around talking, past the Beverage/Gelati truck parked in the square.

The street was one-way, and he was conscious of traffic, cars, trucks and motorbikes coming up behind him, passing by, and the sounds of the city coming alive again after siesta. The strap of the soccer bag was on his left shoulder, angling to the right across his chest, resting against his side.

He and Angela had taken a taxi from Soriano a couple hours earlier and gone to her apartment. He'd gotten Joey's call at 3:15, giving him forty-five minutes to get to the location. McCabe stood at the base of the obelisk, turned and looked up at the twin bell towers of Trinità dei Monti, the French Gothic church with a Renaissance facade, the famous church at the top of the Spanish Steps. He thought he saw something move in the tower on the left, and now a pigeon flew out and glided over the obelisk and disappeared down Via Sistina.

He scanned the top of the steps. There were a couple of black merchants with knock-off purses and umbrellas displayed on a wicker mat, and a painter setting up an easel. He glanced over and saw Angela at a table, drinking coffee at the terrace restaurant. He kept going, walked past Trinità dei Monti, the city of Rome spread out in perfect blue-sky panorama to his left. On his right was a twenty-foot-high salmon-colored wall that bordered Villa Borghese.

He went down almost to the park entrance and came back, studying the scene from a different angle. He walked down the Spanish Steps to the second level and leaned against the balustrade. It was all going to be over one way or the other in thirty minutes. He looked down at the bottom of the steps, always more crowded than the top, people sitting in rows, side by side like they were at a concert, people standing around Fontana della Barcaccia, the boat-shaped fountain, and more people crisscrossing Piazza di Spagna, heading for the shops. There were carriages lined up and he caught the faint odor of horse manure. There were flower vendors and photographers and black merchants selling jewelry, bags and sunglasses.

The Spanish Steps had to be at least one hundred yards from top to bottom, and maybe fifty yards from side to side. He thought they would come from the top. It was a better vantage point, and it was easier to go down than up.

3:48, Joey stood at the bottom of the Spanish Steps, the lower level packed with people, eyes going left to right. He looked up at the balcony on the second level, half a dozen tourists standing there, too far away to recognize. He was more relaxed now after getting out of the hotel, sure he'd lost the agent, and there was no way he was going back. It was time to get out of Rome, too. That's why the ransom money was more important than ever. He had a couple hundred grand in a Swiss account, but it wasn't enough. This was his stake in the future. He'd called Sharon and told her to pack her bag and meet him at the train station, the main terminal, at five.

"First tell me what's going on?" Sharon had said. "You were supposed to come back and get me. We were going to have lunch. Where are you?"

"I can't talk right now," Joey said. "I'll tell you later. Just meet me at the train station. Bring your things and bring mine. There's a bag in the closet."

"Where we going?" Sharon said.

"It's a surprise," Joey said. "For once just do what I ask and don't say anything, okay?" Didn't mention Ray. What was the point? If he was still at the hotel, and that was a good possibility, he might run into Sharon and she'd have to deal with him. Jesus, why was Joey taking all the heat?

He walked up the Spanish Steps, moving along the eastern wall that curved all the way to the top. On his right was an apartment building with an entrance on the square below. Joey had checked it out, walked from top to bottom a couple times earlier that afternoon and noticed the balcony of a second-floor apartment that was only a couple feet from the wall. Christ he could jump to it. He felt his phone vibrate in his pants pocket and took it out, heard Mazara say they were ready, everybody in position. Joey looked up and saw McCabe standing at the second balcony.

3:52, Psuz rested the barrel of an old bolt-action Beretta 501 on top of the metal railing that went around the penthouse patio, seven floors up, looking down at the Spanish Steps. Put the scope on Joey walking up, angled it to the right, saw McCabe at the balcony. Adjusted the scope, put the cross-hairs on McCabe's back about seventy-five meters below him, adjusted again, closing on his head. Psuz could take the shot, drop him, he would never know what happened. But Joey said to wait, make sure he had the money, and also Angela.

It was Joey's idea to have him on the roof of the building. "Psuz, you really a sniper?" Joey said to him. "Let's see how good you are."

But he also had an idea. After his time in the army he had worked for Italgas. He went there, the main office in Rome, and took a uniform from the locker room. First, he was thinking of going in the bell towers at Trinità dei Monti, but to get up there he'd have to go through the convent next door and that would be difficult. There were procedures to follow when dealing with the Catholic Church. So instead he chose the apartment building across Via Sistina from the Hassler Hotel.

In the uniform it was easy to enter with his tool bag, and ride the elevator to the penthouse apartment, ring the buzzer, and when the man opened the door, tell him there was gas leaking in the apartment and the occupants, for their safety, must vacate immediately.

3:57, McCabe saw Joey coming up the steps toward him, breathing hard, gut bouncing under a loose-fitting island shirt with hula dancers on it. "I'd say you're the one in the wrong business."

"We'll see," Joey said. "We all get lucky once in a while. Don't we? I wouldn't count on it happening again."

"You never know," McCabe said.

"Where's my cuz at?"

McCabe pointed to the balcony of the terrace restaurant just above them on the west side of the steps. Angela was standing at the railing. Joey looked at her and waved.

"Where's Chip?"

"Right up there," Joey nodded, indicating the top of the steps, the street level. "Let's do it."

They started up, McCabe leading the way. When they got to the top, Joey glanced at him and said, "I've got a surprise for you."

McCabe could see Mazara standing in front of the silver Opel, and Sisto standing at the rear. Was he talking about them?

Joey said, "Look over there," nodding at the roof of a yellow apartment building rising above them on the right.

He saw someone on the rooftop.

"Know who that is? My little buddy Psuz, turns out he was a sniper in the Italian army. You believe that?" Joey grinned, thinking he was back in control. "Do anything even remotely stupid he's going to punch your ticket, put you out of business. We're going to let you see Chipper, then I want you to hand me the money and walk away, don't say another word."

McCabe moved closer to the car, saw Noto behind the wheel, watching him. Sisto popped the trunk and he saw Chip, bound, gagged and curled up in the fetal position. Chip looked up at him, tried to say something, but Sisto slammed the lid closed. He noticed the little square in front of the Hassler was empty, the taxis and Beverage/Gelati truck were gone.

"I've got a surprise for you too," McCabe said, eyeing Joey. He could see Captain Ferarra and three of his men coming toward them from the left, moving up the street.

*

4:02, Arturo was walking along Via Sistina flanked by Luciano and Gattuso. Next to Gattuso was Borri, a giant at six feet four inches tall. They were coming up next to the convent, the building that joined Trinità dei Monti. Traffic had been stopped on Via Sistina and diverted down Via Gregoriana. The street was deserted.

McCabe had phoned headquarters earlier that afternoon, and Luciano had reached him at his apartment, calling as he was leaving to spend the afternoon with his wife, Arturo trying to make up for the last time he had to cancel his plans, the day they found McCabe's rental car. His wife Teresa was an understanding woman but this was testing her patience.

Luciano explained what he knew. The same gang that kidnapped McCabe now had Chip Tallenger. The ransom exchange was to take place today, 4:00 at the Spanish Steps. The question Arturo had asked himself: where was McCabe, and if he was in trouble, why did he wait so long to contact the police?

He could see the silver Opel sedan parked next to the balustrade at the top of the Spanish Steps, and the men standing next to it. He could see four GIS moving along Via Sistina, approaching from the opposite direction. And then McCabe appeared coming up the steps, carrying a soccer bag, standing next to a bigger heavier man. He saw the sniper on the rooftop, and was bringing the cell phone to his mouth when he heard a rifle shot.

"He hands me the soccer bag shoot him," Joey had said to him. But McCabe did not give the soccer bag to Joey, and Joey was standing close to him, so close he did not have a clear shot. Psuz noticed something else. It was quiet now. No traffic. No car had driven by on the street for some time. He aimed the scope along Via Sistina and understood why. There were police coming, four from the left and four from the right. He put the cross hairs of the scope on one of the men in a suit jacket, running past the church, squeezed the trigger, heard the crack of the rifle echo off the rooftop and saw him fall. He worked the bolt and aimed for a second man, but he was moving, they all were, taking cover behind the stairway that led to the church and he did not have another target.

When the firing started everyone scattered. McCabe popped the trunk and tried to free Chip, but Noto put the Opel in gear, took a hard left, accelerating, driving down the west side of the steps, picking up speed, front end bouncing, trunk lid swinging up and down before slamming closed.

Bullets pinged off the obelisk in front of him. Another bullet ricocheted off the sidewalk next to him. And then someone grabbed McCabe from behind and pulled him back off his feet and brought him down behind the balustrade. McCabe turning now, looking at him, dark hair, late thirties, a guy he'd never seen before in his life, squatting next to him.

"You okay? Stay down. There's a sniper up there."

That's all he said. He was an American and had probably saved McCabe's life, but who was he? The guy glanced up at Psuz on the rooftop and took off, crouching low, moving along the balcony, and disappeared down the steps. The shooting continued, Psuz firing at the police, and the police firing back.

McCabe looked through the balusters, watched the dark-haired guy run down. Below him the Opel lost control, hit the stone railing on the second level, spun out and crashed broadside into the eastern wall. McCabe could hear the whelp of sirens, looked down, saw two carabinieri sedans enter Piazza de Spagna from opposite sides, pulling up at the bottom of the Spanish Steps, more cops getting out of the cars, moving through the scattering mass of panicked tourists. The shooting had stopped.

Mazara was confused. He had seen Angela on the terrace, sitting at a table by herself, sipping coffee. What was she doing? He ran there, hopped the entrance gate, and saw her crouching at the wall, peeking over. All of the customers had gone in the hotel, leaving their cappucini and espressos, their biscotti and cannoli on the tables. There was no one around. He crouched next to her. "What are you doing? Why are you here?" He reached for her hand and tried to pull her up. "Come with me. We have to go." He could see the carabinieri running down the steps, swarming the Opel, pulling Noto out of the vehicle. "There is no time."

She was watching the action below, hardly paying attention to him.

"It's over," Angela said, glancing at him. "Go before they arrest you."

"What about you?"

"I'm staying."

And in that moment he understood, it became clear what had happened. "You and McCabe, uh?"

She looked at him and nodded. He reached behind his back, gripped the Tanfoglio, wanted to take it out and shoot her for betraying him, but he couldn't do it. Two carabinieri sedans drove up Via Sistina and stopped twenty meters away. And now Roberto had no choice but to go. He ran across the terrace and went over the wall, hanging and dropping to the courtyard below.

An ambulance followed two police cars pulling up on the street above them, lights flashing, sirens wailing, and a crowd had formed around the Opel, police holding people back. Angela had come down from the top, put her arms around him, hugged him and then stood close. Captain Ferrara opened the trunk. McCabe could see Chip curled up inside. The EMS techs moved down the steps with a gurney and lifted Chip onto it, untied the gag and freed his hands. His eyes were closed and McCabe didn't know if he was alive or not. Then Chip's eyes flickered open. He looked around and saw McCabe.

"'Are you afraid to die, Spartacus? When one man says no, I won't, Rome begins to fear.'"

"I think he's going to make it," McCabe said to Angela.

Thirty-eight

Joey boosted himself up on the eastern wall, and jumped a couple feet to the apartment balcony he'd seen earlier, going over the railing onto the patio and into the apartment, door unlocked, no idea who lived there, no sign of anyone, and moved down a dark hallway to the front door. He unlocked it and turned the handle, opened the door and went out.

He took the stairs down two flights, opened the door and moved through the crowd that had formed around Piazza de Spagna. He could see Sisto in the square, hands cuffed behind his back, two cops pushing him in the back seat of a patrol car. He walked past store fronts: Rucoline, Byron and Scalinata, all the way to American Express. He looked back. No one was following him. There was a taxi queue down the street. He went there, got in a cab and took it to the train station. It was 4:47.

Sharon had spent the night with Joey at the Excelsior but something was different. He had changed, or maybe she was finally seeing the real him. He seemed crude, vulgar, not the suave, handsome guy she had fallen in love with. It was a big disappointment after all the planning and anticipation, putting her life on hold, flying to Rome to be with him. She was ready to give up her marriage, what was left of it, her job and family to be with Joey. She had been that sure, that confident.

He was supposed to meet her at the hotel, be there when she arrived, but he wasn't, and he hadn't called till the next evening. She'd said, "You know how long I've been waiting for you?"

"I've been tied up. Doing a job for my uncle," Joey had said.

"What, they don't have phones in Italy?"

"Babe, I'll make it up to you," Joey said. "Check out, come to the Excelsior, this cool, classy hotel on Via Veneto, you'll love it."

"Why don't you come and get me?"

"I'm beat," Joey said. "Do me this favor, will you? We'll go shopping. I'll take you to a nice dinner."

That sounded better.

When she got to his room an hour later he seemed preoccupied like his mind was somewhere else.

"What took you so long?" Joey said.

"Hi, Sharon, it's good to see you. I'm glad you're here." Telling him what he should've said.

"I'm sorry," Joey said. "I've got a lot on my mind."

He looked tired, bags and dark spots under his eyes. "You've got a lot on *your* mind? I'm the one taking all the risk." She paused. "Want me to unpack, or what?"

"Yeah, sure. Make yourself at home."

"Why don't you take me to bed," Sharon said. "Show me how much you missed me."

Joey said he was too tired.

Too tired? From what?

His voice woke her up the next morning, Joey talking on his cell phone. He was already showered and dressed.

"I gotta go," Joey said. "Backo shortolo."

"I thought we were finally going to be able to spend time together, not worry about anything."

"We'll have lunch," Joey said. "I'll show you the sights."

He moved to the bed and kissed her forehead like he was her father.

"I'll make it up to you."

We'll see, Sharon was thinking.

Joey didn't come back for lunch, and she was getting antsy. Had been in the room the whole day, waiting, watching CNN. He finally called at 3:30, telling her to meet him at the train station. No explanation. Just be there, he'd said, talking to her like she was the hired help, barking orders, sounding like he was annoyed, irritated.

Sharon wondered what she'd gotten herself into. Was Joey like this before, and she'd missed it? No, he'd been gracious and attentive, a perfect gentleman. She wanted to check his passport, see if he was the same guy. She'd just left a bad relationship and wasn't going to get into another one. She considered cutting her losses, fly home and put it all behind her.

At 4:30, she packed her suitcase, took the elevator down, checked her bag with the bellhop, went outside and got in a taxi.

Joey saw her in the crowded terminal, standing by herself, looking around. Walked up to her, grinned and said, "Hey sexy, you waiting for someone?" He tried to kiss her and she ducked away. "What's the matter?" Joey said. "Where's your suitcase? Where's mine?"

"I didn't bring them."

He shook his head. "I just bought two tickets to Positano, most romantic fucking place in the world, you didn't bring our stuff?"

"I flew 4,600 miles to be with you," Sharon said. "And all I've done is sit in hotel rooms the past three days, waiting for you."

"Well, now you've got my undivided fucking attention," Joey said. He wondered what her problem was. He'd paid for the plane ticket and the hotel room. Maybe it was her time of the month. All he knew, after the day he'd had he didn't need this.

"I made a mistake," Sharon said.

"I make one every once in a while myself," Joey said. "Nobody's perfect. Let's go. Train's leaving in five minutes. We better get on."

"I'm not going."

"You're not going? Come on. We're finally together. Don't worry, I'll buy you some new clothes." He put his arm around her shoulders, tried to move her but she wouldn't budge. You want me to get tough, Joey thought, okay. He grabbed her arm and pulled her.

"Get your hand off me." She said it loud.

People were turning, looking at them. "Take it easy, will you? Jesus. Everything's going to be fine." He tried to smile but it was tough 'cause he was pissed off now. She'd never acted like this and he was trying to figure out what was going on. "Listen, straighten out. Cut the bullshit. You're coming with me. You're going to get on that fucking train if I have to carry you."

*

They were still thirty feet away when Ray saw Joey holding her arms, her biceps. It seemed like they were having a fight. Seeing it sent a blast of adrenalin through him. He'd followed Joey down the Spanish Steps, over the wall to the apartment balcony, through the apartment and across town, losing him in traffic and then seeing his taxi pull up in front of the train station.

Joey was pulling her and Sharon was resisting when Ray got to them. Joey saw him and let her go, and now they were squaring off.

"Come to save the little woman?" Joey said. "I think you're too late."

Sharon looked embarrassed, caught with her boyfriend unexpectedly, and the scene was ugly.

"What're you doing with him?" Ray said to Sharon. "You like being treated this way?"

"I'm not with him," Sharon said. "It's over."

"It's over when I say it is," Joey said.

"You remind me of your father," Ray said. "Same tough-guy attitude with nothing to back it up."

That stopped Joey, got him thinking.

"What're you talking about? You didn't know my old man."

"I met the little guy one night at his house in Bloomfield. We were in that nice paneled room with the fireplace off the foyer. Know the one I'm talking about?" He paused. "I asked him where you were and he said he didn't know. Imagine that? I said okay, you don't want to talk, I'll go upstairs see if Mrs P. wants to be more co-operative. Your little Mafia dad threatened me. Got all worked up. I thought he was going to take a swing. Then he leaned back against the desk, a strange look on his face, grabbed his chest and fell on the floor and died."

Joey glared at him.

"I was surprised you weren't at the wake or funeral. What kind of son are you, you don't come to your father's grave, pay your respects?"

Joey made his move, came at him as expected, threw a big right hand Ray blocked instinctively with his left, his bad arm, and felt the pain shoot up through his shoulder. Joey followed with a left hook Ray blocked with his right, and threw Joey over his hip and saw him land on his back on the hard floor, dazed, turning his body, trying to get up.

"My God," Sharon said. "You're bleeding."

She looked at his arm while Joey got back on his feet. Blood had soaked through the bandage and through his shirt and sport coat, dripping on the tile floor. He could feel a dull throb. "I'm okay."

Joey pulled a gun now, eyes wild, and the people around them shrieked and moved back, moved away.

Sharon stepped in front of Ray and said, "What're you going to do? You shoot him you're going to have to shoot me. Put it down."

"You're coming with me," Joey said.

Sharon didn't say anything. She didn't have to. Four GIS in dark-blue fatigues appeared, aiming automatic weapons, shouting firm commands in Italian. Joey dropped the Beretta and they cuffed his hands behind his back and took him away. That's what happened when you pulled a gun in a public place in a country on terrorist alert.

They each gave police a statement, and thirty minutes later Ray walked Sharon back through the train station and they went outside and stood looking at each other as cars drove up and people passed by with their luggage.

"You going to tell me what's going on?" Ray said.

"I took a vacation," she said. "It's been a while."

"That's it, huh?" His mouth was dry. He ran his tongue over his teeth, shifted his weight, put his hands in his pockets. "How long have you been seeing him?"

"Ray, what're you doing here?"

"You disappeared."

"You did too," Sharon said.

"I know and I'm sorry."

"You're about three years too late."

"Well I've got time now," Ray said. "I quit the Service."

She gave him a puzzled look. "You serious?"

He nodded.

"You think it's going to make a difference?" Sharon said.

"You tell me."

"You really quit, huh?" She shook her head. "I don't believe it." She smiled now, and he did too.

It was a start.

Thirty-nine

Early afternoon, McCabe was glancing out the window at the rolling hills of Lazio, Angela driving the Lancia, smoking a cigarette, window cracked a couple inches, wind at high speed rustling her hair. She took a final drag and pushed the cigarette through the opening and closed the window.

He was replaying the conversation he'd had with Captain Arturo Ferrara, the captain saying, why didn't you tell me you were in trouble?

It was complicated. What could he say? I kidnapped Angela Gennaro and used her to collect the ransom. He couldn't say that so he didn't say anything.

Captain Ferrara said, "I still do not understand. How you recover the money?"

"All I can tell you is it worked out," McCabe said, waiting for the captain to give him a hard time, demand the truth and confiscate the ransom.

He said, "Are you Catholic?"

"Yes," McCabe said, although he hadn't been to mass in three years, confession in five.

"God was looking out for you, uh?" the captain said.

They were at carabinieri headquarters in downtown Rome, the captain loose and relaxed, McCabe sitting across the desk from him, listening to music that sounded like opera. He could see an iPod in a speaker dock on the credenza behind him.

Captain Ferrara packed his pipe with tobacco and lit it, blowing out sweet-smelling smoke that drifted over the table.

"Will you return to the university?"

"My scholarship's been revoked," McCabe said. "Mr Rady kicked me out. I go back there I'll probably get in a fight with him."

"I can speak to him for you."

"I appreciate the offer, but I don't think so."

"What will you do?"

"I'm not sure."

"It is unfortunate you cannot stay in Rome."

McCabe wanted to tell him about Angela, tell him he'd been hit by the lightning bolt, and they were living together, but he obviously couldn't. Ferrara puffed on his pipe. They talked about Chip. He'd gotten out of the hospital, hand in a cast and was back at school. They talked about Mazara and his gang, arrested and in custody in Rebibbia Prison, awaiting trial, all except Psuz, who was killed by GIS marksmen. Nothing about Joey Palermo. The conversation ended. Captain Ferrara stood up and they shook hands.

He looked McCabe in the eye. "I can trust you with the money?"

"I was thinking of buying a villa in Tuscany." McCabe said it straight, then broke into a grin and now Captain Ferrara did too.

"Tell me where, I will visit you." He paused. "Keep the money in Banco de Roma until you transfer it."

McCabe had to admit that made more sense than hiding it in Angela's closet.

*

Now an hour and a half later, he and Angela were approaching her father's estate outside Mentana. He was going to ask the most powerful man in Rome for the missing ransom, the sixty thousand euros Mazara had given him. There was a car blocking the entrance and half a dozen men with guns, standing around. "What's going on? Looks like a scene from *The Godfather*," McCabe said.

"Someone broke in last night," Angela said. "My father has tightened security."

The guards recognized Angela, opened the gates and moved the car and now they were on a pea-gravel driveway that wound through the woods to the villa. Angela parked on the circular drive in front of the house. She turned off the car and looked at McCabe.

"What are you going to say to him?"

"I'll think of something," McCabe said.

"You're not giving me a lot of confidence." She looked concerned. "I want to help you but this is business. You have to do it or my father will not respect you."

They got out of the car and the front door opened and there was Mauro, the bodyguard. He greeted Angela in a shy formal way. She didn't introduce McCabe and he didn't say anything.

Mauro led them through the house to a big room that looked like a museum with all the paintings and statuary. McCabe recognized the don from the night he had seen him outside Al Moro. The man got up from his desk, moving across the room, gray styled hair, black designer glasses and a blue dress shirt with gold cuff links, and a gold watch that looked expensive. He approached Angela, kissed her on both cheeks. He didn't smile but McCabe could see that he liked her. There was affection in his eyes behind the stern gaze.

"You hear about Joey?" The don frowned. "My sister loses her husband and now this."

"Have you told her?"

The don shook his head.

"Where is he?"

"Rebibbia," the don said. "The lunatic pulls a gun in Stazione Termini. He is out of his mind, crazy."

"I never thought he was very smart," Angela said. "What can you do?"

"I agree with you, but he is my responsibility."

"Are you going to use your influence?"

"What influence?" The don flashed a grin.

They stood staring at each other until Angela glanced at McCabe.

"This is the friend I was telling you about."

Don Gennaro turned and looked at him now for the first time.

"Nice to meet you," McCabe said, offering his hand, but the don looked away, his attention back on Angela.

"He has to talk to you," Angela said. "Listen to him, will you? I'll wait in the salon." She gave McCabe a quick glance and walked out of the room.

Now the don focused his attention on him, and McCabe had to admit this gray-haired old dude made him nervous. He was about to say, you owe me sixty thousand euros, but decided he'd better be a little more diplomatic. He could see Mauro about fifteen feet away, watching him. "Roberto Mazara gave you some money," McCabe said. "But it was not his to give. The money belongs to me and I need it back." He thought that summed it up pretty well.

The don stared at him, studying him. "Who are you, come into my house, talk to me this way?"

McCabe shifted his weight, took a breath, thinking it couldn't be going any worse. Walk out right now don't say another word. He looked past the don at the paintings and sculptures behind him. "Forgive me, Don Gennaro. I have nothing but respect for anyone with such an impressive collection of art."

The don eased up, let out a breath, seemed to relax a little.

McCabe looked at the wall. "Is that *Madonna and Child*?" He had seen photos of it, created in marble relief.

The don moved toward it and McCabe followed.

"Do you know who did it?"

"Desiderio."

The don looked at him and nodded.

Next was a bronze porphyry sarcophagus by Verrochio, and an early Renaissance sculpture of David the shepherd boy who killed Goliath. McCabe had seen earlier versions, knew the distinctive style. "Donatello, of course."

Carlo Gennaro grinned. "What is your opinion of this one?"

"It's a Tintoretto," McCabe said. "Unmistakable." It was a Quattrocento action figure stroked out of charcoal, conveying so much energy and emotion. "I wouldn't mind having it in my collection."

"You have a collection?" The don perked up.

"Five days ago I was a student."

"What are you now?"

"A former student."

There was a glint in the don's eye.

"And this one?" He pointed to a painting.

McCabe knew it. "Bronzino's *Allegory with Venus and Cupid.* Commissioned by Cosimo de' Medici and given it to King Francis I of France. But it's supposed to be in the National Gallery in London."

The don smiled. He seemed amused. "Do you understand its meaning?"

"It's a male allegory of syphilis," McCabe said. "Look to the right, you see the face of a beautiful girl, but she's really a monster with a serpent's tail and the legs and claws of a lion."

The don's expression was serious for a beat until he broke into a grin.

Don Gennaro said, "No, I do not think so. The winged creature is Father Time. Look. He pulls back the drape to reveal Cupid kissing his mother and touching her breast, while Jest or Folly toss roses on the incestuous pair." He paused. "Look here," he pointed, "you see the female allegory of jealousy."

McCabe decided not to disagree, tell him it was the old-fashioned interpretation, or tell him the painting was a reproduction.

'How did you do?" Angela said as they walked out of the villa and she closed the door.

"I'm making progress," McCabe said.

She stopped and looked at him. "What does that mean?"

"He's talking to me," McCabe said. "We discussed his art collection."

"Did you ask for the money?"

"I did."

"And?"

"He got mad."

"What a surprise."

"Then things were going good and I didn't want to blow it." McCabe paused. "But your father invited me to come back."

"What do you mean?"

"He's getting a painting he wants to show me."

"So you're going to give it another try, uh?"

"We'll see how it goes," McCabe said.

Acknowledgments

Special thanks to Jeff Posternak, my stateside agent, and Charles Buchan from Wylie UK, Angus Cargill for his fine editorial direction, Katherine Armstrong for her astute project editing, Mattia Carratello for his keen knowledge of ancient Rome, and Gregg Sutter for his research on the US Secret Service.